CHARM SCHOOL

A POWERFUL PROHIBITION
BOOK TWO

RENEE EDWARDS

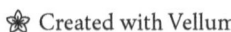

To Nicole,
who I am so grateful to have with me on this journey
#librariantoauthorpipeline

MAP OF DOMAMUNDI

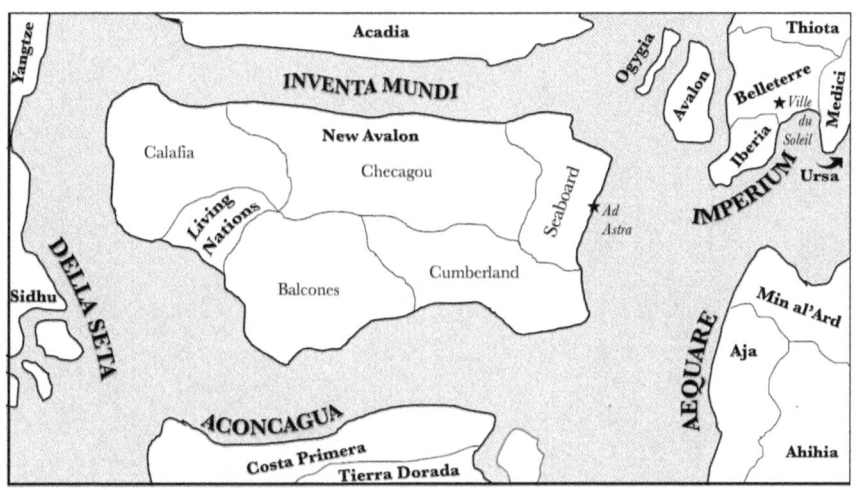

Click here for a larger version of this map.

BENEDICK: Thou and I are too wise to woo peaceably.

— WILLIAM SHAKESPEARE, *MUCH ADO ABOUT NOTHING*

CHAPTER 1

AARON

"*I*'d like a gin fizz with a shot of jubilation, please," a smooth, feminine voice said.

Aaron looked up from where he was polishing an already immaculate glass with a cloth. The girl who had settled onto the barstool in front of him was uncommonly pretty, even for the kinds of patrons he was used to seeing at the Hierophant. She had a delicate, heart-shaped face with a full mouth and wide eyes, but it was her hair that was most noteworthy: a vivid, fiery red that shone like a beacon in the low light of the bar. Her beaded purple dress and jeweled headband tried to muster up some sparkle of their own, but they were no match for those immaculate finger waves.

"Coming right up," he said, flashing her a grin and tossing the cloth aside. As he set about cracking and separating the egg to get the white the recipe called for, the girl glanced out into the main part of the room. Guests were still finishing their meals, so the entertainment hadn't started yet, but even so, he knew it was an impressive sight.

After all, ever since the sweeping law known as the Embargo had gone into effect, prohibiting those with natural magic—like him—from using their abilities, anything related to magic had gone underground. For the tourists who flocked to the bright lights of Ad Astra from around the country, yearning for excitement and adventure, magic was something whispered about behind cupped hands, exotic and dangerous. But if they were clever and willing to walk, however briefly, on the wild side, they would end up at the Hierophant or one of the other "charm schools" around town—nightclubs that offered up magical wonders alongside more pedestrian indulgences to create a uniquely lush and seductive experience. One of Aaron's drinks would have been a showstopper all on its own, but enhanced by his ability to impart and shape desired emotions—well, that was something *really* special.

"New to the city?" he said, scooping ice into a cocktail shaker.

She gave him a sheepish look. "Is it that obvious?"

"Not really," he said. "I've just got the eye." He would have pointed to the eye in question, but since his hands were occupied with pouring and mixing, he settled for waggling his brows, and she chuckled.

He turned his focus to the shaker then, mindful of the liquid sloshing inside, the ice rattling against the sides of the container. At the same time, he thought of the happiest moments of his childhood —blowing out birthday candles, running through unpaved streets under fireworks on Independence Day—and urged those feelings of joy, of jubilation, through the metal and into the chamber where the ingredients were working their own magic, coming together to make the club's most popular cocktail. When he was satisfied that the drink was ready, he strained the concoction into a highball glass, then topped it off with soda and a cherry before sliding it over to the redhead.

"One jubilation fizz," he said with a grin, putting on a bit more of an accent than he came by naturally. It was a tactic that usually worked in his favor.

"Thank you." She picked up the cherry and popped it into her mouth, tugging off the stem and twirling it in her fingers. "You don't exactly sound like a native either."

"Guilty," he said and leaned on the bar. There were no other customers around just then, so he had a minute to chat. "I've been in the city for a few years now, but I spent my boyhood days on a farm down in Cumberland."

"I've never been there," she said. "What's it like?"

"Hot. Good music. Better food." He lifted his chin. "What about you?"

"Just got in from up the coast."

Aaron raised his eyebrows. "What, up by the strait?"

She shrugged. "Thereabouts."

"And what brings you here?"

"Secretarial school. I've been saving up and was finally able to make the move. I'm hoping to get a job at one of the offices downtown."

"Secretarial school, huh? Which one? My aunt moonlights as a typing instructor from time to time."

She opened her mouth to answer, but just then, a couple walked up to the bar, the man signaling to Aaron as they came. Aaron gestured for the redhead to hold on and stepped away to make the couple's drinks. When he finished and turned back, she was giving him a speculative look.

"What?" he said.

"Tell me something... I'm sorry, what was your name?"

"Aaron."

"Aaron," she repeated, and he liked the way it sounded in her mouth. She placed her elbows on the bar and leaned forward. "What's it like working here?"

Aaron mimicked her posture, leaning forward with his hands crossed one over the other, the white of his cuffs bright against his dark brown skin in the near-darkness. "How do you mean?"

"Well, isn't it scary? Knowing what you're doing is illegal and that the authorities could come through at any time?"

Aaron blew out a breath. "Yeah, there's always a chance that we could get raided. But there are ways to discourage that. Coppers are less likely to target us if they're getting fat on what we take in."

"Even so," she said, "is it really worth the risk?"

"It is," Aaron replied, surprising himself with the quick response.

There was just something about this girl that invited confidences—it was in the way he felt he had her whole attention, and the way those wide eyes got even wider at his response.

"Why?" she said.

He shrugged. "I can't speak for all of us, but for me? It's the only place I really feel free"

She looked as if she was going to speak again, but a group of laughing socialites appeared, shouting drink orders over each other. It took Aaron a while to get all of them served, and when he turned back, the girl was taking money out of her fringed handbag and hopping off her stool.

"Leaving so soon?" he said and felt an unexpected sting of disappointment.

"Well, I have a cat at home," she said. "He worries."

"Ah."

"See you around, Aaron," she said with a saucy lift of her chin, and then she strolled down the ramp to the main floor and on to the exit.

Aaron stared after her until the door swung closed in her wake. He was nudged out of his rumination by the band tuning up, indicating that Paloma, the club's headliner and one of Aaron's best friends, would be starting her act soon. Shaking his head, he reached out to clear away her glass, but he noticed something that brought him up short.

There was lipstick on the rim, but as far as he could tell, the glass was still completely full.

THE NEXT MORNING, Aaron had more on his mind than mysterious redheads. Namely, he was concerned with getting to Bauer's Fine Wine and Spirits before the shop got busy for the day. Bauer's was run by the eponymous brothers—elegant, reserved Ernst and charming Felix—who had built quite the reputation for curating the best selection of libations in the city. They did a bustling business, but what most of their customers, even the moneyed, well-connected ones, didn't know was that the owners' grandmother sold exquisite syrups and liqueurs fortified with conjurer magic out of the apartment above the shop.

Aaron did not, technically speaking, need magical ingredients for his drinks—he was fully capable of performing the infusions that had made the Hierophant famous all on his own. But like any true artist, he was particular about his tools, which in his case meant the best ingredients he could find. Grossmutter Bauer, as she was known to everyone in Ad Astra's tight-knit magical community, spoke very little Avalonian and never seemed to smile, but her skill at potion-making was unmatched. She was a conjuror of the old school, trained in the ways of her ancestors rather than the academic approach of the modern practitioners, and she guarded her methods like state secrets. That meant the only way to purchase her wares was to climb the stairs to the dim, cluttered apartment and weather her steely glare as the transaction was completed in near silence. Aaron, who was prone to chattering when he got nervous, had to work extra hard to stay calm and composed, but it seemed to be paying off. On his last visit, she'd carried out their exchange in the same curt, somber way as usual, but also given his hand a little pat as he had collected his purchases—a small thing, but it had left him glowing for the rest of the day.

Aaron stuck his hands in his pockets, taking in the wide avenues and towering office and apartment buildings as he walked. This was what people meant when they talked about heading to "the big city". He'd found it all so overwhelming when he'd first arrived, a scared kid from the country. That had been years ago, though. He'd long since found a place for himself in the great sprawl—in a quieter corner, admittedly, where the streets were narrower and often spanned by clotheslines, where conversations and cooking smells drifted out of brownstone windows to the sidewalks below, but the city all the same. It was home now. Even so, he thought he'd always feel a little thrill coming to this section of midtown. It was a place of endless possibility.

He paused for a moment in front of a hat shop. The cheerful

window display was dominated by new hats for spring, the felt styles of winter giving way to cloches and capelines in lighter materials and brighter colors. One straw number in particular caught his eye—saffron yellow with a black taffeta ribbon circling the crown and matching black trim on the narrow brim. Ebony would love it. He pursed his lips, considering. It might help him get back on her good side. He certainly wasn't above offering a bribe in service to the cause.

It had been a tense breakfast that morning. He'd sat there dutifully eating his scrambled eggs and trying to catch his sister's eye, while she, still in her robe with a silk scarf over her pin curls, sipped her tea and pointedly ignored him.

Aunt Ruth, taking a seat at the table with her own breakfast, glanced back and forth between them.

"What's going on with the two of you this morning?"

"Nothing," they'd said in unison. Ebony had finally deigned to look at him then, but when he'd smiled at her, she'd sniffed and turned away.

"Is something wrong?" Ruth said uncertainly.

Just as Aaron was saying "No", Ebony stood up abruptly, declared, "I need to go get ready," and left the room. Randolph, Aunt Ruth's ancient pug who worshiped Ebony, trundled along after, taking his snorty breathing with him and leaving the kitchen painfully silent.

Aunt Ruth raised her eyebrows. "Want to talk about it?"

Aaron sighed and rubbed his face. "Not particularly."

Aunt Ruth sat back in her chair, considering him. "Seems like things have been rocky between you two lately."

He slumped. "Yes, ma'am."

She gave him a look of such deep compassion, it made his stomach hurt.

"You can't protect her forever, you know."

"I know."

"You're not children anymore," she went on gently. "Maybe it's time to put away childish things."

Aaron had nodded, staring at the remnants of his toast and eggs, but he still wasn't sure if he agreed. Was it really childish to try and keep the person he loved most in the world safe? On the contrary, it had been the first thing that made him feel something like adult responsibility.

Back in front of the hat shop window, Aaron's attention drifted to the bandeaus and embellished headbands, their paste jewels sparkling in the sunlight, and he thought of the redhead from the night before. He remembered the heart-shaped face, the crimson lips smiling at him coyly. There was just something about the girl. The way she'd looked at him knowingly as he'd poured her drink from the shaker into the ice-cold glass. The fact that she'd ultimately left the drink on the bar, untouched.

Shaking his head, he fell back into the flow of pedestrians on the sidewalk, making a mental note of the yellow hat in case it turned out he did need a bribe. But before he'd gone far, there was a flash of purple and orange to his right, and as he watched, stunned, the redhead hurried past him towards the streetlight on the corner.

Surely it couldn't be her, he told himself. It was too much of a coincidence. But he still found himself tugged along in her wake, ensnared by the very improbability of it. She walked quickly and with purpose, as if she had pressing things to do and not enough time to do them. Aaron had just about to caught up with her and was going to call out to get her attention rather than just tailing her like a creep, but just then, the light changed and she melted into the crowd crossing the street toward the imposing building that housed one of the city's preeminent newspapers, the Independent. Suddenly suspicious, Aaron's steps slowed, and he came to a halt before he reached the intersection, keeping his eyes on the redhead's petite form until she mounted the stairs of the Independent offices and went inside.

There were any number of innocent reasons for her to be heading into that building. She could be visiting someone; she could be placing an ad for a room to let or something similar. But somehow, he knew that it was none of those things.

He knew that she was a reporter.

CHAPTER 2

COLLEEN

*C*olleen pushed the glass door of the Independent building open and stepped into the lobby, inhaling the familiar scent of industrial cleaner and tobacco. No matter how many times she walked through this room—which was daily—it still gave her a thrill. There was the high, arched ceiling; the angular chandeliers that felt so bold and modern; the abstract murals by a famous artist that nobody would admit to not understanding. She even loved the sound of her heels clicking against the marble as she walked. It made her feel sophisticated. Significant.

Stepping onto the elevator, she smiled at Jerry, the attendant, and he punched in her floor. He'd long since ceased asking for her destination, a fact that warmed her down to her toes. It was another sign that she belonged here.

"How are you doing today, Miss O'Cremin?" he said as they ascended.

"Like a dog with two tails, Jerry," she said brightly, and he chuckled.

Soon enough, they reached her floor, and she gave him a jaunty wave as she headed out into the wide corridor leading to the newsroom. The moment she opened the glass door, she was hit by a rush of noise—typewriters clacking, voices shouting into telephones, that sweet clamor of the sausage getting made. She stepped in, letting the door close behind her, and took in the state of the place. It was a long room, taking up the complete footprint of the building and dotted with support columns at regular intervals. Between the columns, desks stood in even rows, each occupied by a reporter and stacked with notepads, forgotten mugs of coffee, dictionaries, and anything else that might come in handy as they churned out the day's news. A haze of cigarette smoke swirled above the flurry of activity, stirred into motion by the breeze coming through the tall windows that ran the length of the space; it may only have been early spring, but the newsroom was typically thick with the heat and aroma of so many active bodies, so any bit of fresh air was welcome.

Like the lobby, the newsroom always filled Colleen with a general sense of pride and satisfaction, but today, as she gazed out over the hubbub, she had a particular objective in mind. And as luck would have it, just then the person she needed appeared, walking out of the office situated just to her right.

"Mr. Whitaker!" she called and began walking in his direction. At the sound of his name, the editor turned, but when he caught sight of Colleen, he scowled.

"Oh," he said around the cigar wedged between his teeth, not breaking stride. "It's you."

Undeterred, Colleen hurried after him. "I was just wondering if you'd given any more thought to that story I told you about."

"What, the thing with the missing adepts?"

"That's the one," she said brightly, giving what she hoped was a disarming smile, but he only snorted.

"My opinion hasn't changed since yesterday, O'Cremin."

"But, sir!" she protested, dodging a trash can. "I really think there's something there. This could be front page stuff, a real scoop. If only you'd-"

"Thompson!" Mr. Whitaker bellowed, stopping so quickly that Colleen almost ran into him. "You heard anything about that Vasilyev interview?"

At a nearby desk, a woman in horn-rimmed glasses looked up from her typewriter, her face a picture of exasperation.

"I told you, Whit, it's a no-go. They're not letting anyone near him until after the debut."

"Well, that's just not acceptable."

Colleen crossed her arms and tried to stifle her impatience. Personally, she was sick to death of hearing about Pavel Vasilyev, but she seemed to be in the minority. Vasilyev—or Pasha, as he was known to his legions of adoring fans—had been in the headlines for weeks thanks to his daring defection from his home country of Ursa to New Avalon. Widely considered the greatest ballet dancer of his— or, some said, any—generation, he had made a thrilling cloak-and-dagger escape from his Ursan minders while on tour in Belleterre with the help of New Avolonian intelligence officers and was now settled into his new life in Ad Astra. There were plenty of aspects to this story that would have captured the public's imagination, but the one that stood out, even in that crowded field, was the fact that Vasilyev was an adept and had agreed to comply with the Embargo as part of his asylum agreement. It was seen as a huge win for the Reason and Progress Coalition, the conservative anti-magic group that had been largely responsible for implementing the Embargo in the first place and continued to expand their power on the national stage. The rumor was that Vasilyev had chosen to make a sacrifice of such magnitude because the indignities imposed by Ursa's notoriously autocratic government were even more oppressive and restrictive, but no one knew for sure. Because apparently, he wasn't giving interviews.

And that was all fine and good, but it didn't have anything to do with Colleen's current pursuit, so she could only stand there as Edith Thompson, the women's page editor, and Mr. Whitaker argued about it.

Thompson threw her hands up. "What do you want me to do, break into his hotel room? Hide in the trunk of his limo? They're keeping him under lock and key."

A glimmer of interest crossed the editor's face. "Yeah? Why?"

"Hells if I know!" the woman said. "They say he needs to 'focus', whatever that means."

"Well, stay on it," Mr. Whitaker said. "I don't want anyone else getting that story before we do, you hear me?"

Thompson rolled her eyes but nodded, and as she went back to typing, Mr. Whitaker started walking again. Colleen was hot on his heels.

"So, as I was saying about this story..."

Mr. Whitaker spun on her.

"O'Cremin, there *is no story!*"

Colleen took a step back, stunned. She was used to the editor's mercurial rants, but that had felt oddly personal.

"Look, kid," he said, his voice softening. "I like you. You're smart, and you do good work. But the truth is..." He ran a hand over his thinning hair. "You've managed to ruffle some feathers around here."

A sick knot of dread settled in Colleen's stomach. "What kind of feathers?"

"It's that workplace safety legislation story you worked on with Mills," he said. "Old man Green apparently got a very terse call from MNC Bradshaw's office about it."

Colleen's eyebrows shot up. She and her mentor, Stewart Mills, had known their article on the unpopular legislation might strike some as controversial, but for representatives of a leading Member of the National Congress and de facto head of the RPC to call the owner of the paper...

"Doesn't that mean we're doing something right, though?" she said. "To attract that kind of attention?"

Mr. Whitaker sighed, giving her a pitying look. "Maybe if we were one of those rabble-rousing pro-union papers run out of somebody's basement. But this is a mainstream publication, O'Cremin. We're here to keep the public informed, not incite a riot."

"A phone call hardly constitutes a riot-" Colleen began, unable to stop herself, but Mr Whitaker held up a hand to silence her.

"Listen," he said. "I've been trying to keep the heat off of you. But if you're not willing to listen to reason, I don't know if I'll be able to keep you on. Everyone's got to pull their own weight around here, and you haven't really delivered anything big since the piece that got Green on my back in the first place."

"I can pull my weight, Mr. Whitaker," she said, ~~truly~~ on the edge of panic now. "I can deliver something big, I swear."

"Yeah?" he said, crossing his arms over his chest. "Like what?"

"Well, I'm not sure just now," she admitted, "but I'm certain I can find something..."

He peered at her over the top of his glasses, then pointed a finger at her.

"You know that the big RPC convention is next week," he said. "We'll need a lot of people there to get enough coverage. Bring me something good before then, and you'll be one of those people. If not, you can go ahead and clean out your desk."

Colleen's whole body went cold, but she nodded. All hope was not lost; it was just sort of fumbling around in the dark for the time being. She stood up straight and did her best to smile.

"Yes, sir," she said. "I won't let you down."

He gave her a dubious look, then headed deeper into the office to go yell at one of the sports writers. Once he was out of sight, Colleen's shoulders sagged, and she trudged over to her tiny, battered desk. She dropped heavily into her chair, letting her eyes fall on the small folding picture frame situated amongst the clutter. One side held a photo of a smiling woman climbing aboard an airship, dressed in the height of fashion for the time, which was now three decades in the past. The woman was Amity Bell, pioneering lady reporter and Colleen's idol. While female journalists were still far from the norm, in Amity's time, they had been practically unheard of. That hadn't stopped her, though. Instead, she had kicked down the door of the newsroom with her stylish strap pumps and settled right in—not that she'd stayed put for long. Her taste for adventure had taken her around the world, from revolutions in Tierra Dorada to the confederation council of the newly sovereign Living Nations. It was during these travels that she disappeared, presumed dead, at the age of twenty-nine—but oh, what a life.

The other side of the frame held a clipping from the Independent. It was Colleen's first real story, a piece for the women's page about philanthropists, mostly wives of businessmen and politicians, establishing a new children's guidance clinic on the city's south side. It was hardly the kind of gripping, front-page reporting she'd dreamed of, but it was good work on an interesting topic (the topic being child guidance—the bored socialites could kick rocks). And unlike the countless mundane beat stories she'd written, it had a byline—Lena Crimm. The name Colleen had chosen for herself, inspired by her hero. It was snappy. Spirited. No-nonsense. It made her feel like something more than plain old Colleen O'Cremin, just one of the droves of working class Ogygian girls who came to the city every year trying to make something of themselves.

Because Colleen was not just going to try. Colleen was going to *do*. If she could only figure out how.

"How's it going, sport?" a familiar voice said, snapping her out of her reverie.

Stewart Mills perched on the edge of her desk, finishing a danish wrapped in wax paper. Stewart was an old timer at the Independent, and for reasons she'd never really understood but was nevertheless grateful for, he'd taken her under his wing when she'd first started working in the newsroom. He was the one that had helped her get the guidance clinic story and then recruited her to help on the worker's safety piece, earning her a second precious byline.

Not that it seemed to be helping her out much now.

Without waiting for an answer to his question, Stewart crumpled the wax paper and tossed it into her trash can. "I saw you talking to Whit. Still fighting with him about that magic user story?"

"It's worse than that," she said and recounted her exchange with Mr. Whitaker.

Stewart let out a low whistle. "That's rough."

"Yeah." Colleen slumped lower in her seat.

Stewart dug a pack of gum out of his pocket and offered it to her; when she refused, he took a piece of his own and popped some in his mouth. As usual, Colleen found this habit charming; he was the only writer she knew besides her who didn't smoke like a chimney. As he chewed, he shot a look at the picture frame.

"OK," he said. "Here's your plan. You're going to think about what your old friend Amity would do. The woman was fearless, but she was also cunning. Instead of running into a situation with her hair on fire, she would think through the best way to turn it to her advantage. She worked strategically. That's what you need to be doing, too. Not going off half-cocked on a whim."

It wasn't what Colleen wanted to hear, but she couldn't argue with his reasoning.

"I guess you're right," she said with a sigh.

Someone called Stewart's name, and he turned to wave at someone over his shoulder, but he didn't leave right away.

"Look," he said. "I have to go work on my union piece. But come by and check in later if you want to, OK?"

She nodded, truly grateful for the offer, and he pushed off her desk and left.

Colleen frowned, nudging her rolling chair back and forth with her foot. Stewart *was* right. She really ought to just put her head down, find some middling story that appealed to businessmen and housewives, then move on to her assignment at the convention. And yet...

She hadn't set out to investigate anything pertaining to magic. Coming across reports of adepts going missing from the charm schools that employed them in her regular perusal of police blotters had been pure happenstance. In truth, she still wasn't entirely sure what her personal stance on magic was. Even before the Embargo had gone into effect, immigrant enclaves around New Avalon, like the neighborhood where she'd grown up, had kept magic behind closed doors, reluctant to attract attention from bigots like the RPC. Most homes had some talisman or other stored discreetly, and many of the elderly folks kept to the old ways from the homeland to some extent, but it was understood that magic was something akin to a family secret. With the Embargo, everyone had gotten even more tight-lipped about it.

So when she'd started infiltrating charm schools, she'd encountered things she'd never seen before—things that were thrilling, wondrous, but also unnerving. They made her feel like everything she understood about the world was suspect. If someone could shape light into solid objects before her very eyes, what else could be out there that she'd previously believed to be impossible? It was part of why she'd left the Hierophant before the entertainment started the night before; once she was satisfied that there'd been no incidents there, she'd had no reason to stay, despite the handsome bartender, and she hadn't been up for the simmering turmoil that came with sitting through the show. Or finishing her drink.

But still. She was onto something big there; she could feel it. And whatever Mr. Whitaker had told her, if she had all her ducks in a row when she brought it to him, if he could just see it—surely it would win him over. Besides, no one deserved to just vanish without anyone worrying about where they'd gone.

So there it was. She would turn the magical disappearances situation to her advantage by sheer force of will.

And to do that, she was going back to the Hierophant. Tonight.

CHAPTER 3

AARON

*T*hat night, Aaron was hard at work behind the bar when he glanced up in time to see the duplicitous redhead strolling into the club, as cool as you please. Outrage swelled in his chest, and he instinctively made a move to intercept her. A group of chatty society types were blocking the exit at the end of the bar, so he dispensed with any sense of formality and simply hoisted himself over it to catch her before she disappeared into the crowd.

"Oh, no," he said when he reached her, taking her by the upper arm and steering her back towards the entrance. "I don't think so."

The redhead sputtered. "I beg your pardon! Get your hands off me!"

Aaron said nothing as he pushed through the heavy door into the bare, utilitarian entry hall. The girl went on berating him, and at the coat check, Victor looked up from his book, brow furrowing. He started to open his mouth, presumably to chide Aaron for manhandling the customers, but Aaron beat him to the punch.

"She's a *journalist*."

Victor snapped his mouth shut and took a wrap from a nearby hanger. He held it out with a frown, and Aaron grabbed it as, without breaking stride, he slid open the bolt on the exterior door and dragged the still-protesting girl out into the night. Once the door clanged shut behind them, he finally released her arm and thrust the wrap at her.

The chill from earlier in the day had returned, so she immediately drew the silky fabric around her shoulders, but then she crossed her arms over her chest and glared at him.

"Is that how you treat all your guests here?"

"When they're shameless, sneaky reporters, absolutely."

She scoffed and rolled her eyes.

"I have just as much right to be here as anyone else."

"Sure you do." He cocked an eyebrow. "Who are you anyway?"

She lifted her chin. "Lena Crimm, *The Independent.*"

"So what's your angle, Lena Crimm? Doing some sort of exposé on the Hierophant?"

She snorted. "Hardly. It's not like this place is a secret. I'm pretty sure I saw a city councilman in there just now."

"So what then?"

She gazed at him, considering. Then a bit of her cockiness subsided, replaced by a businesslike candor.

"Have you heard anything about adepts associated with charm schools here in the city going missing?"

"Missing?"

She nodded and began rattling off names, ticking them off on her fingers as she went.

"Sarah Cohen. Giovanni Ricci. Langston Turner. Imogen Parker. All of them were last seen leaving their shift at a charm school, all have not been heard from since."

Aaron's insides went cold. This was just the kind of thing they all worried about—disappearing into the night with no warning, no recourse, because nobody worried about a missing adept. Except this girl, apparently, and that only begged the question of why.

"They probably got caught up in sweep," he said, gauging her reaction, "and are cooling their heels in a containment facility somewhere."

The girl shook her head, eyes intent. "There are no records of sweeps anywhere close to where they disappeared, and they are not registered as detainees in any local facilities. They just vanished. And that's not a fate for anybody."

Now, that was more than upsetting; it was perplexing. If there was anything the anti-magic establishment liked, it was a paper trail. They were proud of how efficient they were in the pursuit of eradicating the plague of magic. But even more than that, it seemed that this girl was concerned about the situation. Not just as a piece of news, but as something involving people who deserved, if not justice, at least acknowledgment.

But as she stood there gazing at him, he instinctively hardened his heart to her. She was an outsider. She had no magic. She couldn't be trusted—not when there was so much at stake. Aaron would not put his home or his friends at risk, no matter how pretty she was.

"Look, that's terrible, but it doesn't concern anybody here, so you can just shove off and go bother some other people who are just trying to do their jobs."

Her face fell.

"Really? That's it? You're not even a little bit interested in what might be going on?"

"Not even a little," said Aaron. "Now start walking."

She gaped at him for a moment longer, seeming like she might try to argue again. Then she snapped her mouth shut, pulled her wrap more tightly around herself, and turned to make her way down the uneven pavement towards the front of the building. He felt a pang of conscience watching her head off by herself, but he knew cabs made regular circuits of the block at this time of night, on the lookout for customers just like her stumbling out of the club. She'd be alright.

Muttering under his breath, he pushed back into the club, almost believing it.

He was still stewing about the interaction later as he closed out the till. Ebony stepped up to the bar, having finished up her own end-of-evening tasks at the card table. She shifted her bag higher up onto her shoulder as she waited patiently for him to finish counting out a stack of bills and jot down the total on a notepad before speaking.

"I just wanted to let you know I have a stop to make before I go home. So you don't worry."

Aaron felt a familiar stirring of irritation and cocked an eyebrow. "This isn't a stop you could make in broad daylight?"

Ebony let out a huff of exasperation, crossing her arms over her chest. "We're really going to do this *again*? Because it is getting old."

Aaron threw up his hands. "Far be it from to question the wisdom of going off alone to a secluded location in the middle of the night. What could I possibly be thinking?"

Ebony gaped at him. "Do you even hear yourself? You are *at this very moment* standing in a secluded location in the middle of the night. Because you are working. As are they."

She didn't need to specify who "they" were. Aaron knew. This was generally how things worked when she went to visit the group of conjurers she'd met through their boss, Esme. It wasn't that he didn't understand why she felt compelled to spend time with them. He'd seen firsthand what could be accomplished when innate magic like Ebony's—or any adept's—was combined with the study and experimentation characteristic of conjurers. It was astonishing. The factions in New Avalon who hated and feared magic had no idea how lucky they were that adepts and conjurers had historically been unable to get past their internal conflicts, because if they had ever managed to work together, they would have been able to dominate the unmagical in a heartbeat. But that wasn't the point.

According to both Esme and Ignotus, her closest friend and adviser among the New Avalon conjurers, Ebony was one of the few adepts in recent times—or, really, ever—who had pursued something like a partnership with practicing conjurers. Even Esme, who valued Ignotus and his comrades' expertise as consultants, typically stopped short of full collaboration. As such, Ebony's role in the magical community was largely unprecedented, which meant there were no established rules or parameters in place for her — or anyone else, really—to rely on in terms of acceptable conduct. No one knew where the boundaries were. And that terrified Aaron down to his bones.

"You don't even know their names," he pointed out, not for the first time.

"It's for their safety," Ebony said. "And mine, too. You *know* that."

"I don't though," he said, his voice rising. "And neither do you! You are assuming that's enough to keep you safe, but you could be wrong!"

Ebony took a deep breath, pressing her hands together in front of her mouth and closing her eyes; it almost looked like she was praying for strength. After a beat, she opened her eyes and gave him a look of pure steel.

"You are not my boss, and you are not my father." Aaron flinched inwardly at that last jab; they both knew she'd chosen it with intent to wound. "You do not get a say in the ways I spend my time. Now, I don't know how long I will be. It could be late, so if you want coffee in the morning, get up and make it yourself."

And she turned on her heel to go.

"Eb," Aaron called out, hating that she was walking away angry, but she paid him no mind. Reaching the exit, she yanked the door hard enough that it hit the wall as she swept through it. Then it swung closed behind her, and she was gone. Exhaling hard, Aaron gave the cash drawer a comparably savage shove, and it banged shut, jostling the register so that the bell inside gave rang softly. No matter what was going on between the two of them, the deposit couldn't wait.

Still seething, Aaron crossed the dining room and made the short trip down a back hallway to Esme's office. Pushing through the office door, he found Esme herself propped against her desk with her arms crossed. She was deep in conversation with Oliver, sprawled in one of the office's leather club chairs, and Daniel, who sat upright like an actual grownup. She gave Aaron a brief nod of acknowledgment as he entered, but quickly returned her focus to the discussion in progress.

"Do we have any solid confirmation on how many disappearances there have been?" Daniel said as Aaron made his way to the safe in the corner. It took a moment for the question to fully penetrate Aaron's awareness, but once it did, he paused with his hand on the dial. Surely they weren't discussing what he thought they were. *Surely* not.

"No," Esme was saying. "You know how it is—all hearsay from a dozen different sources."

"But there's enough talk to suggest that it's a real cause for concern," Daniel said, not a question.

"Yes," Esme said.

Aaron did his best to tune out what he was hearing, but it was a weak effort at best. Spinning the dial to open the safe was basically muscle memory at this point; it didn't make any real demand on his attention. Still, he tried to focus on placing the deposit neatly within the safe's confines, then took special care to close the door soundly and turn the dial so the contents were secure. It still wasn't enough to drown out Oliver's next question.

"Do we think it's related to the Fairchild business?"

"Hard to say for sure, but it seems likely," Esme said. "We never did find out exactly what was happening up at the sanitarium."

With a sigh, Aaron turned to face the group. "I'm probably going to regret asking this, but what exactly are y'all talking about?"

"I've gotten word from a few other charm school proprietors in town that some of their employees have gone missing," Esme said, and any hope Aaron had of being able to just walk away from the discussion and pretend it never happened evaporated.

"But you don't have any details," he tried anyway, and Esme shook her head.

"Not as such. But concerns are mounting. Rumors of it happening once are suspect. Twice is noteworthy. More than that, and we seem to have a real problem on our hands."

By "we", Aaron knew she meant the city's magical community at large, though that was a nebulous entity. Whatever arguments he'd put forth to Ebony, they all knew that secrecy was part and parcel to being a magic user in the era of the Embargo. The charm school owners in Ad Astra made up a loose network of like-minded colleagues, but by design, none of them were especially close. Connections were dangerous, and no one wanted to become a point of vulnerability for the group as a whole. If none of them had extensive knowledge of what the others were up to, it couldn't be bribed, blackmailed, or—gods forbid—tortured out of them if the authorities came calling. Every charm school in the city had coppers on the payroll, but kickbacks were hardly a foolproof insurance plan, especially for places like the Hierophant, which existed not only as a money-making venture (though it was certainly that) but a safe haven for adepts and their associates.

"So what are you going to do?" he said finally.

Esme turned her palms up in a shrug. "I'm not sure there's much we *can* do besides take steps to increase security around the club—make sure none of you are left alone in vulnerable situations."

Aaron thought of Ebony stalking out the door just minutes before, and his stomach turned. "That's it?"

"Well, what else are we supposed to do?" Oliver burst out, throwing up his hands. "Investigate every case individually? Trek all over the city visiting affected charm schools? That could take days, and there's no guarantee we'd even turn up anything. Unless we happen to stumble upon someone who's already collected and cross referenced that information, I'd say we're at a dead end."

Aaron sighed and dragged a hand down his face. "Actually, I think I might know someone who fits that description."

CHAPTER 4

AARON

*T*he next day found Aaron leaning against a low brick wall outside the Independent offices, waiting to catch a glimpse of Lena Crimm. He'd made a point to approach the building around the time he'd seen her before, then waited around until the hustle and bustle of morning rush hour had subsided to see if she appeared, but the attempt had been fruitless. He thought about walking in and simply asking for her, but considering how their previous interaction had ended, he wasn't sure how well that would go over, and the last thing he needed was for her to make a scene in front of the paper's entire staff. So he'd taken the opportunity to pick up a novel from a nearby book shop and spent the morning reading and drinking coffee at a nearby diner. Now he was back, hoping to catch her on her way to lunch.

At least it was a pleasant day. It was warm enough that he'd taken off his jacket, draping it over the wall next to him. Some pigeons hopped around on the pavement, picking at stray berries and leaves that had been jostled out of the nearby ornamental trees, and he was pretty sure he heard a barrier owl off in the direction of the sprawling downtown park. This was what passed for spring in the city, he thought ruefully—watery sunshine and birds heading north again.

There was nothing wrong with it, per se, but it was a far cry from the turning of the season back in Cumberland, where the trees leading down to the river sang with green and came alive with animals, the returning warmth and rain causing crops to practically burst from the earth. He wondered idly if he would ever see that kind of spring again.

So caught up was he in his musings that he almost missed Miss Crimm as she strode down the steps in front of the Independent building, making her way towards the corner; by the time his brain finally registered what he was seeing, she was already melting into the crowd. Cursing under his breath, he snatched up his jacket and hurried after her.

"Miss Crimm!" he called as he wove between bodies, trying to keep her in his line of sight. "Miss Crimm!"

At first, she didn't seem to hear him, and he worried that she'd cross the street and be lost in the crowd before he caught up, but then he saw her pause and glance over her shoulder. He could tell the moment she caught sight of him, because she rolled her eyes in disgust before turning away. Aaron kept at it, though, and arrived at the corner just behind her. As luck would have it, the light had just changed, sending autos careening past them down the street. He had at least until it turned red, giving pedestrians the crosswalk, to talk to her.

"So it occurred to me that we might have gotten off on the wrong foot last night."

She snorted. "You think?"

"And I was wondering," he went on, "if maybe we could start over."

She turned to him with a look of stupefaction. "Are you serious right now?"

"I'm just saying, I may have been a bit hasty in dismissing your concerns. After all, what you're describing is a serious matter."

She snorted and looked away, clearly indicating that she thought of the conversation. Before Aaron could try again, the light changed, and the crowd surrounding them surged into the intersection. Aaron hurried along with them, doing his best to keep up with her.

"I can see where you may have reservations-" he started as they reached the sidewalk.

"Go away, please."

"But I think we may be able to come to some sort of mutually beneficial arrangement."

She came to an abrupt halt, rounding on him. He pulled up short to keep from running into her, leaving grumbling pedestrians to maneuver around him.

"Listen," she said. "I don't know why you tracked me down, and I don't care. Frankly, it's more than a little creepy. So I'm going to turn around now and be on my way, and you are going to go back to whatever it is you do when you're not standing behind a bar, and we're never going to think about each other again. OK?"

They had reached one of the tiny parks that dotted the city, barely more than a garden with a path down the center providing a shortcut from the thoroughfare where they stood to a cross street, and now she set out along this path without a backward glance. Seeing her go and considering the prospect of returning to the club, only to tell Oliver and Esme (but especially Oliver) that he had failed, he felt a surge of panic. Which is why he called out, "What if I told you that I had information to give you in exchange?"

This was a risky move. He had not actually been cleared to tell her anything, and there was a chance he'd catch hells for offering, but he'd deal with that later. For now, the ploy seemed to be working, as Miss Crimm had stopped walking away. Slowly, she turned to face him.

"What kind of information?" she said, seemingly against her better judgment.

"Well, I can't tell you now," he said. "If I did, what motivation would you have to agree to work with us?"

She raised her eyebrows. "Us?" But Aaron said nothing, leaving the ball in her court.

She worried at her lower lip with her teeth. "How do I know what you have is actually worth anything?"

"You don't," he said. "But I bet you one shiny nickel that it's more explosive than what you have."

She glowered at him. "A whole nickel?"

He took a step forward onto the path, into the full shade of the trees. "It's *very* shiny."

She was quiet for a moment, clearly turning the proposition over in her head. Aaron was beginning to worry that he'd lost her when she finally said, "All right. You're on."

"Oh," Aaron said. "Well, good."

"Good."

"Fine,"

"Fine."

They both went silent.

"Let's shake on it," she said at last and extended her hand, but not, to Aaron's complete horror, before spitting in it. She kept her gaze on him steady, a challenge. He hadn't come this far only to quit now, so swallowing down his revulsion, he took her hand and shook it.

Miss Crimm gave a satisfied not and crossed her arms. "So, where do we go from here?"

"I have a car," Aaron said. "I can take you back to the club to speak with my associates."

Her eyebrows shot up. "What, now?"

"Well, yes," Aaron said, and once more, she started nibbling at her lip. Aaron realized suddenly how that proposal must sound, coming as it did from a strange man. He was about to open his mouth to propose an alternative when she dropped her arms and straightened her shoulders.

"Fine. Let's go." She pointed a finger at him, waving it at his face. "But don't get any big ideas." She used the finger to poke him in the shoulder. "I have a pistol in my handbag."

He stared at her. "Is that true?"

She gave an exaggerated shrug, and he scowled.

"So how do I know you're not going to shoot me as soon as we're alone together?"

"You don't," she said and turned in the direction he had indicated for the auto. Frowning, Aaron scrubbed his hand against his pant leg and followed.

He quickly fell into step next to her, and they walked in silence for a while. Her stride was confident, despite having no real idea where she was going. He suspected that was how she typically navigated the world, and he found that he was a little envious.

"What changed your mind?" she said at length and without preamble.

"Pardon?" Aaron said.

"Last night, you wouldn't give me the time of day. Now, you seem dead set on enlisting my help. So what changed?"

"I got confirmation of your story from someone I trust," he said.

She gave him a look of such outraged affront that he almost laughed. "I don't strike you as credible?"

He realized that as a journalist, that must be a sensitive subject, but she really had no one to blame but herself. "By your own admission, you approached me under false pretenses."

She sniffed dismissively, but she didn't argue. Because she couldn't. They walked on for another block or so before she spoke again.

"If we're being candid, I should probably tell you that Lena Crimm is just my nom de guerre."

Aaron raised his eyebrows. "Oh?"

She nodded. "You can call me Colleen."

"All right then... Colleen." They had almost reached the auto at that point, and Aaron took the keys out of his pocket, twirling them around his finger. "And I'm Aaron. But you already knew that."

"Yes," Colleen said. "I did."

Aaron stepped off the curb to open her door for her. "Isn't this supposed to be where one of us says 'Nice to meet you'?"

Colleen gave him a smile with both actual and metaphorical teeth. "Candid, remember?" And she folded herself into the auto, pulling the door shut before Aaron had a chance to.

He would never have admitted it, but as he rounded the auto to take his own place in the driver's seat, the corner of his mouth quirked up against his better judgment

CHAPTER 5

COLLEEN

The Hierophant looked different in the daylight. At night, the building had the seductive pull of the forbidden. There was a thrill in knowing the secret of the place, that the nondescript building concealed a haven of glamour and ease, something wholly apart from the dreariness of the mundane world. During the day, it was just a warehouse, indistinguishable from the dozens she'd seen every day in her neighborhood growing up.

As they approached, the illusion was further dispelled by Aaron leading her not to the "discreet" entrance she'd used as a customer—ostentatious in its own way, with its metal slot and required password, all in keeping with the charm school experience—but to a truly unassuming door that opened onto the kitchens. Once inside, he took her down a hallway past a small staff dining area and some other rooms devoted to club business, finally pausing before a door labelled "Office". He gave a quick knock, then opened the door without waiting for a response, ushering her through.

They stepped into a tasteful, well-appointed office. The warm color scheme and elegant furniture stood in stark contrast to both the shabby exterior of the building and the lush glamour of the main dining room. But all of that was parenthetical to her primary observation—that the room was packed with people.

Colleen took an involuntary step backward as she took all of them in. When Aaron had proposed meeting his colleagues, she had assumed he meant two or three people and decided it was an acceptable risk. Now, though, she was facing a host of strangers, some of whom were likely very powerful, and there wasn't a soul in the city who knew where she'd gone. If she was honest, it did seem to demonstrate a rather galling lack of good sense on her part.

But even as the rational part of her brain was encouraging her to turn around and walk right back out the door, another braver, hungrier part started berating her. Would Amity Bell be intimidated in a situation like this? No, she would not. The woman had stared down queens and dictators, pirates and freedom fighters. If she could do that, Colleen could handle this. There was a phonograph playing one of her favorite records softly in the corner, for heaven's sake; how dangerous could this situation really be with such a mundane detail?

Taking a deep breath, she straightened her shoulders, pulling a renewed sense of calm around her like armor. She'd had a rough moment, but now she felt ready. Cool, professional, unruffled.

That sense of self-possession was obliterated a moment later when a door at the back of the office swung open, and a young woman strode in.

"Paloma said you wanted to see me," the woman was saying, and to Colleen's eternal mortification, she let out an audible *meep* of surprise. Because the woman was Cecily Dearborn—one of the most notorious figures in the city who had only recently been accused (and cleared) of a brutal magical murder.

Cecily paused when she caught sight of Colleen, cocking her head. "Hey, do I know you?"

"Um, I don't think so?" Colleen stammered. "That is, I-"

"Oh, wait," Cecily said, snapping her fingers. "I remember. You were with Stewart Mills at that farce of a press conference we held for my 'homecoming' after the trouble with Dr. Fairchild."

Colleen's eyes widened in surprise. "Actually, I was, yes."

Cecily nodded. "I remember you had a really nice hat. And you were also the only woman in the crowd. Good for you."

"Thank you," Colleen said, feeling completely off balance, and then unsettled by that. It wasn't that she didn't put effort into being noticed. It was why she'd adopted purple as her signature color, why she was always quick to speak up and put herself in places people didn't necessarily want her. But she did those things to take control of situations, to make sure she was in a position to chart her own course. Going somewhere with the intent to observe only to be observed in turn was a development she had not considered, and she was not at all sure that she liked it. It made her feel ominously exposed.

"Well, now that that's been established," Aaron said, oblivious to her disquiet, "let's get the other introductions out of the way."

He proceeded to do just that, making his way around the room. The man standing closest to Cecily, a stoic, ruggedly handsome type in a vest and flat cap, was Daniel. Though they weren't so much as touching, Colleen thought she detected a connection between him and Cecily, a notion that she filed away for later. Next came Oliver, a debonair smooth-talker with a gold-topped cane, and a pretty, poised middle-aged woman named Esme. Standing next to Esme was a slightly stocky man with a shock of prematurely white hair and wire-framed glasses who was introduced as Leo. Finally, there was the dark-skinned girl Colleen had seen at the card table on her first visit, who bore such a strong resemblance to Aaron that Colleen was embarrassed she hadn't noticed it right away. She was intrigued but not surprised when Aaron identified the girl as his twin sister, Ebony.

"And this," he said finally, gesturing to her, "is Colleen." Her name came out with an uncertain lift at the end, a question—had he chosen correctly, or did she want to be Lena Crimm here? She gave him a quick nod, and he seemed to relax a bit.

"It's very nice to meet you, Colleen," Esme said, and Colleen could tell by the others' respectful deference that this woman was the one in charge. "Thank you for coming, Would you like to have a seat?"

Colleen nodded and settled gingerly into one of the leather club chairs. Aaron sat in the one next to hers, and the others in the room moved to take their own seats, or at least lean against a convenient piece of furniture, settling in for the duration.

"Now," Esme said. "Why don't you start from the beginning?"

So Colleen did. She explained how she had stumbled upon the disappearances but been unable to find any information explaining them, how she had started haunting charm schools to see if there were whispers of similar things happening that hadn't been recorded in official channels. As she spoke, she decided Esme would have made a good journalist. The older woman listened intently, as if there was nothing in the room more important than Colleen, jotting down notes from time to time and asking insightful follow-up questions. When Colleen finished, Esme stared down at the paper on her desk, brow furrowed.

"And you really couldn't identify anything they had in common?" she said. "Not where they lived or worked, not their powers?"

Colleen shook her head, reaching into her handbag. She withdrew a tiny notebook, riffling through the pages. "Like I said, they were from all over the city, all worked for different clubs. As for powers..." She found the page she was looking for and scanned her hasty penmanship. "Cohen is a telekinetic. Ricci can levitate and has some enhanced movement—he was working as an acrobat. Turner can perform any action perfectly after observing it once. And Parker controls fire." She closed the notebook and tucked it back into her purse. "Those are just the ones I've been able to learn the most about. There are others, but I don't have as many details."

Esme and Oliver exchanged a look that seemed to encompass an entire conversation. But Colleen was not quite finished.

She cleared her throat. "Aaron said that you had something to share with me as well."

Oliver made a sound of consternation, his eyebrows shooting up. "Oh, did he?"

Colleen glanced at Aaron and noticed he looked a little sheepish. Ah. He hadn't gotten permission to tell her that. She felt like a fool.

"It's only fair," he said, trying to look nonchalant.

"It's not about fair," Daniel jumped in, his voice gruff. "It's about making sure adepts are safe."

Cecily laid a hand on his arm, and he subsided. Colleen decided she had been right about the two of them.

"Yes, it is," Esme said thoughtfully. She kept her gaze on Colleen steady, then gave a single nod, seeming to make some sort of decision.

"May I speak off the record?"

Colleen had to fight not to roll her eyes. She *hated* talking to sources off the record. But she suspected it was the only way she was going to get any information at all, so she nodded.

"I'm sure you're familiar with the scandal pertaining to Dr. Fairchild," she began.

"Of course," Colleen replied. It had only been the biggest story of the year. Dr. Fairchild, a "harmonic therapist" who claimed he could cure natural magic, had been murdered by an adept using precisely that type of magic—and Cecily had been the primary suspect. In the end it was determined that Cecily had been framed and Dr. Fairchild had been killed by an adept he had double-crossed as part of a plot involving Ad Astra's RPC Member of Congress Thaddeaus Vandermark, but the whole thing had seemed pretty fishy. She shot a quick look at Cecily, whose face remained impassive.

"The first thing you must understand is that the information that was made public regarding that affair was not, strictly speaking, accurate."

Colleen felt hairs stand up on the back of her neck. "Oh? How so?"

"The part about Vandermark and Erasmus Stone conspiring to frame Cecily for Farichild's murder was true," Esme continued. "But that didn't have anything to do with conflict in the RPC—or at least not the way we made it sound."

"We?" Colleen said. Esme nodded, but before she could say more, Oliver jumped in.

"Well, together with Cecily's bonehead brother." Colleen glanced once more at Cecily, to see if she took offense, but the socialite looked much the same as before. "That was a rather unforeseen twist, honestly, but thanks to Herbert's involvement, we were able to jump in and control the story that intrepid word-slingers such as yourself shared with the masses."

"OK," Colleen said slowly, prickling at the not-so-subtle dig at her profession. "So what was the actual story?"

"From what we have been able to gather," Esme said, "Dr. Fairchild had isolated the part of the brain responsible for giving adepts their powers. In essence, unlike the other sham 'therapists', he really had figured out how to control magic."

Colleen gaped. "But... that's..."

"Impossible, unprecedented, paradigm-shifting?" Oliver said, waving a dismissive hand. "We all did the stunned incredulity thing, too. It seems to be true, however."

"That would be huge, though!" Colleen finally managed. "There's no way a discovery like that wouldn't be on every front page in New Avalon—hells, in all of Domamundi. Word would surely have gotten out."

"We suspect word was about to," Daniel said darkly. "And that's why Dr. Fairchild is dead."

Colleen looked at him sharply. "So someone wants it kept under wraps? Who? And why?"

"Thaddeus Vandermark," Esme said. "And it seems he got his wish. After a fashion."

Colleen stared at her, trying to sort all this new information into some sort of order. "Hold on—so Vandermark had Fairchild killed, and then he was killed in return? Was it..." She trailed off, letting her gaze drift around the room.

"No!" Oliver snapped. "We didn't have anything to do with that! Well, not intentionally, anyway."

"Oliver," Daniel said warningly, and Oliver subsided.

"But if Fairchild really made this discovery," Colleen said, "there must be proof. Research or notes or something."

"We've been looking," Esme said. "Cecily got verbal confirmation of the discovery from Vandermark before he died, but we haven't been able to find concrete proof. Apparently, Fairchild was paranoid enough to take the precaution of hiding his work, even if that caution didn't extend to his personal safety."

"OK," Colleen said, pressing her fingers to her temples. She realized she was not responding to this situation in a very Amity Bell fashion, but in fairness, she suspected Amity Bell had never had a conversation quite like this. "Let's say I believe you. Which I'm not sure I do, but let's pretend. What does any of this have to do with me and the missing adepts?"

"As we were investigating Fairchild," Esme said. "We discovered that MNC Turner-Hoff is a primary investor in a sanitarium up the coast called Ocean Serenity. The sanitarium is also connected to an organization called the Center for a Flourishing Humanity, which Fairchild was working for. We believe that members of the RPC were hoping to use Ocean Serenity as a testing ground for 'therapies' based on Fairchild's research."

"So it's a containment center," she said.

"No," said Oliver. "Or at least not an official one. Containment centers mean oversight, red tape, *lots* of paperwork. This place is designed to go unnoticed. If the RPC is responsible for taking these adepts, which seems possible, if not likely, it's probably where they're being stashed."

Colleen frowned. "If you know all this, why haven't you done anything? Told someone?"

"I took a trip up there a few months back," Leo said, perhaps a touch defensively. "Scoped the place out. But then we got distracted by other developments, and with the scrutiny the RPC was under with the whole Fairchild mess, we figured they would lay low for a while, not push their luck. Looks like we were wrong."

"So, what now?" Colleen said, and Oliver shrugged.

"Now someone else needs to go up there and figure out what's going on. Leo and his poor Credenza would be remembered for sure, so it needs to be someone else." Leo shot Oliver an irritated look at this jab, which seemingly had some history between the two of them, but Oliver looked entirely unbothered.

Again, Esme gave Colleen that assessing look. "I don't suppose you'd be willing to do it? As someone with no existing ties to the magical community, you'd be the least likely to be made as a spy."

"I would absolutely be willing," Colleen said. "Though I should probably tell you that some of my work has attracted Eleanor Bradshaw's attention, and not in a good way. That could pose a risk."

"Your nom de guerre may have attracted her attention," Aaron piped up. "But do you think she'd recognize your face?"

"Probably not," Colleen conceded.

"Plus," Oliver said, "even if she would, it's *highly* unlikely she'd be anywhere near the place herself. I think you'd be safely anonymous."

"That's all well and good," said Daniel. "But she can't go alone."

"No," Esme agreed. "Oliver, would you be up for going with her?"

"No!" Colleen blurted, surprising everyone, including herself. She was starting to get her feet back under her, but the idea of taking the journey to this mysterious sanitarium with Oliver was somehow a bridge too far. "It should be Aaron."

Aaron stared at her in open shock, which was fair. They weren't friends. Even calling them acquaintances was glamorizing things. But they had established some kind of connection, however tenuous. And it felt like a lifeline in the midst of these strange new revelations.

Esme was the first to recover. "All right. Aaron, does that work for you?"

With visible effort, Aaron collected himself and nodded. "Um, sure. OK."

Off to the side, Ebony made a dismissive noise, then slipped out the back door. Aaron frowned, but quickly returned his attention to the conversation, drumming his fingers on his knees.

"Daniel, I guess we'll need an auto."

"No problem," Daniel said. "We'll get you taken care of."

Esme smiled, looking again at Aaron and Colleen. "Well, all right then. Tomorrow, the two of you are heading behind enemy lines."

CHAPTER 6

AARON

There was a bit more discussion to work out particulars, and then Aaron drove Colleen back to the Independent offices, a tense, silent ride that didn't bode well for the long journey to come. When he returned to the Hierophant, Cecily had left Esme's office, but Leo, Oliver, and Daniel were still there, sitting in chairs around Esme's desk.

Esme looked up as Aaron walked through the office door. "Everything all right? Get her dropped off at the newspaper?"

Aaron nodded. "Yep. All squared away."

Esme sat back in her chair, eyeing him thoughtfully. "What was your take on that meeting exactly? How would you say it went?"

Aaron dropped into an unoccupied chair next to Daniel. "I'm more concerned with how you'd say it went."

"Well, as I've *already* said," Oliver cut in. "I don't see how we're all that much better off than we were. We already knew adepts were missing, we already knew that was likely connected to the RPC, so what... Now we really, *really* know it? It doesn't seem like she brought much to the conversation."

"Yes, Oliver," Esme said evenly. "You've made your position abundantly clear, but now I'm asking Aaron." Her brow furrowed. "Do you trust her?

"I trust her to go after this story like a bloodhound until she uncovers the truth," Aaron said. "But we'd be naive to assume that her interests would necessarily align with ours after that."

"And I still think you're being generous in giving her that long," Daniel said. "There's literally nothing stopping her from taking what we told her straight to her bosses at the paper, and it's not in our interest for any of that to become public just yet."

"No," Aaron said, surprising even himself. "I don't think she will."

Daniel raised an eyebrow. "Yeah? Why not?"

Aaron thought for a minute, trying to find words for what was essentially a gut instinct. "She's slippery, but I think she abides by some code of her own. If she said it was off the record, she won't do anything with it. At least not until she was some other source to verify the story."

Daniel sank deeper into his seat. "I wish I had your confidence."

"Well, for the time being, this is all hypothetical," Esme said. "And in answer to Oliver's question, what Colleen gave us was specifics. We have names now, powers, clubs. Just because we can't find a connection between them now doesn't mean there isn't one. Maybe some of us can dig into the facts a little deeper while Aaron is gone tomorrow."

Speaking of, Aaron had a hypothetical of his own to clarify. "Once we get up there to the sanitarium," he said, "what are we actually supposed to *do*?"

"Well," said Leo. "Look around. Ask questions. See if anything seems fishy or out of place."

"How much are we really going to be able to find on what amounts to a glorified day trip?"

"Case in point," Oliver muttered, pointing his cane at Leo to indicate the last futile fact-finding trip. Leo scowled.

"I'm not as good as the covert stuff as the rest of y'all," Aaron went on, knowing better than to let Oliver sidetrack him. "And even if I were, I'll have a reporter snooping along after me. She'll see whatever I see, whether we want her to or not."

"Just do what you can," Esme said with her usual implacable—and in this case infuriating—calm. "We can't make a plan until we know what we're dealing with, and we can't figure that out until we have eyes inside. Even something small could prove extraordinarily helpful. Just lock it all away in your brain and brain and bring it back here."

She was right. Aaron knew she was right, and not just because she was Esme and she was always right. Going in blind with delusions of heroic grandeur would be stupid in the extreme. In addition to putting the missing adepts—if there were even there—in greater danger, it would blow any strategic advantage Daniel, Esme, and Oliver were working hard to build against the RPC. it was just that it felt so... flimsy to do what Esme was describing. Drive hours up the coast to a location where all kinds of terrible things could be happening, just to give the place a once-over, then turn right around and come home? If he was going to get involved in this mess, he wanted it to be for something worthwhile.

But he was just the bartender. There were definitely people in their network who were better qualified for these sorts of things, including two who were in the room with him right then.

"All right," he said, then did his best to subtly change the subject. "By the way, did anyone notice where Ebony went?"

Aaron was used to Oliver having uncanny insight into what was on his mind—that came with the territory of being friends with a reader—but it was Esme who gave him a knowing look now. He couldn't tell whether Ebony had confided what was going on between them or if Esme had picked up on it because she was, in her own way, almost as perceptive as her son, but either way, he wasn't sure he liked it. There was no judgment in Esme's look, but somehow her scrutiny prodded him to judge himself.

"She wanted to go look at some new cards at the gaming shop," Oliver said. "Said she'd be back later."

Aaron nodded, picking up on what Oliver hadn't said. For Ebony, the gaming store served the same purpose as the liquor store did for him—it allowed her to immerse herself in familiar materials and colors, easing her mind as she perused the tools of her trade. Which did not exactly paint a rosy picture of her state of mind when she'd left the club.

"Maybe you should take the night off, Aaron," Esme said. "After all, you'll have a long day tomorrow."

"No," Aaron replied, almost too quickly. The idea of sitting in his empty apartment fretting about Ebony and the trip the next day seemed too grim to contemplate. "No, I'll be fine. Truly."

Esme looked unconvinced, but she nodded, so Aaron left, letting Esme and Oliver's voices fade behind him.

He made quick work of his preparations for the evening, then asked Daniel if he could use the car again to go grab his clothes from home; because he'd been out looking for Colleen all day, he hadn't brought his work suit to change into, which he could see now was an oversight. Heading out the back door, he very nearly tripped over Claudia, who was sitting on the back steps, arms around her knees.

With everything that had been going on, Aaron hadn't even noticed it had been a couple of days since he'd seen Claudia. She was a quiet kid, the polar opposite of her older sister Paloma, and he tried to keep an eye on her, make sure she didn't get lost in the shuffle of the bigger personalities around the club. She was dressed in her usual outfit for doing odd jobs around the place—a simple dress with a half-apron tied over it—though she'd thrown a light jacket around her shoulders. And she looked very put out.

Aaron dropped down next to her on the steps, shoving the car keys into his pocket.

"You OK?" he said.

Claudia just shrugged. Aaron mimicked her pose, pulling his knees closer and propping his arms on them.

"Come on," he said, leaning in conspiratorially. "You can tell me."

Claudia shot him a sideways glance, clearly trying to maintain her air of annoyance, but after a second, the corner of her mouth quirked up.

"My sister is infuriating," she said finally, and kicked at a loose splinter with the toe of her shoe.

Paloma was one of Aaron's very favorite people, but even he had to admit she wasn't someone he'd want to cross. And she and Claudia seemed to be butting heads over something more often than not these days.

"What is it this time?" he said, and Claudia scowled.

"She's gone all starry-eyed over the stupid dancer who left Ursa to come here."

Aaron raised his eyebrows. "You mean that Vassilyev guy?"

"Yes," she practically hissed. "Everything lately is 'Pasha this' and 'Pasha that'." She pulled a disgusted face. "As if he isn't a rotten traitor. We all know so many adepts who just want to be left alone to be magical in peace; we're all working so hard for it, even those of us like Daniel and me who don't have powers. And he gave his magic up like... like it was *nothing*."

Aaron was surprised that of all things, this is what she was upset about. As of yet, Claudia had not demonstrated any natural gift for magic, so Vassilyev's defection wasn't a betrayal of her personally. But maybe it made sense. The vast majority of the people who were important to her were adepts, so it did strike pretty close to home for her. And she was at that age where a lot of kids started getting angry about the state of the world, something that he understood more than liked.

"No one really knows why he did it," Aaron said. "Maybe he had a good reason."

Claudia snorted.

"What reason would justify it? He came here so he can, what— make some more money here than he can at home? Have more 'artistic freedom'?" She said the last two words disdainfully, but she still sounded uncannily like her sister. "Paloma doesn't care, because he's handsome and talented and all that, and she tells me to leave her alone because I am being a wet blanket, but I don't want to leave her alone. She shouldn't like him so much."

"I hate to tell you, kiddo," Aaron said. "But you don't get to tell her what she can and can't like."

Claudia scowled again, shooting him a sidelong glance.

"Why are you defending her?"

He shrugged, stretching his legs out in front of him. "We older siblings have to stick together."

Claudia's expression turned dubious. "What do you mean, older sibling? You came out what, five minutes before Ebony? That doesn't count."

"It's eight minutes," Aaron said loftily. "And every single one of them counts." He leaned forward, pointing at his head. "Look at this. I'm already getting gray hairs, and they're all because of her. She's a *menace.*"

Claudia rolled her eyes good-naturedly and bumped him with her shoulder.

"But seriously," he said. "Try to cut Paloma a little slack. There are too many people out there who bear us ill will. We shouldn't be fighting with each other."

Claudia's mouth twisted, but she nodded. "I guess you're right."

"Of course I'm right. I'm the older sibling."

At that Claudia gave him a shove, and he used the momentum to roll off the steps and to his feet, laughing.

"If you see Ebony, will you tell her I went home to change?"

"Maybe," Claudia said. "Or maybe we'll start making younger sibling plans to take our older siblings down a few notches?"

Aaron gave her a wounded look, pressing a hand to his chest, and Claudia laughed.

"I should probably get back to work," she said, getting to her feet. "Thanks, Aaron."

"You're welcome, kiddo," he said as he watched her head up the stairs and back inside.

If only he could make things right with his own sister so easily.

CHAPTER 7

COLLEEN

When Colleen got back to the Independent offices, she was a little worried she'd get in trouble, but it seemed like nobody had really even noticed she was gone. She wasn't sure if this was a good or a bad thing.

As she made her way to her desk, she saw that Mr. Whitaker was talking with Edith Thompson again. While she'd sought him out earlier in the day, now she just wanted to slip past unnoticed. She still overheard part of their conversation as she passed, though.

"Vasilyev still isn't talking," Thompson was saying.

Mr. Whitaker harumphed.

"What is he, a mime?"

Edith gave him a flat look, "Hilarious. The people at the ballet keep saying he'll make his first 'public' appearance at a reception on the ballet's opening night, but then they won't give anybody credentials to get in."

Mr. Whitaker glowered at her. "Since when do we wait on credentials? We don't ask permission to cover the news; we just put ourselves where the story is."

Edith snorted. "Good luck. That place is going to be locked up tight as a drum."

"What place? Where is this reception?"

"Oh, you know—that monstrosity over in Hartley Center."

Hartley Center was still a fairly new addition to the city, having only opened a couple of years earlier. The brainchild of industrialist Benjamin Hartley, it was a sprawling complex of shops, restaurants, offices, luxury apartments, even a prestigious private school and a park, complete with band hall and petting zoo. It had been conceived as a tribute to "the spirit of Ad Astra," which seemed to boil down to extravagant wealth and rampant self-regard, and none of the buildings that had been erected had been more controversial than the Ad Astra Performance Hall. A massive, modern hulk of a building, it was home to not only the Ad Astra Ballet but also the opera and the symphony, and besides the theater space, it boasted an array of cafes, cocktail lounges, smoking rooms, and other luxurious spaces, topped by a ballroom with floor to ceiling windows that gave patrons dazzling views of the city. In theory, the performance hall was meant to enrich the lives of all Ad Astrans, it reality, it was the domain of the city's elite, and Edith had the right of it in thinking that the muckety-mucks wouldn't want any reporters infiltrating the exclusive reception and getting their inky fingerprints all over the pristine white marble. Especially if Eleanor Bradshaw, honorary co-chair of the city's arts council would be in attendance.

Bradshaw, who was seemingly connected to the very story Colleen had been investigating.

It was rather uncanny, how things were falling into place. She'd uncovered the lead on the adepts while digging through a police blotter, something she did sometimes on her lunch breaks or even her days off. It was tedious work with no guarantee of any kind of return, but she lived in hope that she'd uncover something juicy that other reporters might have overlooked. It was better than staking out the morgue, a tactic many of her colleagues relied upon. She always prided herself on the fact that she wasn't that desperate. Yet.

In this particular instance, she had been perusing the blotter at a station near the Independent offices when she came across a report that said a library employee at a local branch had gone missing after closing time the week before. It caught her eye because she had noticed a similar report at a different precinct on one of her recent visits. The first one had seemed oddly specific in addition to just being generally odd—one didn't typically expect the library to be the scene of nefarious wrongdoing. But two... two was suspicious. Two had promise. She jotted down the details and headed over the front desk. It was quiet for the moment, so she caught the eye of one of the clerks she'd gotten friendly with.

"Hey, Joe," she said. "You know anything about this report I found about an employee going missing from the 14th Street library a few days ago?"

Joe, a tall, gangly guy only a year or two older than Colleen, had flushed a little and hurried over to her. "Hey, keep your voice down, huh?"

Colleen felt a thrill of triumph in her chest. She'd *known* there was something to this. "Why? What's the story?"

Joe had swallowed, Adam's apple bobbing, and glanced around for bystanders before leaning in closer to her. "Nothing happened at the library. That's just a code some of the boys use for the books."

Colleen leaned in, too. "A code? For what?"

Joe bit his lip. "This is off the record, right?"

Colleen sighed. Gods, but she despised going off the record. Still, she made a twirling motion with her finger, indicating that he should keep talking.

"It's for whenever something goes down at a charm school," he said, barely above a whisper now. "Putting it down like that in a report gives the officer cover, but also makes them look busy, which keeps the captain off their backs."

"Why would anyone at a charm school go to the police for a crime?" Colleen said. "I'd think they'd want to keep as low a profile as possible."

"I'm just the messenger," Joe said, taking a step back and holding up his hands. He was clearly still uncomfortable with the conversation, however susceptible he usually was to Colleen's charms. "If you want to know what those magic folks are thinking, you'll have to ask them. But I'd really stay away from it, if I were you. One working stiff to another."

Colleen had, of course, disregarded that advice. She'd gone back to the precinct where she'd found the first library report, then visited several more, compiling a list of disappearances, then she'd set about finding the locations of charm schools in the designated neighborhoods. It hadn't been all that difficult; they really were open secrets once you put some effort into looking. Her receptions at the different establishments had been mixed, but she'd picked up a few useful tidbits. That pretty much every charm school had coppers on the take, and the employees all knew which officers were, if not safe, at least reliable when it came to taking a bribe. That they never liked going that route, but when the stakes were high enough, they were willing to take the risk. That all the incidents had followed the same pattern: the victim in question was last seen leaving their place of employment at closing and never heard from again. Was someone staking out charm schools? Who would do such a thing? And why?

Now, possibly, she had her answer. And she needed time to pursue it.

When she reached her desk, she shuffled through the piles of paper to gather her notes on the disappearances. She had more at home, and she really wanted to put them all together and get everything straight in her mind for the next day. These would serve to get her through until quitting time, though.

All that remained was figuring out how to keep herself from getting in trouble when she didn't show up to work the next day. Based on how Mr. Whitaker had reacted—or, more accurately, not reacted—to her absence that afternoon, it might not be an issue, but better safe than sorry.

Just then, Stewart came in from she could only guess where and took a seat at his desk. In a fit of inspiration, she jumped up and hurried over to him.

"Stew, I need a favor."

He looked up at her, brows raised. He'd told her that he hated it when she called him Stew, but she suspected that he secretly found it endearing. That would be helpful in this instance.

"A favor?" he said. "And what might that be."

"I need you to cover for me tomorrow if Mr. Whitaker comes looking for me."

"And where exactly will you be that needs covering?"

"Following a lead," she said demurely, but he wasn't fooled.

"You're going to be pursuing that adepts story, aren't you?" he said, sitting back in his chair with a sigh. "The one that he explicitly told you to drop."

"I'm on the cusp of something big here," she said, wishing she could share some of the details she'd learned with him, but not daring to just yet. "So close, I can taste it. I just need a little more time."

He frowned. "This is a bad idea, kid. You're going to push Whit to the edge of his patience. Why can't you just drop it?"

Colleen scowled. "You're the one who told me I should think strategically. So that's what I'm doing."

He returned her look. "This isn't what I meant, and you know it." His face softened. "Whit can be an ass, but he knows what he's doing. There's not an editor in the city that would assign a story like that. Not with public opinion being what it is."

The two faced each other in silence for a beat before Colleen sat down in one of the chairs and moved closer to Stewart, putting them eye to eye. "Stew, this isn't just about missing adepts. It's bigger than that. We could blow something wide open here."

He gave her a searching look. "You know something you're not telling me, don't you?"

"I might," she said, keeping her gaze steady. "If everything plays out the way I think it's going to, I'll tell you all about it." Stewart still looked dubious, but after a moment, he sighed.

"Fine. I'll try to keep him off your scent for as long as I can."

Colleen let out a squeal of delight and leaned over to kiss Stewart on the cheek. He frowned and made a show of pulling out his handkerchief and scrubbing at the lipstick she'd left behind. "Hey, now—you're going to get me in trouble with the missus."

Colleen smirked. "You don't have a missus."

"Yeah, well..." He tucked the handkerchief back into his pocket, his face turning serious again. "Just... be careful, OK?"

"I will," she said. "I promise."

CHAPTER 8

AARON

*B*right and early the next morning, Aaron pulled an auto up to the curb outside the Independent offices. Rush hour was not yet in full swing, so it was easy to pick out Colleen waiting in front of the building. She was hatless today, her red hair aflame in the sunshine, but even from a distance he could tell that she looked more understated than usual. She had forgone her customary purple for a drop-waisted navy dress with a demure white collar and matching trim on the short sleeves. The only note of embellishment was the row of gold and pearl buttons running down the front. Even her shoes and handbag seemed to have been chosen for their unfettered ordinariness.

She had begun making her way over to the auto as soon as she had spotted him, but a driver idling behind him had already honked by the time she opened the door and got in. As soon as he was sure the door was closed securely, Aaron pulled out into traffic, earning a squeak of protest from Colleen, who hadn't fully settled into her seat.

"Where's the fire?" she grumbled as she shifted to a more comfortable position.

"I *was* blocking traffic, you know," Aaron said, checking the rearview mirror to change lanes. "Why was I picking you up there again, rather than, I don't know, wherever it is that you live?"

"The landlady at my rooming house is a horrible snoop," Colleen said. "If she'd seen me getting into an auto with a strange man, I'd never hear the end of it." She took a compact out of her handbag, checked her lipstick—as with her clothing, it was a more subdued shade than he'd seen her wear before—and, sighing, snapped the compact closed and returned it to her purse.

"Are you sure you know where we're going?" she said, and Aaron had to fight down a swell of annoyance.

"Yes," he said. "I went over the route with Leo before I left." He shot her a sideways glance. "This isn't the first time I've done something like this, you know."

This was perhaps an exaggeration, considering his previous involvement in covert operations had largely consisted of sitting in the back seat of a parked auto with a bird call in his hand, but it was the principle of the thing. For her part, Colleen just tutted skeptically and looked out the window as the streets slid by.

It was going to be a long day.

As they drove out past the vestiges of the city and the landscape became more rural, Aaron was surprised by the emotions that swelled up inside him. Once he'd arrived in Ad Astra, he'd never really felt the need to leave its confines. The rhythms of the streets and blocky silhouettes of buildings had become the things that felt like home to him. Now, as he returned to the domain of fresh air and fluffy clouds, trees and grass and wide open sky, he felt memories closing in around him—some good, others decidedly less so.

He was so wrapped up in his musings that at first, he didn't notice that Colleen had likewise turned contemplative. It was only when a train whistle sounded off in the distance that he realized how profound the silence had become. He began watching her from the corner of his eye, taking note of how she gazed out the windshield pensively, seeming to take in every detail with those keen journalist eyes.

"Is this your first trip up this way, too?"

"No," she said, eyes still straight ahead. "What I said about being from up north was true."

Something about the cavalier way she said it grated on Aaron, and his hands tightened on the wheel.

"Ah," he said. "So it was just everything else that was lies."

She did turn to him then, scowling.

"I didn't lie about everything."

"Oh, no?"

"No."

"Are you in secretarial school?"

She shifted, looking both contrite and annoyed. "I mean-"

"Do you own a cat?"

"Maybe not *technically*," she hedged. "It's more of a roommate situation." If roommates only showed up every three or four days and did their best to drink all her milk.

"Well then, *technically*, those are lies," Aaron said.

Colleen crossed her arms. "I was undercover. It comes with the territory."

"And why did you feel the need to go undercover exactly?"

She raised her eyebrows. "You found out I was a reporter and bodily removed me from your club. Why wouldn't I go undercover?"

"So it wasn't because you wanted to make sure you had an easy out? Because you thought being around magic users was scary and dangerous?"

She blinked at him. "No. Why would you say that?"

"I didn't say that—you did. When you asked me what it was like working at the club."

Colleen rolled her eyes. "Oh, come on—you know that was about risking arrest, not the magic itself."

"Oh, yeah?"

"Yes," she said. "I don't have any problem with magic users, as long as they don't have a problem with me."

A look of bitter understanding crossed Aaron's face. "Oh, so you're one of those types."

She bristled. "One of what types?"

"You know—the enlightened ones who never have a bad word to say about adepts, until they are confronted with magic personally, and it becomes a matter of public safety or common decency or whatever makes them feel better about their fear and disgust."

"I'm not disgusted by you," she said. "And I'm not afraid of you either."

"Oh, no?"

"No."

"Is that why you didn't actually drink any of your gin fizz the other night?"

He could tell he'd caught her off guard. She opened her mouth, then closed it again and turned to look out the window.

"I just... don't like the idea of someone having that kind of power over me," she said finally.

Aaron arched an eyebrow. "What kind of power?"

Her gaze snapped back to him. "You know—taking away my free will. Making me feel things that aren't really my feelings."

His hands tightened on the wheel. "That's not how it works."

"Isn't it?"

"No. Everyone who buys a drink from me knows what they're getting into. I'm not forcing them to do anything."

"And that makes it OK to use your power to manipulate them?"

"Yes, as a matter of fact."

She let out a dumbfounded laugh. "Seriously? That's how you justify it to yourself?"

He scowled. "Where is this self-righteousness coming from? Aren't you the one who decided to become some kind of champion for these adepts that went missing from charm schools? How can you claim to be on their side and then accuse me of being some sort of evil puppet master?"

She dropped her eyes to her lap, smoothing her skirt. "That's different."

"Yeah? How?"

"It... just is."

Aaron snorted. "Because you stand to gain something. That's the difference."

"You're gaining something, too," she muttered, but Aaron suspected it even sounded weak to her own ears. They drove on in silence for a long time.

The sun was high in the sky when they reached the turnoff Leo had given him earlier that morning. Trees enveloped them almost as soon as they left the highway, the leafy canopy casting diffuse shadows over them as they drove. The first sign of the sanitarium was an imposing wrought-iron fence that began long before any buildings came into view. Eventually, the trees thinned, and Aaron was able to make out a stately, many-gabled structure of at least three stories. It was painted a soothing blue-gray with white trim, presumably in keeping with the nautical theme implied by the name, and the uppermost turret was crowned with a pole bearing the New Avalon flag, which snapped crisply in the salt breeze coming up off the beach. As they got closer, smaller buildings appeared, painted in the same color scheme as the main building; some seemed to be various types of functional outbuildings, but others were tidy little cottages, with small gardens and net curtains in the windows. It made for a quaint scene, but Aaron didn't see people anywhere, and that absence gave him a sense of foreboding.

They finally reached the entrance, where a wooden sign proclaiming "Ocean Serenity—Where All Humanity May Flourish" in elaborate script was flanked by shrubs. The gates had been thrown wide, and Aaron turned carefully into the drive that arced up towards the main building. He parked in what he assumed was the designated area, though it was hard to tell since there were no other autos in sight, heightening the feeling of isolation. As they got out of the car, he started to wonder if they had made a mistake by deciding to come here.

Colleen, however, seemed to have no such qualms. She and stood staring up at the building, with her head to the side, taking its measure. After a moment, she squared her shoulders and smoothed her already immaculate hair.

"Right," she said, her voice taking on a note of absolute confidence. "Just follow my lead."

She may have been speaking figuratively, but she didn't give him much choice in complying literally as well, walking briskly to the front steps without a backward glance. Aaron hurried after her, mounting the steps and crossing the wide porch to reach the door. The porch was clearly meant to instill a sense of comfort to those arriving at the sanatorium. Wooden rockers had been arranged at intervals along the porch's length, along with sets of white wicker tables and chairs; each table sported a bud vase filled with wildflowers, and in the chair closest to the door, a cat was curled into a ball, napping. Aaron caught up to Colleen as she paused in front of the door, scanning it and the nearby wall for a knocker or bell; neither were in evidence. She shot him a quick glance, and at his shrug, reached for the knob, which turned easily in her hand.

The picturesque quality of the porch only intensified once they stepped inside. The room was light and airy, filled with comfortable furniture upholstered in calm pastels. A stone fireplace took up much of one wall, empty now with the warm weather, with a pleasant if bland painting of sailboats hanging above it. Framed photos—of staff perhaps, or past patients?—were arranged artfully on the mantle, while a table nearby displayed the day's newspapers from Merrimack and Ad Astra. The far wall featured a built-in welcome desk, with graceful arches on each side that formed niches filled with plants and little painted screens. There wasn't anything *wrong* with the place, per se, but something it struck Aaron as contrived. Like someone trying too hard to make a good impression.

He couldn't tell if Colleen shared his opinion, or if she had taken time to form an opinion at all, because she had walked purposefully over to the reception desk and given the service bell a sound whack. After a moment, a petite middle-aged woman with a pinched face came out to the desk.

"Can I help you?" she said, in a tone that suggested she was really hoping they'd say no.

"Well, I sure do hope so," Colleen said brightly—and in a spot-on

Cumberland accent. Aaron had to force himself not to do a double take. "My name is Veronica Keith, and this here is my husband, Logan." She twined her arm through Aaron's, tugging him close. "We've heard some wonderful things about your establishment here and were hoping to get some information."

The woman gave the two of them an assessing look. "And what is the nature of your interest? Would it be one of you taking up residence here?"

"Oh, no!" Colleen said, waving the notion aside with her free hand. "We're looking for somewhere that might be able to help my brother Joseph, you see. He's, you know, an *adept*." She leaned forward and whispered the final word, though they were the only people in the lobby.

A spark of interest kindled in the woman's eye. "I see. What exactly are the particulars of his, erm, affliction?"

"Well, sometimes, he makes things move just by, you know"—she wiggled her fingers meaningfully—"*thinking* about it. Especially when he gets upset, which seems to happen quite a lot at family gatherings. He positively wrecked our last Independence Day celebration—ham and potato salad all over the place, isn't that right, hon?"

Aaron cleared his throat. "It certainly is, sugarpuss." Behind the counter, Colleen dug her heel into his toes, and, suppressing a hiss of pain, he shook her off. The woman didn't seem to notice anything amiss, however; she was too intent on Colleen's description.

"Well, it sounds like he might be a good candidate for treatment here at Ocean Serenity," she said, her voice notably warmer than before. She reached into the desk and pulled out a pen and a clipboard bearing a stack of typed forms. "If you could just give us some information, I can have one of our representatives reach out to you to discuss your situation."

Colleen's face fell, her lips twisting into a pout. "Oh, but we were really hoping to get a feel for the place today. You know, find out a little about the methods of treatment, maybe take a look around..."

The woman frowned. "I'm sorry, but that is not typically something we offer on such short notice. Our doctors are very busy, you know, and the privacy and comfort of our clients are paramount-"

"Oh, but it wouldn't take long," Colleen said, her voice taking on a plaintive note. "Just a few questions. After all, we've come so far."

The woman looked both annoyed and uncertain. Rather than addressing her again, however, Colleen turned to Aaron. "Maybe you were right, sweetie. That place down the coast *was* awfully nice. So much closer to home, and they were so welcoming, you know with the coffee and those little cakes I liked so much." She sighed happily.

The woman set her clipboard aside, frown deepening. "You've visited other sanatoriums?"

"Oh, yes," Aaron said, just because he felt he should say something as part of this charade. "My wife is very concerned with her brother's welfare, so she's done her homework. She's a busy little bee." He gazed down at Colleen with what he hoped was convincing fondness. In turn, she beamed back up at him, then tilted her head in thought.

"And those doctors were so patient, explaining everything to us like that. Maybe we should just head back down there."

The woman stood. "You know, I think we might be able to work something out. If you'll just wait here a moment, I'll go consult our director." And with that she strode through a door in the wall behind her.

After a moment of silence, Aaron murmured. "What place down the coast?"

"I don't know," Colleen said. "I mean, there's got to be one down there somewhere."

Aaron struggled to keep his face placid, conscious that the woman could return at any time. "These people talk, you know. They're going to realize you're lying."

"Maybe," Colleen said. "But hopefully not until we've got what we came for and are on our way back to Ad Astra."

Aaron let out a long breath. "And if they catch on before that?"

Colleen shrugged. "It's a calculated risk."

Aaron opened his mouth to retort, but just then, the door opened, and the woman returned, accompanied by a tall man in a snappy blue suit. Aaron wasn't much of one for sports, but the man instantly put him in mind of a linebacker, with his barrel chest and broad shoulders; he also had the vigorous, tanned look of someone who spent a lot of time outside. His wavy blonde hair had been slicked back with pomade, and he had one of the narrow mustaches currently in fashion. As he approached, Aaron could also see an RPC pin attached to his lapel.

"This is our hospital administrator, Dr. Hayward," the woman said, beaming at him. "As it happens, he has a bit of room in his schedule today, so he can answer some of your questions."

"Oh, that's wonderful," Colleen gushed. "Thank you so much, doctor."

"It's my pleasure," Dr. Hayward said, extending a hand. "And I'm sorry, Mildred didn't catch your names."

"Well, I'm Veronica, and this is Logan," Colleen said as they each shook his hand in turn. "And we're here on behalf of-"

"Your brother," Dr. Hayward cut in. "If I'm not mistaken."

"Yes, that's right," Colleen said, still perky, but looking a little taken aback by the doctor's intensity. If he noticed, he didn't comment, instead motioning for them to follow him.

"Please come on back to my office," he said. "We can talk there."

Dr. Hayward led them down a narrow hall and opened a door with his name on it. The office was by no means opulent, but the decor did represent a departure from the folksy charm of the lobby. The wallpaper was patterned with a soothing composition of greens and blues that mimicked ocean waves, and a rug on the floor featured similar colors. The furniture seemed to be predominantly made of oak, less ostentatious than mahogany or teak, but solid and well made. One wall was given over to bookshelves, while another boasted a large window that had been thrown open to let in the spring air; lace curtains swayed gently in the breeze.

"Please, make yourselves comfortable," Dr. Hayward said as he rounded the desk to sit in the plush leather chair behind it. Aaron and Colleen each took one of the more modest seats intended for visitors.

"Mildred didn't mention if she'd offered you any refreshments. Can I get you some tea or coffee?"

"That's so kind of you," Colleen enthused, crossing her legs demurely. "But I don't think it's necessary. We stopped to eat on the drive, didn't we dear?" Again, she looked at Aaron adoringly, and he nodded, trying to look sufficiently smitten.

"Fine, fine," Dr. Hayward said, leaning back in his chair and tenting his fingers. "You certainly picked a beautiful day for it; you will get to see our facility at its best. And where did you say you drove up from again?"

Aaron had to admire the smoothness of the question, because they hadn't said, and he was certain the doctor knew that. Colleen had to be aware of it, too, because she blithely said, "Oh, you know, down the coast some, not too far from the Cumberland border. This is actually day two of our trip. Last night we stayed at just the cutest little inn, didn't we, sweetie?"

Aaron nodded again, noting how neatly she'd accounted for their accents while also establishing a vague but credible back story. Truly, watching these two jockey for advantage was like sitting courtside at a tennis match.

"And what was it that brought you so far afield?" Dr. Hayward said.

"Well, your reputation precedes you," Colleen said in a tone of such blatant flattery, Aaron had to fight back a snort.

"I'm happy to hear it," Dr. Hayward replied, and Aaron couldn't read his expression. He didn't have long to think about it, though, because the doctor sat forward and opened a desk drawer, withdrawing a pair of leather-bound folios. He handed one to Colleen and the other to Aaron, who opened his to find a page printed with the sanitarium's name, along with the motto from the sign out front.

"Those documents contain all the pertinent details regarding our work here," he said, and Aaron could tell he'd slipped into a rehearsed sales pitch. "You'll find that our treatment programs are based on the most up-to-date scientific research related not only to medical interventions, but also diet, exercise, and moral and intellectual pursuits. We offer a broad range of services. Our patients come here seeking relief for a variety of respiratory ailments, as well as maladies of various internal organs and the skin, and the vast majority see improvement in very short order. Much of this salutary effect is attributable to the riches of the natural environment, from the fresh sea air to the healing waters of the local mineral springs. Our facilities, meanwhile, provide all of the best comforts and amenities, from steam-heated rooms to improving lectures to therapeutic massage. Our mantra here is 'Health by Right Living.'"

"Very impressive," Colleen said, flipping the pages eagerly. "But of course, we're especially interested in the more specialized regimen." She closed the folio and looked up at Dr. Hayward. "I've heard such wonderful things about this Partners in Progress initiative sponsored by the RPC. Can you tell us a bit about how you're incorporating that into your mission?"

Dr. Hayward smiled tightly, and Aaron got the feeling that he was parsing his words carefully. "I should stress that our work on that program is still in the nascent stage, but we do have high hopes for it. We have a slate of successfully rehabilitated adepts in place to serve as mentors to our patients who are enrolled in the program." Aaron had to fight to keep his hands from curling into fists at the word "rehabilitated", but he succeeded in maintaining his composure. "We only have one such patient on the grounds at the moment, but she has been working with her mentor twice a week, and we have seen some real improvement in her mental well-being and ability to sublimate her magical urges. I'm sure she would be happy to speak to you to give you her own perspective." He paused, presumably for dramatic effect. "I think she may have some particular insight into your brother's struggles."

"Yes, I think I would like that very much," Colleen practically purred, giving the doctor another beguiling smile.

"Wonderful," Dr. Hayward said, getting to his feet. "Shall we take a stroll around the grounds?"

He led them out onto the wide lawn, which was almost laughably idyllic. In the time they'd been in the building, patients had begun coming out for fresh air and recreation. Some sat on the front porches of nearby cottages, in wheelchairs or rockers like the ones in front of the main building. Meanwhile, a sanitarium employee was leading a group in a round of archery, the patients taking wobbly aim at paper targets that had been attached to hay bales. As they walked. Dr. Hayward held forth on the landscape, detailing the history of the cliffs in the distance and the native flora that dotted the campus. Aaron listened with half an ear, devoting the bulk of his attention to the layout of the premises. Aside from the main fence, most buildings were encircled by a smaller one, each of them largely concealed by landscaping. Every so often, he thought he caught the sound of dogs barking on the breeze—big ones, like some kind of shepherd. Then, as they made a turn back towards the main building, he caught a glimpse of what looked like a guard tower tucked back into the trees. He didn't say anything, but he squeezed Colleen's arm where it was tucked into his, and she glanced at him, he tipped his chin ever so slightly in its direction. She followed his gaze and, catching sight of the tower, gave a tiny nod before turning an attentive face back towards Dr. Hayward.

It was minutes later, when Dr. Hayward paused in his monologue, that she finally said, "I notice you haven't said much about security, doctor. What measures have you taken to keep the patients here safe?"

Dr. Hayward seemed caught off guard by her question, but he recovered quickly enough. "We have, of course, taken steps to address anything that would threaten the atmosphere of rest and relaxation we've established. Our facilities boast the latest innovations for protection from fire and extreme weather. As you saw when you came in, we have protocols in place to ensure no one with any kind of malicious intent is able to access the patients. I think you'll find that your brother would be quite safe with us."

Colleen's placid expression took on a slight hint of distress. "Let me be frank, doctor. There have been occasions in the past where Joseph was… resistant to our interventions, even though they were for his own good. I appreciate the lengths you've gone to to keep bad actors out, but what about to keep your patients *in*?"

"Ah," said Dr. Hayward, his own face taking on a look of sympathetic understanding. "I see. We do sometimes run into such difficulties with patients. Often these recalcitrant attitudes can be addressed through psychoanalysis. In more extreme cases, medications may be utilized to ease strain on the nervous system. As a last resort, we do have orderlies on duty throughout the day, as well as discreet security personnel in place at night."

As he looked towards the main building, Colleen shot Aaron a dark glance, and he pressed her arm in acknowledgment. "Discreet security personnel" covered a lot of ground, but it seemed noteworthy that he had not explicitly addressed the tower.

Dr. Hayward seemed to be looking for something in particular ahead of them, and when he found it, he clapped his hands in front him. "But you've been listening to me prattle on long enough. You'll really be able to get the best sense of what we can offer your brother by talking to our other recovering adept. Please let me introduce you."

He led them up a set of stairs to a section of the main building that they hadn't yet visited. It was a sunroom that ran the length of the building's rear, connecting to the porch at either end. However, unlike the porch, which was open to the elements, the sunroom was screened to keep out bugs and bad weather, with ceiling fans spinning lazily at intervals along the ceiling. The sunroom boasted more of the white wicker tables and chairs where various patients were seated, engaged in sedate activities like reading or playing cards. The doctor led them to a far corner where a woman in a broad-brimmed hat sat working on a jigsaw puzzle. She did not look up as they approached, leading the doctor to clear his throat gently to get her attention.

"Mrs. Paulson, you have some visitors."

CHAPTER 9

COLLEEN

*C*olleen's concerned sister act almost slipped as she took the woman in. Based on Dr. Hayward's description, she'd been expecting someone her own age or possibly younger. This woman was in her 60s at the very least. Soft grey curls peeked out from beneath the brim of her hat, looking oddly of a piece with the neat but faded floral day dress she wore. Her face was pale and lined, and she gazed up at them with vague, watery blue eyes.

"Oh, but I wasn't expecting visitors today." She cocked her head but maintained an air of pleasant haziness. "I'm sorry, but I don't recall making your acquaintance. Have we met before?"

"No, Mrs. Paulson," Dr. Hayward cut in gently before Colleen or Aaron could answer. "These nice people are here to learn about the services offered by our institution. I thought they might like to hear directly from someone who has benefitted from treatment."

Mrs. Paulson gave a drowsy smile. "Oh, but of course. Would you like to sit down?" With swift, silent deference, Dr. Hayward pulled one of the other chairs at the table for Colleen, gesturing to Aaron to take a third. For his own part, Dr. Hayward hovered at Mrs. Paulson's shoulder, the picture of an attentive caregiver.

"The doctor has been remiss in making proper introductions, I'm afraid." She cast a fond look of reproof over her shoulder, and Dr. Hayward looked appropriately contrite. "My name is Mrs. Abigail Paulson. Whom do I have the pleasure of addressing?"

"My name is Veronica, ma'am," Colleen said. "Veronica Keith, and this is my husband, Logan." A bit of her disquiet must have shown through despite her best efforts, because Aaron took her hand under the table. It was more comforting than she might have guessed.

"Now," Mrs. Paulson said. "Which of you is thinking of joining us here by the sea?"

"Oh, not us," Colleen said. "It's my brother Joseph."

Mrs. Paulson nodded in understanding. "Oh, yes. It *is* hard on families, the magic."

Colleen felt her face flush. "Oh, but I didn't mean-"

"Please don't fret, dear," Mrs. Paulson said, waving away her concern. "It is only the truth. When my son and daughter were young, I used my power frequently. Not for anything big mind you—just hurrying chores along, sometimes doing something to amuse the children, like making their toys dance in the air." She smiled sadly at the memory. "But the time for that sort of thing has passed. There's nothing to be done but to comply with the Embargo. And yet, sometimes, that's so hard."

Mrs. Paulson's eyes welled with tears. Dr. Hayward laid a comforting hand on her shoulder, and she seemed to draw strength from it, lifting her chin.

"It upset my children so when I slipped and used my powers. They're not magical themselves, thank the Creator, but it means they don't understand. We used to have such rows about it. But then we met Dr. Hayward." She glanced up at him, smiling. "He, and everyone here, knows what it is we face, and they do not judge us. Franny, my mentor, drives up from Merrimack to see me twice a week, and she helps me master the urges that still plague me from time to time. Being here is such a relief. I don't think I have ever known a deeper peace."

She smiled again, but it didn't strike Colleen as peaceful so much as empty. Physically, she seemed perfectly healthy, but mentally, she was… flat. Almost mechanical, like one of those robots from the pulps her youngest brother had always left lying around the house, or a toy that had been wound up with a key and set on a predetermined course. It chilled her. If this was the face of the sanitarium they chose to show to the world, what were they doing to the patients who weren't on the tour?

Again, Aaron seemed to pick up on her hesitation. He reached forward to pat Mrs. Paulson's hand.

"I'm so sorry for your struggles, ma'am," he said. "Thank you for sharing that with us. We truly do appreciate it."

As a consummate fast talker, Colleen had a keen sense of when someone was faking sincerity and when they were exhibiting the real deal. This was entirely the latter. If Colleen wasn't mistaken, there were tears in his own eyes as he withdrew his hand. It made her feel a quiver of shame. She'd been disturbed by Mrs. Paulson's condition, but Aaron had felt compassion. Her reaction seemed weak in comparison.

"Well, we won't take up any more of your time, Mrs. Paulson," Dr. Hayward said, perhaps realizing this interaction wasn't having the effect on this nice young couple that he'd been hoping it would. "Please enjoy the rest of your afternoon. Mr. and Mrs. Keith, shall we?"

Colleen and Aaron got to their feet, murmuring their farewells to Mrs. Paulson. The old woman gave them a small wave and turned back to her puzzle, looking for all the world as if she hadn't been fighting to not cry only moments before. Colleen shivered as they crossed the sunroom towards the door.

Dr. Hayward had slipped easily back into his salesman patter as they made their way back to his office. Colleen was only listening with half an ear, but as they approached a staircase, she had a flash of inspiration.

"I can't help but notice that we haven't visited the upper floors yet," she said brightly, interrupting his monologue about the benefits of cold water immersion. "Would it be possible to pop up there before we go?"

If Colleen hadn't been watching the doctor very carefully, she might have missed the startled flicker in his eyes, but she was, so she didn't. For the first time since he'd emerged from his office to greet them, she'd caught him off guard. Which meant that whatever was up there was the thing they'd come to find.

"I'm sorry," he said, recovering quickly. "But those areas are off-limits to everyone except patients and staff."

"But why?" Aaron said, projecting a fairly convincing an air of abashed wonder. "I'm sure they must be just as impressive and instructive as everything else we're seen so far."

"Some of our more... sensitive treatments are conducted up there, many of which are proprietary and exclusive to Ocean Serenity. It would compromise patient privacy and the efficacy of the therapies in question to have outsiders present."

"Oh, come now," Colleen said cajolingly, going so far as to bat her lashes. "Just a peak couldn't do any harm, could it?"

The doctor's smile tightened, and his face went hard in a way he hadn't shown them yet. "I'm sorry, but the answer is no."

Colleen could tell that this tactic had hit a dead end. Pushing any more would only result in putting Dr. Hayward's guard all the way up, so she settled for pursing her lips in a moue of disappointment and looping her arm through Aaron's.

They continued on to Dr. Hayward's office, where he tried to nail down a plan to get the elusive Joseph on the premises for an assessment and they continued to deflect his questions with noncommittal answers and straight-up lies, but Colleen was really going through the motions at that point. Her mind had already skipped ahead to what she was going to do with everything they'd learned. With the bit of awareness she was using to keep up with the conversation, she began to worry that Aaron would expire from the effort of keeping up the charade, but eventually, they were able to extricate themselves from the meeting with a folder of promotional materials and a handwritten letter from Dr. Hayward to "Joseph", inviting him to come experience Ocean Serenity personally. Colleen trilled a cheery goodbye to Mildred as they left, but she was just as relieved as Aaron seemed to be once they were finally back in the auto.

"Well," Aaron said as he steered them out the gates and back onto the narrow road, tugging at his necktie to loosen it. "That was... something."

"Those upper floors," Colleen said, unable to keep it in any longer. "That's where the key to all of this is hiding."

Aaron nodded "Yeah, I think you're right." He shot her a sideways glance. "You're very good at that, by the way."

She arched an eyebrow. "Good at what?"

"Just..." He gestured vaguely over his shoulder. "*Wrangling* people like that. Getting them to do things for you, tell you things. I've seen Oliver do stuff like that, but he has his power to draw on. You just seemed to wing it."

"Not that well, apparently," she said morosely. "I couldn't get us upstairs."

"Maybe not," Aaron replied. "But you still got him to show his hand. We have confirmation that there is something shady going on there." He glanced at her again. "How do you do it?"

She felt her cheeks warm. "I guess I just have a knack for under-standing what it is that people want. If I can give it to them, the rest is easy."

His brow furrowed. "What do you mean?"

"Well, those people at the sanatorium, you can tell they have a high opinion of themselves. They think the work they're doing is impor-tant; they're fixing what's broken. And because they're not magical themselves, they're the opposite of broken. They're whole. Virtuous. Superior. So I walk in, all naïve innocence and heavy accent, and they see a hick who's maybe not too bright and needs their help. It's too much for them. They slip into the characters they've created for themselves without even thinking. And because I am somebody who is below them, who makes them feel smug and righteous, they maybe overplay their hand. Because they're showing off to an audience of one—themself."

Aaron was quiet for a moment. "You think I sound like a hick?"

Colleen's eyebrows shot up. "Out of everything I just said, *that's* what you latched onto?"

"It just seemed kind of unnecessary," Aaron retorted, a note of defensiveness entering his voice. "You know, as a piece of description."

Colleen sighed. "No. I don't think you sound like a hick."

Aaron gave a single nod, seemingly mollified. "I will concede that otherwise, that was a nice bit of strategy. Where did you pick it up?

Colleen shrugged. "I grew up with four hot-tempered Ogygian brothers. We spent a lot of time roaming the streets, and the unspoken rule was, if one of us fought, all of us fought. You may have noticed that I'm not exactly imposing. I didn't want to fight if I didn't have to. So I learned to talk my way out of hot situations before they blew up."

He nodded, seeming to mull her words over. They drove in silence for a few minutes, and then Colleen brought up something that had been on her own mind.

"That woman—Mrs. Paulson." She swallowed. "She seemed... wrong. Do you think she'd been drugged?"

Aaron shrugged. "It wouldn't surprise me. But that's also just how it goes with some of the older adepts"

Colleen furrowed her brow. "How do you mean?"

"Well, for those of us who were kids when the Embargo passed, it's pretty much all we've ever known. We hate it, obviously, but it's what we're used to. Middle-aged adepts, like Esme, have mostly been able to adjust, too. But the ones who spent their whole lives – five and six decades, some of them—using their powers and suddenly couldn't..." He shook his head. "It did something to some of them. The loss was more than they could bear."

Colleen toyed with a loose thread on her handbag. "Did you use your power on her? When you patted her hand?"

She could see some of his defenses go up, still sensitive from their earlier conversation. But she only sat quietly, waiting, and he must have decided she was asking in good faith, because he finally said, "Yes. Just a little."

"How?" she said, careful to keep her voice neutral.

"I leaned into that nostalgia she mentioned," he said. "Of those times when her kids were small. Tried to give her some of the comfort of those memories without the baggage they've given her."

His voice turned hard at the end, but she could hear the sadness underneath the anger.

"That was kind of you," she said quietly. From the corner of her eye, she saw him look at her sharply, but she pretended not to notice. As he turned back to the road, he glanced at the rearview mirror, and whatever he saw made him tighten his hands on the wheel, muttering a curse under his breath,

"What is it?" said Colleen.

"We're being followed."

"What?!" Colleen went rigid and started to turn, but Aaron barked out, "Stop!" and clamped a hand on her knee. The contact did far more to arrest her movement than the shout did, and it seemed to surprise him just as much as her based on the way he snatched his hand back. He took a deep breath and continued more calmly.

"Don't turn around. It will only tip them off that we've noticed them."

Colleen took a deep breath of her own, using every bit of her will not to look over her shoulder. "So what do we do now?"

"Well," Aaron said. "We'll be coming up on the turn-off for Merrimack soon. We can take that; I need to find somewhere to stop for gas anyway."

"OK," she said slowly. "And then what?"

Aaron shrugged. "And then we go to Merrimack. It will be easier to lose them in a city than it will on these country roads. It'll delay us quite a bit in getting back to Ad Astra, but I'm not sure what other options we have."

Colleen slumped in her seat. "I'm sorry. I guess I wasn't a very convincing actress after all."

"Hey, no," Aaron said quickly. "This is not on you. You did a good job baiting the hook. They may just want to make sure their fish doesn't have a chance to slip away."

She found that his words warmed her. He'd tossed the assurance off casually enough, as if he was just stating a fact rather than trying to reassure her, but it felt significant that he'd withheld blame when he would have been well within his rights to dish it out.

"Now," he said, face turning serious as they passed a mile-marker for Merrimack. "We just need to figure out where to kill some time in Merrimack until we can sneak away."

Colleen sat back in her seat, gazing out at the fading afternoon sunshine and doing her best to ignore the queasy roil of inevitability inside of her. If she'd learned anything about Aaron today, it was that he was resourceful, able to think on his feet. Left to his own devices, he would surely come up with a good plan. Except he didn't know the ins and outs of Merrimack like he did Ad Astra. He didn't know the personalities of the neighborhoods, the twisting warrens of streets that made up the older parts of town.

Not like she did.

She let her head fall sideways against the window, sighing. "I know a place."

Aaron glanced at her, but he didn't push. For a long time after that, they drove on in silence.

The closer they got to the city, the more depressed Colleen felt. She had been more than happy to see the back of it, once upon a time, and she'd had no real intention of coming back so soon, if ever. As they reached the outskirts, pangs of deep recognition, almost fondness, bubbled up inside of her, but so did unpleasant memories. Merrimack was different from Ad Astra, older and more staid. Where Ad Astra's name conjured pictures of glass and steel, Merrimack was all brick and stone. Even the most modern, bustling parts of the city looked more like the neighborhoods near the Hierophant than they did the commercial district where the Independent's offices were located. Aaron listened carefully as she gave directions, but he stayed quiet, seemingly picking up on her mood, and she was grateful. She didn't think she could have held her own in a conversation just then.

She made sure they took a scenic route to their destination, one that would have the greatest chance of losing their tail in the snarl of rush hour traffic. Finally, she directed Aaron to pull the auto to the curb on a quiet street lined by budding trees and unassuming clap-board houses. She could hear kids playing in the distance when she got out of the auto, and parents shouting that it was almost time to come in for dinner; if she closed her eyes, she could easily imagine she was eleven years old again. She pushed the thought away, turning her mind instead to girding her loins for battle.

Aaron had really displayed an amazing degree of restraint up to this point, but she could tell he was dying of curiosity. She couldn't bring herself to satisfy it; she wouldn't even know where to start. Still, it wouldn't be sporting to let him go in completely unawares, so after she led him to a house in the middle of the block and knocked on the front door, she laid a hand on his arm.

"I should warn you," she said, her voice grim. "This probably won't go very well."

Aaron's eyebrows shot up. "Won't go well? What do you-"

The door opened to reveal a plump, harried-looking woman in a brown day dress wiping her hands on her apron. The woman's face was lined and careworn, and her hair, gathered into a bun at the back of her neck, had largely gone gray, though a few threads of red managed to peek through. At her neck, she wore a religious medallion popular among High Church Ogygians. A pair of yapping terriers circled her feet, but she paid them no mind, instead staring at Colleen goggle-eyed.

Colleen slumped. "Hi, Mam."

CHAPTER 10

AARON

*A*aron blinked at Colleen in surprise. The woman—*Mam*—also blinked in surprise. Colleen, meanwhile, looked expectant and cautious, as if she were bracing herself for whatever came next. She didn't have to wait for long.

"Oh, my darling!" her mother exclaimed and stepped forward to gather Colleen into her arms. Colleen was not what anyone would describe as tall, but Mam was shorter yet, and the act of pulling her daughter down to her level, coupled with Colleen's obvious shock, threatened to knock both of them off balance. Colleen managed to catch them before they toppled over, but then, she seemed stumped as to how she should proceed. Her arms were rigid at her sides for a moment, before she slowly raised one to give her mother a tentative pat on the back.

Mam finally stepped back from the hug, moving her hands to Colleen's shoulders and gazing at her.

"Oh, you are a sight for sore eyes," she said with a little sniffle. "But let's not stand out here all night—come in, come in!"

She turned and walked back into the house, the dogs still yapping their ratty little heads off. Colleen followed, looking vaguely stunned, and Aaron brought up the rear, closing the door behind him. The entryway, dim and pleasantly cool, opened into a modest but cozy dining room. While the lobby of the sanitarium had felt contrived in its use of creature comforts, this place simply felt comfortable and lived in. The sofa and chairs all boasted doilies that Aaron was 99% sure Mam had crocheted herself, as well as needlepoint pillows and worn quilts. The walls were decorated with photographs and religious prints, and rag rugs were scattered across the floor. One one of these, a group of children, all sporting aggressively red hair, sat playing with blocks and dolls.

"Brigid," Mam said as she passed the children, "run and tell your daddy that his sister's come home."

The oldest child jumped up and ran to the front door, orange pigtails bobbing.

"I've got a stew on," Mam went on as she led them further into the house. "You two arrived just in time for dinner! The others should be here soon." Aaron wasn't sure who "the others" were, but Colleen seemed to. She continued to follow her mother wordlessly, but her shoulders slumped.

In the kitchen, a massive soup pot was bubbling away on the stove; the smell was divine. Mam gestured for them to sit at the small breakfast table near the back door, which they did as she picked up a ladle and gave the contents of the pot a stir. She shot Colleen a look that was both affectionate and assessing.

"I don't know what you've been eating down there on your own; you look like you could use a good meal. I know it's fashionable to be thin these days, narrow hips don't do you any favors when it's time for birthing babies."

"Mam!" Colleen said, and the fair skin of her cheeks turned dark pink.

Mam glanced at Aaron looking sheepish.

"Oh, I'm sorry—I can see why you wouldn't want me bringing such things up in front of your fella."

"Oh, no," Aaron jumped in, just as Colleen said "He's not-", the two of them falling silent as they realized the other was speaking. After a beat, Colleen cleared her throat.

"Aaron is just a friend, Mam."

"Oh, aye?" Mam said, a note of skepticism in her voice as she turned back to the stove. "My mistake then."

Aaron felt his own cheeks burning, but just then, one of the children toddled into the kitchen. As a rule, Aaron didn't spend much time with children, so it was hard to tell how old this one was; the best he could do was "not very." The little one was wearing a dress, so presumably a girl, but he wouldn't have been able to tell otherwise. She seemed cheerful enough, though, walking right over to Colleen to beam up at her and pat the navy skirt with chubby hands.

"You remember Molly, don't you?" Mam said absently. "She'd only just been born when you left. Now look at her, getting to be such a big girl."

Colleen nodded, her face full of some emotion Aaron couldn't identify. Still without speaking—seriously, this was the longest Aaron could remember her going without talking, he was starting to get worried—she reached down and lifted the little girl into her lap. Molly was instantly fascinated by the buttons running down the front of Colleen's dress and began toying with them as Colleen smoothed a hand over her wispy red hair and kissed the top of her head.

"Yes," she said finally, barely more than a whisper. "Such a big girl."

In the living room, the dogs started barking again, followed by the sound of the front door opening and closing. Aaron heard the children calling out greetings as the floorboards creaked under heavy treads, and then two men appeared in the kitchen door.

"Da!" Molly shrieked in delight. She wiggled down from Colleen's lap and ran none too steadily across the room, where the smaller of the men scooped her up, pressing more kisses to her face. The other, who stood in front, a step or two closer to the table, was very tall, well over six feet, and lanky with wire-framed glasses, but Aaron could see the resemblance between him and Colleen; the features were remarkably similar, and his hair was the same color, though it was cropped nearly to the scalp. He blinked at the two of them as Colleen got to her feet. "Hi, Tim."

For a moment, Tim just stared, but then he stepped forward and pulled Colleen into a tight hug. He was so much taller that even bending down, the movement pulled Colleen up onto her tiptoes. Just as with her mother, Colleen looked surprised at first, but then she seemed to melt into the embrace, closing her eyes and pressing her head into his shoulder. When they finally pulled apart, Tim's eyes had gone a little red. Aaron was sure that Colleen noticed, but she didn't comment on it. Instead she looked past him at the man holding Molly.

This one, while shorter than Tim, was stockier, and his demeanor was far less welcoming. Rather than coming into the room, he hovered in the doorway, scowling at them over his daughter's head.

"So, you're back," he said flatly, and Colleen's eyes narrowed. She crossed her arms, mirroring his stance.

"Well, don't wear yourself out getting all sentimental about it, Joey."

"I would never," he said, and Colleen's fair skin flushed again, this time in anger. Aaron braced for an argument, but in one smooth motion, Mam spun around, brandishing her ladle at the two of them.

"Stop it, the pair of you. Acting like this when you haven't seen each other in so long, you should be ashamed." She turned a sharp gaze on Joey. "I'll not have it on the day your sister's returned, do you hear me? You're not too old for me to turn over my knee." After waiting a moment to confirm that peace had been successfully established, she turned back to the stew. Behind her mother's back, Colleen sent Joey a smug, satisfied look. Snorting in disgust, he turned and stalked back into the living room.

Mam tutted and turned to Aaron apologetically. "You'll have to forgive Joey. He can be a bit temperamental."

"I can think of a few other words for it," Colleen muttered, but not, Aaron noted, loud enough for her mother to hear.

As it turned out, Tim and Joey's appearance was just the beginning of a sudden rush of people descending on the house. A third brother, Tommy, wandered in, kissing his mother on the cheek and ruffling Colleen's hair; she put on a show of protest, but Aaron could tell it lacked any of the real tension he'd seen between her and Joey. Next came a trio of women, all quite pretty, two holding tiny babies. These, Colleen explained, were her sisters-in-law: Mona, who was married to Tim; Robbie's wife Agnes; and Siobhan, who was paired with Joey. Aaron despaired of ever being able to keep all of that straight, but he smiled and nodded anyway. Finally, the last brother, whip-thin and barely more than a teenager, came through the door and pretended to faint at the sight of Colleen. She just smirked and introduced him as Robbie, the only one who was younger than her. He greeted Aaron cordially enough, then made a beeline for the kitchen, where Mam had to chase him away from the stove with her ladle.

"But, Mam, I'm *starving*," he moaned.

"That's no reason to forget your manners," she said and pushed a basket covered with a cloth into his hands. "Go put that on the table so we can eat like civilized people."

Colleen steered Aaron into the dining room, where someone had put a leaf in the table; this provided more room for the diners to gather, but also made the already snug space more cramped. A mismatched collection of chairs had been assembled by raiding the other rooms in the house, which just allowed all the adults to squeeze in together; the children had been banished to the living room to eat around the coffee table. Aaron could hear them chattering as Mam brought the final serving dishes to the table and took her seat.

"Timothy, will you say grace for us?" she said, and Tim nodded. As one, the members of Colleen's family reached for each other's hands, and for a heartbeat, Aaron wondered if he would—or should—be included in the moment of devotion, but then he felt Colleen's delicate fingers slide into his right hand and Robbie's rougher ones into his left, and it became something of a moot point. He felt an odd sting of nostalgia as everyone bowed their heads, thinking of a thousand other dinners at crowded tables from his childhood, and then Tim began to speak.

"Majestic Creator, bless these gifts that we are about to receive for the nourishment of our bodies. Thank you for this time we have together and thank you for the return of your daughter Colleen to this house." Aaron felt Colleen stiffen next to him, but she didn't make a sound. "Let everything we do this day be to your glory. Amen."

"Amen," everyone murmured, and most made the holy sign of the High Church. Then they ate.

The stew tasted just as good as it had smelled on the stove and was served with wedges of fresh-baked soda bread and glasses of dark beer. From the corner of his eye, Aaron noticed the look on Colleen's face as she took her first bite—it was pleasure and sadness together, almost more emotion than he thought she could stand. Everything about this place was complicated for her. If he ever went back to Cumberland, he thought he'd probably feel much the same.

"So, Aaron," Agnes said as everyone tucked in. "How did you and Colleen meet?"

"Um, through work," Aaron said, sneaking a look at Colleen to make sure this was an acceptable answer. She gave a small nod as she blew on a bite of stew.

"Ah, yes," Joey piped up from across the table. "Colleen's quest to become the next Amity Bell." He took a swig of beer. "Never mind that the first one died alone with no family to even miss her."

In his peripheral vision, Aaron saw Colleen pause briefly, but instead of responding, she took a deep breath and continued to eat. Other members of the family, meanwhile, were exchanging anxious looks, while Siobhan was outright staring daggers at her husband.

Aaron cleared his throat. "This stew is delicious, Mrs. O'Cremin. I'm sure my aunt would love the recipe, if you don't mind sharing." In his experience, matriarch-types loved to be asked for their recipes, even if they ultimately declined, determined to take their secret ingredients to the grave. Mam showed no such compunction, however, flushing with pleasure at the compliment.

"But of course," she said. "I'll write it out for you before you leave." She took a sip of beer then, giving him a speculative look. "Do you live with your aunt?"

He felt a prickle of unease at her tone, but there wasn't much to do but brazen through it. "Yes, ma'am. My sister and I. Aunt Ruth has no children of her own, so it works out well for all of us. We take care of each other."

Mam's expression turned sympathetic, sincerely, he was pretty sure, but her gaze was still alert. "Oh, are your parents deceased then?"

She'd caught him with his mouth full, and he swallowed, dabbing his mouth with his napkin. "No, ma'am. We just don't see them much." Or ever. "They're still on the farm down in Cumberland."

'Well, that's a shame," she replied, not unkindly.

"It is a shame," Joey piped up, eyes on his bowl. "There's nothing more important than family."

"Stop it, Joey," Colleen said, her voice low but sharp.

"Why?" he scoffed. "Am I pricking at your conscience?"

"Pricking at my patience, more like," Colleen retorted.

"It's not our fault if you're not getting the welcome you were apparently expecting," he went on as if she hadn't spoken. "If you wanted something different, you should have acted better, instead of coming across all wounded because nobody threw you a bleeding parade when you turned your back on us."

Colleen dropped her spoon into her bowl with a clatter. "I didn't turn my back on anyone."

Joey got a malicious gleam in his eye. "Oh, no? Davey's brother-in-law went down to Ad Astra for his job, and he said you aren't even using your real name. He said he saw a story by someone named Lena Crimm and thought, 'That sounds like the O'Cremin girl, but surely not? Why would she try to hide herself like that?'"

Colleen sucked in a breath. Joey looked triumphant, realizing, as Aaron had, that the statement had hit its mark. For the first time since they'd sat down, Colleen didn't look irritated or indignant; she looked guilty. The others at the table likewise seemed more uncertain than they had. Suddenly, it seemed they had more on their hands than a simple case of sibling rivalry.

"Is that true, Colleen?" Mam said, hurt plain in her voice.

"I-" Colleen stammered. "That is-"

"Don't try to pretty it up," Joey said. "You're ashamed of where you came from, pure and simple."

Some of the steel came back into Colleen's expression. "I'm not."

Joey's eyes narrowed, and somehow, Aaron knew he was going in for the kill.

"I'm just glad Da isn't here to see this. It would break his heart."

Colleen leapt to her feet, making the whole table shake.

"I need some air," she declared, then turned and stormed out of the room.

The silence at the room was heavy, with silverware suspended between mouths and eyes turned to Colleen's departing back. Joey, meanwhile, took a long sip of beer, apparently satisfied with his work.

"I'm sorry you had to see that, Aaron," he said, not sounding sorry at all. "Though it's probably best you know what you're getting into with her. She's a smart girl, our Colleen, but she can be a bit of a martyr."

Aaron was starting to understand why Joey was the brother Colleen had selected for confinement in the nefarious sanatorium.

Robbie glared at Joey. "You just couldn't help yourself, could you? You couldn't even give us all one day with her?"

Joey opened his mouth to argue, but Tim beat him to the punch.

"Shut up, both of you, and eat your dinner," the eldest O'Cremin said. "You're upsetting Mam."

He hadn't raised his voice, but he still conveyed a certain confident authority, and his brothers subsided. For several moments, there was no sound in the dining room besides the clatter of silverware, but eventually Agnes made a comment about the quality of the beef in the stew, which set Mam off into a story about visiting the butcher that day, and the group fell into an easy rhythm of inane small talk. Aaron was at something of a loss as to what he should do, so he just kept eating, thinking Colleen would reappear at some point or that someone would go to check on her. Neither of those things happened. The closest anyone came to acknowledging her continued absence was Robbie collecting her dishes as he carried his own to the kitchen, with the kind of mindless ease that suggested he'd done it many times before.

Aaron cleared his own place and offered to help wash up—Aunt Ruth would have murdered him if he'd even thought of doing otherwise—but Mam just waved a dish towel at him, shooing him out of the room.

"You're our guest," she said. "You sit back down and make yourself comfortable."

It was a nice suggestion, but the fact was, he and Colleen needed to go. He'd been surprised by how dark the sky had gotten when he'd glimpsed it through a window on the way to the kitchen and even more disconcerted when he'd glanced at the wall clock. They'd presumably thrown the guys following them off the scent for the time being, and Esme was going to be worried if they didn't check in soon, never mind Ebony and Aunt Ruth. He really needed to collect Colleen and head back south.

In the dining room, the brothers had reclaimed their seats and were drinking coffee out of delicate china cups, but rather than joining them, Aaron made his way to the living room where the children, finished with their own dinner, were gathered in front of the wireless. Aaron crouched down next to them.

"Brigid," he said, for the sole reason that she was the only one whose name he knew, and the girl looked up at him with wide eyes. "Did you happen to see where your Auntie Colleen went?"

Brigid nodded and, wordlessly, pointed to the staircase leading to the second floor. Aaron thanked her and stood, facing the stairs. The thought of leaving the public rooms of the first floor for the more private upstairs rooms felt strangely presumptuous, almost intimate to Aaron. But he needed to find her sooner or later, so he took a deep breath and started to climb.

When he reached the landing, he saw four doors, two on either side. Three of them were closed up tight, but one was open a crack. Keeping his footsteps light, Aaron went to that door, nudging it open a few more inches, and peeked inside.

The lamp in the room was off, but there was enough light coming in through the open window for him to get a sense of the layout. It was a crowded space. There was a crib wedged into one corner and a rocking chair in another, presumably placed there for the legion of grandchildren going in and out of the house. But the rest of the room bore the clear marks of belonging to a teenage girl. There was a dresser with a doily and a collection of bottles and jars on top, as well as a desk with a small shelf nailed above. The shelf looked to have held books once, but was now largely empty; the few objects that did still reside there appeared to be trophies. The wall next to the shelf was adorned with ribbons and what looked like certificates of some kind, together with pictures cut from moving picture magazines and a world map that had been stuck through with pins bearing a variety of paper labels. Next to the window, there was a narrow, wrought iron bed, and on that bed was Colleen. She had kicked off her shoes and pulled her knees up to her chest, gazing out into the night. The look of melancholy on her face went straight to Aaron's heart.

It felt intrusive to just stand there watching her, so Aaron cleared his throat. Her head snapped towards the door at the sound, and the look on her face suggested she was ready to fight, but when she saw him, her face softened.

"I thought you might be one of my brothers," she said. "Or Mam, coming to tell me I should go down and apologize."

"Nope," Aaron said. "Just me." He took a cautious step into the room. "You OK?"

"Yeah," she said with a sigh and went back to looking out the window. "It's just... this is why I left, you know?"

"I think I do," Aaron replied and stepped in further. Despite his sense of urgency, he felt oddly reluctant to hurry her out when she was clearly upset; they could probably afford a few minutes. He gestured to the rocking chair. "May I?"

CHAPTER 11

COLLEEN

*C*olleen shrugged. "Be my guest."

Aaron stepped forward and lifted the needlepoint cushion out of the rocker. As he sat, he held the pillow out, reading the message by the streetlight.

"Grand," he said, with just a bit of questioning upturn at the end.

"It was my father's favorite word," Colleen said. "He used it for everything. Sunny day? Grand. Butterfly passing by? Grand. Seeing his brother who he'd left back in Ogygia for the first time in a decade? Grand." She smiled, even as the familiar ache rose in her chest. "It was all the same to him. Everything was a blessing."

"He sounds like a good man," Aaron said softly, placing the pillow in his lap and crossing his arms atop it.

Colleen sighed. "He was."

"When did he pass?"

"Eight years ago," Colleen said. "Dropped dead of a heart attack behind the bar. He was alone; no one found him until the next morning." In her peripheral vision, she saw Aaron wince.

"I'm sorry," he said.

"Mam always says he died doing what he loved," Colleen said, "but... I don't know."

"You don't think so?"

"The bar wasn't supposed to be a family business," Colleen said, "at least not like some of the others around here. Da didn't see it as his legacy. He was a teacher back in Ogygia, and he wanted to be one here, too. But nobody would hire him. All he had to do was open his mouth, and they clocked him as fresh off the boat—too old-world, not good enough for their precious New Avolonian youth." She scowled at the memory. "So he opened the bar. And he insisted that all of us get an education so we could go on to do whatever we wanted. But then he died, and we closed ranks, because that's what we always do. I don't think any of us expected it to be permanent, but..." She shrugged. "That's just how things go sometimes."

"What happened?" Aaron said.

"Tim has always been our leader—keeping an eye on us, making sure we stayed out of trouble. Well," she amended with a crooked grin, "out of any trouble he didn't have a hand in starting." She sobered again. "It weighed on him, becoming the man of the house, but it suited him, too. He saw taking over the bar as taking care of us, so he was more than willing to do it, but I think it surprised him how much he actually enjoyed it. Because he was taking care of the customers, too, making it a place they felt at home. What he wasn't any good at taking care of was the finances, but that's where Tommy came in. He's always been a whiz at numbers. He helped keep the place afloat and then better than afloat."

"Do you think he felt pressured to stay for Tim's sake?"

She shrugged. "I don't think so. It's a good living, and that was what he needed to marry Agnes. He's been in love with her since we were kids. I think as long as he gets to go home to her at the end of the day, he doesn't really care what he does. Robbie's pretty much the same. He's good with the customers; he gets to run his mouth and be charming, which he enjoys, and then he gets to play his music at night. It's enough for him for now, and if he ever changes his mind, he doesn't have any big responsibilities tying him down."

"Like Joey," Aaron said, not entirely a question.

"Like Joey," Colleen confirmed.

"He strikes me as a fairly belligerent person in general," Aaron ventured, and Colleen snorted in agreement. "But he also seems to be really angry with you in particular." He waited for a response, but Colleen went quiet wrapping her arms around her knees. "Have the two of you always butted heads like that?"

"No," she said quietly. "In fact, when we were kids, we were inseparable. Strangers usually assumed we were twins." She smiled at Aaron. "We had some of that deep connection, you know—the kind you must have with your sister."

Aaron shifted in his seat, and she thought she saw him frown, but he motioned for her to go on.

"I think it might actually be because we're so alike that things have gotten so hard between us," she continued. "Because we had the same dreams when we were young, of adventure, of new places and new people and never staying in one place for too long." Her face darkened. "In the end, though, I was the only one who pursued those dreams, and he's never forgiven me for it. In his mind, I deserted the family—deserted him—but it was never about that. Even with Da gone, nobody pressured Joey to stay here except Joey. He could have gone, too, but he was a coward. I mean, look at you. You and your sister came up here all by yourselves. Yeah, it takes courage, but people do it all the time."

Aaron was quiet for a long moment. "Sometimes it's not about courage. Sometimes you just don't have a choice."

"Oh," Colleen said. The word hung in the air between them, solitary and awkward. Her regret at the misstep was at war with her curiosity, and it left her adrift over what to say next. After a moment, though, she heard Aaron huff a soft laugh in the darkness.

"You can ask. I know it must be killing you."

Colleen narrowed her eyes at his wry tone, but well, it was killing her, so she asked.

"What happened?"

"Well, Ebony and me – people usually assume we are fraternal twins," he began. "Which I guess is fair, all things considered. But when we were born, everyone said we were identical, exactly alike in every particular. As in, they all thought Ebony was a boy."

"Oh," Colleen said, more than a little surprised. "But she isn't?"

"No."

"When did she, uh... figure that out?" Her face warmed. "Or do you think she'd mind you sharing that kind of thing with me?"

"No," Aaron said. "She wouldn't mind. It's not something she advertises, but it's not a secret either." He shrugged. "She told me just before we turned thirteen, but I suspect she knew for a long time before that. She was just worried that I'd judge her or tell her she was delusional."

"But you didn't?"

Aaron shook his head. "Ebony is the most honest person I've ever met. If she said it, it was true, pure and simple." His eyes went soft, and Colleen saw sadness there, as well as regret. "She was so relieved when I didn't recoil from her or argue with her. It was humbling, realizing how much my opinion meant. But it turned out she was right to worry about what people would think."

He paused, taking a deep breath.

"I was the one who convinced her to tell our parents." The words came out in a rush, followed by silence. Colleen was likewise silent. It was a trick she used when conducting interviews—people typically hated the tension that came without speaking and rushed to fill it. This time, though, she wasn't angling for something that would make good copy. She was genuinely interested in what came next, and she wanted to give Aaron the space to share it in his own time.

"I thought I was so smart," he said finally. "She knew, somehow, they wouldn't be able to accept it, but I was sure—*sure*—that she could make them understand. They were our parents, after all. They loved us."

"But they didn't understand," Colleen murmured

Aaron shook his head again, rubbing his hands together slowly. "They told her that what she was saying was an affront to the Creator, and if she wanted to stay under their roof, she had to repent. But she'd come too far at that point; she couldn't go back. So they told her she had to leave. And I wasn't about to let her go on her own, so I left, too." He sniffed. "That made it even worse in their minds. They kept shouting prayers of lamentation as we were leaving, saying that she was stealing me from them. But Ebony just kept walking. I was so sick with anger and grief that I could barely keep up with her, but she didn't look back once."

"What happened to you then?"

Aaron shrugged. "We rode the rails up and down the coast for a while. That's when Ebony started running poker games, to get us food money. She had always been a dab hand at cards, even before we got our powers; she barely even had to cheat."

Colleen cocked her head. "What is her power, exactly? I'm not sure You've ever told me."

"It's like mine, but with thoughts," Aaron said. "So if, say, she sees a player at her table debating which card to lay down, she can nudge them in the direction she wants."

Colleen nodded, satisfied, and Aaron continued.

"Anyway, that's when she started living as a girl. That made a lot of things harder for her, in terms of keeping herself safe, but it actually worked to her advantage sometimes, too; the big, cocky guys always underestimated her."

"But you couldn't do that forever."

"No," he said. "We thought we might have to. Because what else would we do, two little country kids with no money, no skills to speak of, and very little education? But then Ebony got sick. And not sick like we usually got from huddling in cold box cars and eating scraps, but really, really ill. She got this wracking cough that just got worse and worse, no matter what we tried.

"I decided we should head north to Ad Astra. I don't know exactly what I expected to happen when we got there. I think I just had an idea of it being a place with good doctors and medicine, never mind that we couldn't afford any of those things. We made it, but she kept getting progressively worse. I was terrified she was actually going to die."

"So what did you do then?"

"While we were growing up, our parents talked about my mother's sister, Ruth, who was always putting on airs and got it in her head to go to the big city to make something of herself." He glanced at Colleen; he didn't say *Like you*, but he didn't have to. "They always made her sound so mean and selfish. I didn't have any reason to think she'd be willing to help us, but I knew she was in the city, and I was desperate. I found her address in a phone directory, and I took Ebony to see her, just hoping we could have a safe place for the night or a hot meal.

"I've thought about that night a lot over the years, and I can only imagine how we must have looked to Ruth when she opened the door. We were two filthy, malnourished little scarecrows, and Ebony was hanging off my shoulder, looking about half-dead already. I started babbling something about being family and how we didn't mean to bother her but I didn't know where else to go. She just stepped forward and pulled both of us into her arms, and I started bawling like a baby. Then she took us inside, and we've been with her ever since."

"And she understands? About Ebony"

Aaron nodded.

"Ruth is just as devout as our parents, but her faith is different. She says that the Creator made all of us just as we should be, and Ebony knows what that means better than anyone else."

"So, I guess Ebony isn't the name she was born with? It's one she chose for herself."

Aaron nodded again. "Yeah, she started using it when we were living rough and made it official when we started living with Ruth. We actually thought about changing our last name, too, but Aunt Ruth talked us out of it."

"Oh?" said Colleen. "How so?"

"Well, she knew Ebony's name was a given," he said. "And she told us it was our choice if we wanted to make a really fresh start and change our last name. But she also said that name belonged to us as much as it did our parents, and we shouldn't let them take that away from us, too, if it was important to us. So we decided not to make the change." The corner of his mouth quirked up then, but the rest of his face suggested that whatever memory had surfaced was bittersweet. "We used to do this thing where we would put a fist over our heart"—he demonstrated—"and shout 'Dozie'. Like we were laying our claim to it. Confirming that we were still family through it all." His half smile faded. "We haven't done that in a long time."

"How did you end up at the Hierophant?"

"It was after we finished high school—Ruth insisted on that, like your dad. She knew Esme through some complicated chain of acquaintances and heard there might be some work opportunities for us at the club—she thought it might be good for us to be with other adepts, and she was right."

"So, that's when you started tending bar?"

Aaron barked out a laugh. "Oh, gods, no! They wouldn't have even let me look at the bar at that point."

Colleen's cheeks warmed, but she pushed on.

"Then what did you do?"

"A little bit of everything. Custodial work, maintenance... once they even had us sewing costumes. We had to show that we were trustworthy. Then they started offering us more important things. Like, I started in the front of house as a barback. I was fascinated watching the head bartender, Ray, work—he wasn't an adept, but he was still incredibly good at his job. He taught me virtually everything I know, and then we started experimenting with infusions of my power. By the time he left, it seemed natural for me to step in."

"What about Ebony? How'd she get her job?"

Aaron chuckled. "She played cards with Oliver. Once. She took him for more than a week's pay before he even knew what happened, and the next thing either of us know, she was the backup dealer."

"You're proud of her," Colleen said, and Aaron nodded.

"I am. She's come so far, and she's accomplished so much..." His voice trailed off.

Colleen couldn't quite make out his expression, but she heard a wistful note in his voice. "Sounds like there's a 'but' in there."

Aaron sighed. "We've always gotten along so well, but lately, we just can't seem to get on the same page. She thinks I'm being overprotective."

"Are you?"

Aaron huffed a laugh. "Maybe. But how can I not be? The threats to us are so real. You got a taste of it today."

"Just a word to the wise," Colleen said. "On behalf of sisters everywhere: when she tells you what she needs and doesn't need, listen." She inclined her head towards the floor and the family gathered underneath it. "I know they mean well. But it's hard."

Aaron turned his face to her sharply, but he didn't say anything. Eventually, he nodded. She returned the nod, realizing as she did so that it had started to ache. She had been so absorbed in Aaron's story that she hadn't noticed her muscles getting stiff. How long had she been up here? As she stretched her neck and rolled her shoulders, she realized Aaron must be wondering, too, because she saw him squint at the clock sitting on a shelf over the crib.

"It's time for us to go," she said, not a question.

Aaron nodded. "I think we're safe now. We've probably lost them, and even if he haven't, it'll be harder for them to keep eyes on us in the dark."

Colleen pushed herself off of the bed, indulging in a luxurious, full-body stretch before putting her shoes back on. It was odd—she had been positively dreading coming back to this house, but now, she felt a nagging reluctance to leave. Was it because her family—Joey excepted, obviously—had actually been happy to see her? Or was it something to do with sitting together with Aaron in this dark, quiet room, sharing secrets without judgment?

Honestly, probably best not to think about it.

"Come on," she said. "Let's go get this over with."

CHAPTER 12

COLLEEN

Saying goodbye went about as well as she expected.

"Leaving?" Mam said, reaching up to clutch her medallion, as she always did when she was distressed. "You only just got here!"

"I know," Colleen said, pushing down a pang of guilt. "But we need to get back to Ad Astra tonight, Mam. We have work. And Aaron needs to check on his aunt."

Perhaps it was the invocation of Aunt Ruth that did it—for all that her mother had an Ogygian work ethic, Colleen couldn't believe that citing her job would have been entirely compelling on its own—but Mam closed her mouth on any further argument. Colleen was robbed of any satisfaction she might once have derived from this triumph by the way Mam's shoulder's sagged in resignation. Quickly enough, though, she rallied.

"I'll make you some sandwiches," she said, straightening her shoulders and crossing to the counter, where the remnants of dinner still sat, waiting to be packed into the icebox. "For your drive."

Colleen sighed. "Mam, you really don't need to-"

"Nonsense," he mother said briskly as she picked up a bread knife and began sawing off thick slices of soda bread. "It won't take a minute. Of course, then you'll have to wait for me to jot down the recipe for Aaron's dear aunt. But after that, you'll be on the road in no time."

Knowing she was beaten, Colleen slumped into a chair at the kitchen table much as she had earlier in the day. Come to think of it, she did recall spending a lot of time slumping into that chair back when she'd still lived there. She'd forgotten; by design, there hadn't been as much call for slumping since she'd moved to Ad Astra.

Aaron sat down next to her, and they watched Mam work, her movements neat and precise. Laying out the slices of bread on a piece of wax paper, she piled two pieces high with bits of roast, then slathered the other pieces with a thick layer of butter from the crock on the counter. Mam had been buying that butter, thick and yellow, from the same local dairy for years, and Colleen hadn't been able to find anything quite like it in Ad Astra. Another memory surfaced then, a sudden, vivid flash of sneaking downstairs as a girl, long after she was supposed to be in bed, and sitting at the kitchen table next to her father, eating a piece of soda bread heavy with that butter, while he worked on the books from the bar, the two of them the only ones awake in the house. She felt a sudden pang of homesickness, even while she was sitting in that home.

She shook her head, shifting in her seat. She had to get out of there. Her head was getting all muddled.

At the counter, Mam began wrapping the sandwiches in the wax paper, tucking in the ends to make a neat parcel. She handed these to Colleen without making eye contact.

"Back in a tick," she said and went out to the living room, presumably to Dad's desk which still stood there, inevitably stocked with writing paper and his fountain pen in the top drawer.

Colleen stared at the package in her hands, holding it as one might a bomb: gently, but with the appropriate amounts of respect and fear. She'd felt so liberated when she'd left here from Ad Astra, casting off the confines of her old life for a new start. Now she was wondering if she'd made the break too clean.

But she could also feel Aaron's eyes on her and knew that she didn't really have the time to think about it just then. Taking a deep breath, she got to her feet and followed Mam into the living room. While they'd been upstairs, most of the family had left, needing to get the children to bed, so only Tim and Robbie lingered on the sofa. Mam was just putting the cap back on her pen and waving the paper in the air to dry the ink as they approached.

"Here you are, dear," Mam said, folding the paper in half and handing it to Aaron. "Give it to your aunt with my compliments."

"I will," Aaron said solemnly, tucking the recipe into his jacket. "Thank you."

With a nod, Mam turned to Colleen.

"Well," she said. "Don't be a stranger now, aye?" And to Colleen's horror, her lip began to tremble, and her eyes filled with tears.

"Oh, Mam," Colleen said, and she felt tears prick at her own eyes. She reached out and pulled Mam into a tight, one-armed hug, the sandwiches pressed in between them. They stood like that for several seconds, then Colleen let her mother go, and Mam dabbed at her eyes with the corner of her apron. The brothers stood, Tim stating it was time for them to head out anyway. The two of them walked out to the street with Colleen, Aaron, and Mam, Tim blocking the door with his foot to keep the dogs from escaping.

Robbie hugged Colleen and shook Aaron's hand before heading off down the street to his apartment, while Tim put his arm around Mam, who now had an embroidered hankie clutched tight in her hand.

"Hope to see you soon, little sister," he said. Colleen, for once, couldn't think of a single thing to say, so she just went up on tiptoe to kiss him on the cheek, then took Aaron by the elbow and all but ran to the auto

Once they were settled and Aaron was making his way back through the winding Merrimack streets, Colleen once again stared at the wax paper bundle. Why did her mother have to do that? Leaving would have been much easier without having this clumsy gesture of affection literally dropped in her lap to make her wonder if maybe, just maybe, Joey had a point.

"You didn't finish your dinner," Aaron said out of nowhere.

Colleen looked up. "What?"

"You didn't finish eating," he said again, nodding toward the bundle. "Before. If I noticed, you can bet she did. She didn't want you to be hungry."

Colleen stared at him, then looked back down at the sandwiches that were causing so much turmoil. The symbol of her mother's love. Neither of them mentioned the notion of love being smothering, because neither of them had to.

Without a word, Colleen opened the package, pulled out a sandwich, and began to eat.

They drove on in silence, but it was a comfortable silence this time. After a while, Aaron began to hum softly, something that probably would have grated on her nerves earlier in the day, but now, it just seemed nice. She listened, chewing slowly, and tried to make sense of her jumbled thoughts.

There was Mr. Whitaker's warning. Aaron's disdain, and his grace. The emptiness behind Mrs. Paulson's eyes that afternoon. And this fragile, wriggling thing inside of her that had been her deep-seated desire to rub her family's face in her success and now might be growing into a longing for them to be proud of her. They kept shifting in her estimation, sliding and spilling over each other, but in the end, they all led her to the same place. It was still vital that she break something big, perhaps even more than she'd thought. And if she wasn't careful, it was going to slip through her fingers.

But she had an idea. One that might even help Aaron, too.

As they approached the junction with the highway and Aaron slowed the car to take the turn, Colleen laid a hand on his arm.

"Wait," she said.

Aaron looked over at her, eyebrows raised, but there must have been something in her tone that caught his attention. Easing the car over the shoulder, he shifted into park and turned to her.

"What is it?"

"If Dr. Hayward was suspicious enough to send someone after us," she said slowly. "It means he's going to be on alert—especially when they don't catch us."

"From your lips to the Creator's ears," Aaron muttered, but she ignored him.

"So when—if—anybody goes back, security will be tighter, right? They'll be taking additional steps to keep whatever's going on up there a secret."

Aaron scowled, but she could tell that it was more at the general state of affairs than it was at her. "Yeah, sounds about right unfortunately."

"But maybe they wouldn't have time… if we went back tonight."

Aaron let out an incredulous laugh. "Are you *nuts*?!"

"Come on," she said. "Think about it—you know I'm right."

"You're certifiable is what you are," he said. "That is the absolute last thing we should do."

"It's the absolute last thing they'd *expect* us to do," she corrected. "So all things considered, it's probably pretty safe."

Aaron pressed his palms into his eyelids, making some vaguely hysterical sound. Dropping his hands, he turned to her, brows lowered.

"Listen," he said. "This has already gotten way out of hand. We were supposed to just drive up there, take a quick look around, and head back. No evasive action, no detours, *definitely* no breaking and entering. Just a boring bit of reconnaissance and home."

She raised a challenging eyebrow. "Are you saying you're not up to a little breaking and entering? Don't have the stomach for it?"

He threw his hands up in dismay. "I'm saying this entire conversation is ludicrous! And I'm not indulging it one minute longer—we are going back to Ad Astra, and that's final."

As he turned back to the steering wheel and reached for the gear shift, Colleen realized she wasn't going to be able to brazen this one out. So she made one last attempt to convince, using a tactic that did not come naturally to her—subtlety.

"Aaron," she said quietly. "Don't you want to do something real to help those people?"

Aaron paused then, looking like he wanted nothing more than a strong drink and a good long sleep. Then, with a growl of frustration, he put the car into gear and steered them out onto the northbound side of the highway.

AARON KILLED the headlights as they approached the sanatorium, navigating his path by moonlight. He did not approach the gate this time, instead turning off the road into a stand of trees near the iron fence, easing the auto to a stop. Wordlessly, he reached into the back seat and pulled out an electric torch, flipping the power switch a few times to make sure it was working.

"So what's our play?" Colleen said.

"As far as I can tell, our only real option is going over the fence," Aaron replied.

Colleen slumped in her seat. "I was afraid you'd say that."

Aaron gave her a sidelong glance. "If you don't think you're up to it-"

"I'm up to it!" she snapped, then heaved a sigh. "I'm not particularly dressed for it, but I'm up to it. What about getting inside the building?"

"Daniel's been teaching me to pick locks," Aaron said. "I brought my picks with me, just in case."

Colleen raised an eyebrow. "In case of what, exactly, Mr. We Just Came to Look Around?"

"I don't know," Aaron said, throwing up his hands. "A random opportunity for some light burglary? In any case, I should be able to get us in.

"All right, then," Colleen said. "Let's go."

They both got out, closing their doors softly behind them. As they approached the fence, Colleen could see Aaron looking up and down the length of it, trying to find the best entry point. The ironwork boasted a frankly unnecessary amount of decorative finials and scroll-work along the top, which made scaling it a dicey proposition, but every so often, the iron gave way to a brick pillar that was more or less flat on top. Aaron lifted his chin to the closest of these, and Colleen nodded.

When they reached the column, Aaron put the torch down and leaned forward, making his hands into a cradle that he held out to Colleen. Taking a deep breath, Colleen wrapped one hand around a fence post and stepped into Aaron's grip. The climb itself didn't bother her; she'd spent years scrambling up and down the fire escapes in her neighborhood, after all, but she'd done it in her brothers' hand-me-down dungarees and boots, not a fashionable dress and delicate pumps. Nevertheless, when Aaron hoisted her up, she planted her other foot on a crossbeam in the fence and maneuvered herself into a sitting position on top of the pillar, hoping he hadn't caught a glimpse of her unmentionables as she went.

Swinging her legs to the inside of the fence, she gazed down into the shadows, thinking that the drop seemed much longer than it had on the way up. It wasn't like she had a choice, though. Even if she hadn't been desperate to find out what was on that upper floor, which she was, there was no way she was going to let Aaron see her back down. Taking the marginal precaution of removing her shoes so she didn't turn an ankle, she tossed them to the grass ahead of her and then eased herself off the pillar to the ground.

She realized in an instant just how far removed she was from her fire escape days. She hit the ground harder than expected, and her foot slipped, causing her to land flat on her ass. She let out a whispered stream of profanity as she shifted to her knees and felt around for her shoes. She had just gotten them back on her feet when Aaron dropped down next to her with infuriating grace. He was decent enough not to be smug about it as he held out a hand and helped her to stand.

"You OK?" he whispered, and she took a few experimental steps. Her right hip throbbed, and she knew she'd have a wicked bruise there the next day, but otherwise, she seemed more or less all right. She gave Aaron a nod, and the two of them started off towards the main building.

They picked their way carefully across the grass, ears pricked for any sounds of movement on the grounds. The lawn hadn't seemed especially large to her earlier in the day, but now it felt impossibly vast, bathed as it was in moonlight that exposed their every step.. Eventually, though, they reached the safety of the main building's shadows. While the darkness concealed them, it also obscured any hint of the rustic charm the staff had been so careful to cultivate for the public. The structure loomed over them, prodigious and forbidding, the bulk of it blotting out the sky as they made their way to the door of the screened-in sunroom.

After a few moments of whispered conversation, they decided Colleen would wait in the bushes next to the stairs while Aaron went up to pick the lock. Crouching as best she could with her sore hip, Colleen couldn't see much of what Aaron was doing, but she could see the tension in the way he held himself, the taut set to his jaw as worked the picks. As the interminable seconds ticked by, she felt the first stirrings of panic. He'd admitted, after all, that he was still learning. What if all of this was for nothing? What if he ended up alerting someone to their presence, and they got caught?

She was becoming increasingly torn between asking him what was taking so long, which would only break his concentration and prolong this ordeal even more, and keeping her mouth shut, which had never come naturally to her, ever, when she heard the soft click of the lock giving way. She hadn't really needed to hear it, though; Aaron's body practically sang with relief. At his downward glance, she scrambled up the stairs. Taking care to close the door soundlessly behind them, they slipped inside and made a beeline for the central hallway.

Suddenly, Aaron froze, holding up a hand in warning. At first, Colleen couldn't tell what had grabbed his attention, but then she heard it, and her stomach sank. Footsteps. They weren't terribly close yet, but with every stride, they came closer; soon enough, whoever they belonged to would be upon Aaron and Collen.

Springing to the left on his toes, Aaron grabbed the knob of the nearest door, but it refused to budge in his grip. Colleen tried the closest door to the right, but her luck was no better. They each moved on to the next door on their side of the hall, but those were also locked up tight, and the footsteps sounded as if they would turn the corner at any moment. Colleen felt a panicked sob rising in her throat when the third door Aaron tried swung open into absolute darkness. He grabbed Colleen's arm and yanked her inside, shutting the door just as the torch beam swept into view at the hallway junction.

For a moment, all Colleen could focus on was her rapid breathing and hammering heart, but gradually, she came back to herself enough to realize that the room they were in wasn't a room at all, but some sort of supply closet. She couldn't see a thing in the pitch black, but she felt the hard wooden handles of brooms and mops pressing into her back and caught a whiff of disinfectant; raising a tentative hand, she could feel glass bottles lined up on shelves to her left. Also, the space was sufficiently snug that Aaron was pressed flush against her, close enough to feel that he was barely breathing.

The proximity was startling. She'd known Aaron was handsome, obviously, with his bright smile and lean, muscled physique, but being able to feel that physique along every inch of her own body... well, in a day filled with surprises, this one might take the cake. Not that it was entirely unpleasant. Not at all...

But, she reminded herself fiercely, they had bigger things to worry about at the moment. Since her eyes were useless, she squeezed them shut, straining to hear what was happening out in the hallway. The footsteps were getting closer. Their pace remained steady, leisurely, not suggestive of any suspicion. As they seemed to come even with the closet, she couldn't help herself anymore. She cracked an eye just in time to see the edge of the flashlight beam slide past the crack under the door, and the footsteps continued on down the hall.

She closed her eyes again, this time in relief. Aaron let out a silent gust of air and some of the tension left his muscles, which had the unfortunate side effect of settling more of his weight on Colleen. The shift knocked her off balance, and while there wasn't much of anywhere to go, she frantically braced herself against the door so as not to rattle any of the bottles. It worked, though it seemed she'd somehow knocked one of the brooms over; she could feel the handle pressing into her hip-

Wait. Was that...

Oh. *Oh.*

She went very still, and Aaron must have realized she noticed, because he immediately tried to arch his body away from hers, a futile enterprise in the tight space. Colleen felt a hysterical urge to laugh, but instead she bit her lip, counting silently in her head. When she got to sixty, she reached out and turned the doorknob. Aaron all but fell out into the hallway, tugging at his clothes, as she stepped out after him and pulled the door quietly shut.

"Apologies," he said in a hoarse whisper, running a hand over the back of his head. "It's just... the friction..."

With some difficulty, Colleen shook off the smothering fog of mortification, smoothing her skirt and ignoring the warmth from his body that lingered on her skin.

"It's fine," she whispered. "We're all adults here. And the clock is ticking, so are we going to stand her jabbering, or are we going to get to work?"

Looking almost painfully relieved, Aaron nodded, and without another word, they resumed their long, fraught journey.

CHAPTER 13

AARON

They climbed the stairs slowly, heedful of any creak or rattle as they set down their feet. Finally—blessedly—they reached the second floor, and Aaron paused.

"Stay here or keep going?" he whispered, looking at the stairs that continued to spiral upward. When he turned his gaze to Colleen, he saw that she was worrying at her lip.

"Stay," she whispered finally. "We may find something here that will help us know what to expect as we go on."

This was fairly sound reasoning, as there was absolutely nothing in their current surroundings that hinted at what they were walking into. The hall extended to both the left and right of the staircase. In each direction, the walls were lined with identical, nondescript doors. No signage, no decorations—there wasn't even a runner on the floor. Upon closer inspection, Aaron could see small brass numbers mounted above each doorknob, but those were the only distinguishing features.

Also, each knob boasted a very secure lock. The kind that suggested the administration really, *really* wanted to keep nosy visitors out of these rooms. The kind that would be hard as hells to pick. Aaron started to sweat.

"Where should we start?" Colleen said, and after a moment, Aaron picked a door more or less at random. Pulling the lock picks out of his pocket again, he crouched to examine the lock in the scant moonlight coming in the windows at the far ends of the hall.

It was, as he'd guessed, a rather complex lock, but not too different from the tricker ones Daniel had made him practice on, so he stuck the picks in and got to work. He made a concerted effort to keep his breathing steady and even, in order to transfer that steadiness to his hands, but the rhythm of the air entering and leaving his lungs sounded very loud to him in the dark silence of the hall. It didn't help that Colleen was standing almost as close as she'd been in the closet, only now she seemed to be directing all of her energy to making him hurry by sheer force of will.

"Come on," she said, her foot starting to jiggle with anxiety.

"I. Am. Trying." Aaron gritted out. "And you are not helping."

In his peripheral vision, he saw her physically struggling to keep from arguing, and he found that he was precariously close to losing the battle as well, but just then, the lock clicked. If he'd thought his breathing was loud, the click sounded like a gunshot, and he and Colleen both froze, ready for guards to descend at any moment. But they didn't. Cautiously, he rose from his crouch and turned the knob, sliding the picks out and back into his pocket. Then he slipped into the room with Colleen on his heels and eased the door shut behind them.

The curtains on the room's lone window were open, admitting more moonlight than those in the hallway had. Aaron could make out two empty beds that had recently been slept in, and he had just enough time to be surprised about that before he caught a flash of movement off to his side, which then registered as a metal chair careening towards his head.

He managed to get an arm up in time to deflect, but he still had to bite down to keep from crying out as pain radiated from wrist to elbow and even up into his shoulder. He had to content himself with cursing a blue streak in a choked whisper while Colleen leaped forward to close and lock the door and the chair clattered to the floor.

Aaron, still cradling his arm, looked up at his attacker. She was a slight figure, with bobbed hair that had gone ragged at the ends, so blonde it almost looked white, and for all that she was tiny, her expression was one of seething rage.

"Who in the hells are you?" she spat, but she kept her voice low just as Aaron had.

"We're friends," Colleen whispered. "We're here to help."

"Kirby, put it down," the girl said.

For a moment, Aaron was confused by the non sequitur, but then he realized with a start that there was someone else in the room.

A boy with hair almost the same color as the girl's had picked up the chair and was holding it above his shoulder, ready to strike. He was small, heartbreakingly so; Aaron would have put him at 8, possibly nine. He had the lean, hungry look of a street kid, so it was possible that malnourishment made him look younger than he actually was, but still—too young to be in a place like this.

"Kirb," the girl said again. "Put the chair down."

"But what if they try something?" the kid said. He was clearly trying to keep his voice quiet like the others, but it still came out louder than Aaron would have liked. The girl glowered at him, jaw set.

"I *said* put it down."

The boy wavered for a moment, debating whether to obey. Then his face twisted into a fierce scowl and he let go of the chair, which hit the floor with a crack. As the others cringed at the sound, he threw himself onto one of the beds, curling in on himself and facing the wall.

The girl sighed and turned back to Aaron and Colleen, apparently ready to continue her interrogation, but just then, there were footsteps outside. The doorknob jiggled slightly, as if someone had put a hand on it, though there was no sound of a key in the lock.

"Parker?" a voice said. "Everything OK in there?"

The girl closed her eyes, looking pained. "Yeah, Murphy. We're fine."

"I just thought I heard some banging. You sure you're alright?"

"Yeah. Kirb just had a bad dream is all—I've got it under control."

"OK," Murphy said, still not sounding entirely convinced. "Give me a shout if you need anything."

"Will do," the girl replied, and they all stood frozen as they listened to Murphy's footsteps get further away.

"Parker?" Colleen whispered urgently when they were confident he was gone. "Do you mean Imogen Parker?"

The girl looked taken aback, but then her expression settled into suspicion.

"Yeah. How do you know me?"

"We've been looking for you," Colleen said. "And some other adepts who went missing from charm schools in the city."

Imogen's face went strangely blank. Aaron suspected it was because there were too many emotions warring inside of her, and none of them were quite strong enough to subdue the others.

"I didn't think anyone even noticed we were gone," she whispered.

"I did," Colleen said, and there was no smugness in her tone—only empathy and reassurance. Aaron wondered if that was new or if he was just getting better at reading her.

"Are you here to get us out?" Imogen said, an almost bitter twist to her words. The question of a jaded person who, against her will, had started to feel the stirrings of hope. It broke Aaron's heart.

"Well, no..." Colleen began, but she broke off when she caught sight of his face. "What?"

"We can't leave them," he said.

Both girls stared at him wide-eyed. "What are you talking about?" Collen sputtered. "You're the one who said coming back her to look around was dangerous. What's going to happen when they realize they're short two patients?!"

"We need them," Aaron said, mind spinning. Colleen wasn't the only one with tricks up her sleeve when it came to persuasion. He suspected she didn't like the idea of leaving these two behind any more than he did, but he knew now that a pragmatic argument was more likely to sway her than a sentimental one. "They know far more than we would be able to take back to Esme ourselves. They can help us figure out what to do next. And help you find the most compelling angle for your story." When she hesitated, he pushed forward. "Are you trying to wriggle out of paying off our bet? Because that hardly seems sportsmanlike. I want my nickel."

Aaron could see in Colleen's face that she was wavering. She shot a sideways look at Imogen, then threw a glance over her shoulder towards Kirby's huddled form on the bed and sighed.

"Fine," she said. "But let's go now. We don't have much time."

Aaron and Imogen locked eyes, and the blonde girl hurried to the bed, bending over to give Kirby a gentle shake.

"Kirb," she said. "Come on. We're getting out of here."

The boy shook her hand off of his shoulder and muttered something Aaron couldn't hear. Imogen closed her eyes for a second before speaking again.

"If you don't come now," she said, teeth gritted. "I will leave you here by yourself, and I won't feel bad about it. I'm not giving up my chance to leave this hellhole behind, so get with the program or get used to surviving this place alone."

For a long moment, Kirby didn't respond, seemingly deciding if he should call her bluff. Because it was a bluff—Aaron could tell by the look of agony on her face. But Kirby couldn't see that look, and her voice hadn't wavered as she'd issued her threat. With a growl, he threw himself upright and faced them, scowling.

Aaron took a deep breath. "All right. We have a car outside the perimeter fence. We just need to get out of the building and across the lawn without alerting any of the guards." He looked at Imogen. "Is there anything you can tell us to help with that?"

She shook her head. "We're always locked up in here. I don't know anything about what they do out there all night."

This made sense, for all that it was supremely unhelpful. "OK then, we just go fast and quiet and hope for the best."

On the bed, Kirby snorted, and even Imogen looked dubious. Colleen scowled.

"Look, it got us this far," she hissed, and whatever the other two thought, they didn't argue.

With a sharp gesture from Imogen, Kirby finally got off the bed and joined the others by the door. Then, the four of them set about retracing Aaron and Colleen's steps to the auto. Aaron wouldn't have believed it, but the trip down the stairs seemed even longer and more perilous that ascending them had. They all made it without incident, though, and Aaron couldn't help but breathe a small sigh of relief. That was one obstacle down; now they just had to focus on getting out of the building.

He should have known he'd jinxed them by even having the thought. Because they hadn't made it ten yards before a guard turned a corner ahead of them, catching them in the light of his torch.

Behind Aaron, Imogen sucked in a sharp breath. Aaron had a hard time making out the man's face behind his flashlight beam, but he could see the pistol at the man's belt well enough. When he spoke, Aaron recognized his voice as the one he'd heard through the door upstairs.

"Parker?" the man said, and behind the censure in his voice, Aaron thought he detected a note of... disappointment? Hurt?

"Murph, I can explain," Imogen began, but Aaron could see the man's hand twitching toward his pistol, so he didn't wait to see what she had in mind. Instead, he lunged forward and seized Murphy by the wrists.

This effectively kept the guard from reaching his gun right away, but that was not Aaron's primary goal. It was difficult using his power through touch without skin-to-skin contact, but when his emotions were heightened, as they were now, he could make it work even with the cloth of the uniform jacket in the way.

Pushing away his fear, he made himself focus on the time Oliver had acquired a batch of particularly excellent reefer, and a group of them had gone up to the roof of the club to smoke it. It had been a balmy summer night with a clear sky and a full moon, and they had sprawled across the cast-off furniture that adorned the roof, passing around the joint and talking nonsense. The world had gone soft around Aaron, all starlight and distant laughter. It was perhaps the most relaxed he had ever felt.

Before him now, the guard's eyes started turning glassy, and his hands went slack in Aaron's grip. Aaron didn't release his hold, though, urging more of that remembered serenity, that calm, into the guard's consciousness. He was almost there. He only had to push a little bit further.. just a tiny bit more-

The guard slumped in his arms, unconscious. Aaron caught him, stumbling slightly under the sudden weight, then eased the slack body to the floor. When he looked up, Colleen, Imogen, and Kirby were gazing at him wide-eyed, their expressions both shocked and relieved.

"We don't have long," he whispered. "Let's go."

Their urgency made them less careful, but they still made it out of the building without encountering any other guards. Aaron led them past the trees and cottages closest to the main building. When they reached the clearing, they took turns sprinting across the open expanse until all four of them huddled at the foot of the pillar Aaron and Colleen had used to scale the fence the first time.

Aaron boosted Colleen up first, and she once again took off her shoes and dropped to the ground, though this time, she managed to keep to her feet. Next came Imogen, and then Kirby, with Colleen helping them over, though both were so agile, she suspected they didn't need it. All seemed to be going well until Aaron reached for the fence—and all the lights in the main building came on at once. Half a moment later, a siren wailed, and the sound of dogs barking drifted across the lawn.

"Hurry!" Colleen said, but Aaron didn't need to be told twice. He scaled the fence in half the time he'd taken on the way into the compound, and as soon as his feet hit the ground, the four of them were sprinting to the auto.

Aaron and Colleen scrambled back to their places, while Imogen shoved Kirby ahead of her into the back seat. Dispensing with any attempt at stealth, Aaron revved the engine and hooked a sharp U-turn back towards the road, spraying dirt and grass behind them.

As the auto hit the pavement of the road, Collen spun to look behind her, joining Imogen and Kirby in squinting through the back windshield at the receding sanatorium.

"What have we got?" Aaron said, hands tight on the wheel.

"People spreading out all over the grounds," Colleen said. "A few with dogs. Don't see any autos yet, though." She faced front once more, face grim, eyes on the road. "Drive."

Aaron drove. When they hit the highway, he turned north based on some vague notion of getting the pursuers off their back before heading in the direction they actually wanted to go. As he sped along, Aaron kept his eyes open for some kind of turnoff—not another road or trail, but an opening in the trees where the car would be hidden from passersby. Finally, one flashed in his peripheral vision, and he cut the wheel sharply to the right.

The auto's occupants lurched with the transition from smooth pavement to uneven terrain. Stray branches scratched the auto's roof and sides as they moved; Aaron suspected he'd get an earful about the state of the paint when they got home, but he'd just have to deal with that then. Eventually, he came to a point where the trees closed in too tightly for them to progress any further. Deciding they were reasonably safe, shifted the car into park and killed the engine and the headlights.

"Hey, now, what are you doing?" Imogen said, alarmed. "You didn't just bring us out here to murder us or something, did you?"

"No," Aaron said patiently. "I just wanted to get us somewhere safe so we can make a plan for what to do next."

"Aren't we going back to Ad Astra?" Colleen said, and he shook his head.

"I'm not sure anybody got a good look at the auto, but at this time of night, we'd be some of the only ones out on the road. They'd find us in a heartbeat. We need to wait until morning, when we wouldn't be quite so obvious." He looked over at Colleen, nodding toward the glove compartment. "I think there might be a road map in there. You probably have a better sense of the area than the rest of us. Want to take a look?"

Colleen swallowed and nodded, but she didn't look especially confident. Reaching forward, she popped the door of the glove compartment open, revealing a jumbled collection of maps. Squinting through the gloom, she managed to find one depicting the stretch of land north of Merrimack. She shoved the others back into place, nudging the door shut with her knee, and spread the map out on her lap. Then she scowled out the window at the clouds partially obscuring the moon. "I can't see anything like this. Maybe you could turn the headlights on and I could get out and read by-"

She stopped abruptly at a soft flare of brightness from the back seat. The next thing she knew, Imogen was leaning forward and extending her arm, flames dancing on the tips of her fingers.

"Oh," Colleen said haltingly. "Thank you." She lifted a hand, then glanced at Imogen. "May I?"

Imogen nodded, and Colleen took her wrist, adjusting the angle to best see the map.

At first, she seemed to just let her eyes roam, orienting herself. The map was one of those promotional things gas stations stocked for tourists; local landmarks, hotels, and other businesses were labeled in tiny red letters. She placed a finger next to Ocean Serenity and ran it up the highway, gauging how far they'd come. Unsurprisingly, there wasn't much nearby; Aaron suspected that was more or less the entire point of Ocean Serenity. But then she moved her finger up and to the left.

"Here," she said decisively, tapping the map. "That should give us a good place to lay low."

Aaron leaned over to see where she was pointing. "Houseman's Hideaway? What's that?"

"I'm pretty sure it's a bungalow colony," she said. "There are dozens of them up this way. We should be safe there, at least for a while."

Aaron looked dubious. "Are you sure we can get in there without anyone noticing? The last thing we need is some angry tourist shouting at us in his pajamas."

Colleen shook her head. "It's too early in the season. The colonies are typically closed up until families start traveling in the summer. I think it's our best bet."

She looked up, and the two of them locked eyes. Aaron could sense her trepidation, but she really was the one most capable of making the call. He didn't have any better ideas, and he was acutely aware of the two terrified adepts in the back seat watching them, depending on them for safety. So he decided to trust her judgment.

"All right," he said. "Houseman's Hideaway, here we come."

CHAPTER 14

AARON

*A*aron drove to Houseman's Hideaway slowly, while Colleen murmured directions and Imogen and Kirby sat gazing out the back window, craning their necks to detect any hint of pursuit. He realized that all these gestures towards alertness were ultimately empty; if anybody stumbled upon them at this point, they would certainly be outnumbered and would vanish even more completely than adepts in the back seat had the first time. But the alternative was to break down from the strain, which wasn't an option, so on he drove at a snail's pace.

"What did you say this place was again?" he said, mostly just to break the silence.

"A bungalow colony," Colleen said absently, watching the trees slide by outside the window.

"Which is?" he prompted when she didn't continue.

Something about this second question caught her attention where the first hadn't and she turned to look at him.

"It's a vacation spot," she said. "Families from the city come out to spend the summer in the fresh air. Sometimes the dads stay in the city to work, then come out to join the families on the weekends."

"Just people from Merrimack?" he asked.

"Mostly, but there are a few from Ad Astra and even from the south or out west, if it's a family tradition."

"I've never heard of these places," he said. "How do you know about them?"

"When I was a kid, my best friend Miriam's family went to one, and one summer, I was allowed to go with them for a little while." She sighed, biting her lip thoughtfully. "Never thought I'd be heading back to one as a fugitive."

Aaron was about to point out that they weren't technically fugitives yet, assuming the sanitarium staff hadn't contacted the authorities—and they probably hadn't, considering they were hiding a secret whatever-it-was up there—but then she said, "There is it" and gestured to the left side of the road. Without the heads-up, he probably would have driven right past it, but now he could see a slight break in the trees and a wooden sign with "Houseman's Hideaway" carved into it with what looked like more enthusiasm than skill. Feeling the car slow even further for the turn, Imogen and Kirby faced front, the four of them hushed with anticipation for what awaited them.

In an odd way, the colony's layout mimicked that of the sanitarium, if both less grand and less forbidding. At the center of the property, there was a long, low building with a paved area out back; upon closer inspection, the paving proved to be a tennis court, though there were no nets in evidence at the moment. Gravel paths extended from the building in both directions, curving back from the entrance to form two lanes lined by tiny bungalows. Off in the distance, there was a faint gleam of moonlight on water—presumably a pond or creek. Once more, Aaron pulled off into the trees to ensure that the auto was hidden from any prying eyes.

Leaving the car behind, the four picked their way through the scraggly grass around the central building until they came to a back door. Aaron pulled his lock picks out again, making quicker work of this lock than he had back at the hospital (he couldn't help but think that he actually was getting quite good at this) and eased the door open.

The moonlight filtering through the trees revealed a spacious kitchen. Colleen ushered Imogen and Kirby inside, and Aaron followed, closing the door behind him. Turning on the electric torch, Aaron swept the beam around, revealing some ancient cabinets and counters paired with a jarringly new kitchen and stove, but the space had an air of disuse; it was clean, but almost clinically so, as if no one had actually cooked in it for some time. A swinging door at the far end of the room ostensibly permitted access to the rest of the building, though Aaron couldn't make anything out through the small window embedded in it.

No one spoke, but the setting seemed to make an impression anyway, because Kirby's stomach let out a mighty growl. He crossed his arms, self-conscious, and Imogen gave him a concerned look.

"It's been a while since dinner," she said, glancing at Colleen and Aaron.

"There's a roast beef sandwich in the car," Colleen said, but Kirby hunched defensively.

"I, um, already ate it."

Colleen and Aaron stared at him, but Imogen jumped to his defense.

"He's a growing kid!"

"Could we see if there's any food?" Kirby asked in a small voice that hit Aaron right in the heart. He gestured at a door off to the left labeled "Pantry". "Please?"

"All right," Colleen said, and when Aaron opened his mouth to suggest that maybe they should think about it, she continued, "We can leave some money on the counter to cover it". Which did seem a perfectly reasonable strategy, so Aaron closed his mouth.

Not needing to be told twice, Kirby and Imogen went to the pantry and began rummaging around. Colleen found a wall switch and turned on the overhead lights for them, then she and Aaron pushed through the swinging door to see what else the building had to offer.

It was a large space, but Aaron couldn't tell much else about it. The only windows he could see had been installed up near the ceiling around the perimeter of the room, not much wider than they were tall, and they let in only a meager bit of moonlight. Pointing the torch beam at the wall, he found another light switch and flipped it.

A handful of fixtures mounted on the ceiling flickered to life, revealing a comfortably shabby dining area with a small stage at one end and a frankly tragic excuse for a bar at the other. Round dining tables and chairs were stacked on and around the stage, seemingly to allow for the deep cleaning and polishing of the wooden floorboards, which, like the appliances, stood out in contrast to the worn-in feeling of the room at large. A few other random pieces of furniture were distributed through the space, including a battered velvet sofa and a half-empty bookcase. The walls were hung with photos featuring smiling groups of people gathered outside a building that must be the one they were standing in, as well as endearingly amateurish paint-ings, presumably done by some of the people in the photos. All in all, it could have been a lot worse.

By unspoken agreement, Colleen and Aaron stepped into the room to get a closer look at the state of things. A few moments later, Kirby came bursting through the kitchen door with a jumble of items in his arms, while Imogen proceeded more slowly, trying to preserve her tentative grip on four glasses of water.

Kirby went to a relatively clear spot on the stage and dropped his loot. Stepping closer, Aaron could see that he had managed to scav-enge a puzzling hodgepodge of snacks: a box of crackers, home-canned jar of pickles, store-bought jar of peanut butter, and partial link of dry summer sausage. Some of Aaron's confusion and distaste must have shown, because Imogen explained the haul as she set the glasses down carefully next to the food.

"It was mostly dry ingredients in the pantry; these were the only ready-to-eat foods we could find. The refrigerator wasn't even plugged in. There were dishes, though, and silverware." Reaching into her back pocket, she pulled out some of the latter and handed it to Kirby, who immediately pried the lid off the peanut butter and dug into it with a spoon. That only held his attention for a moment though, before he spotted a battered velvet sofa across the room.

"That looks comfy," he said, gathering up an armful of food and a glass. "I'm going to go eat over there." Then he shuffled over to the sofa and flopped down, spilling half his water down the front of his shirt. Soon, though, he was settled enough to begin shoveling food into his mouth.

"He's quite, um, exuberant," Colleen said, and Imogen laughed.

"He's a terror. But most kids his age are."

"Is he your... brother?" Colleen hazarded. "Or son?"

This only made Imogen laugh again, harder this time.

"Gods, no. I'd never laid eyes on him until he showed up at the asylum a few weeks ago."

"Really?" Aaron said. "You two seem close."

Imogen shrugged. "He was practically feral when they brought him in—screaming, biting. They kept having to sedate him. I had an empty bed in my room, so they stuck him in there with me. Said I'd be a calming influence on him. I guess they thought, being a woman, I'd have some sort of maternal instinct to draw on or something." Her tone made it very clear what she thought of this assumption.

"It does seem like it sort of worked," Colleen said, glancing at Kirby, and Imogen's expression turned rueful.

"I guess it did," she said and took a sip of water. "I do have a brother; I guess Kirb sort of reminds me of him. I was good at calming him down when we were young."

"Did he have powers like Kirby's?" said Colleen.

Imogen shook her head. "Nah. He was just a kid. Sometimes, kids get upset for no reason."

Aaron and Colleen exchanged a glance. They both knew that well enough.

"Speaking of powers," Aaron said. "What exactly is Kirby's?"

"He can see inside of people," Imogen said.

Colleen cocked her head. "What, like he can see through their skin to their internal organs?"

Imogen gave her a despairing look. "No. I mean he can see into people's heads." She tapped her own skull for emphasis. "Sometimes it even feels like it's into their souls. He can tell what their worries are, what makes them happy, all kinds of things."

"Like Oliver," Aaron murmured, and Imogen looked at him sharply.

"Who's Oliver?"

"A friend," Aaron assured her. "One who sent us to find out what happened to you and all the others who were taken. You'll meet him tomorrow, once we think it's safe to travel."

Imogen raised her eyebrows. "You're going to take this kind of heat to his door? How do you think he's going to take that?"

"He'll adapt," Aaron said easily. Imogen nodded, but she still looked dubious.

"Where did Kirby come from?" Colleen asked. "I don't remember seeing a report on him in any of the police blotters, although I'm sure there were reports I'd missed. Ad Astra's a big place, after all."

Imogen shook her head. "Kirby didn't come from Ad Astra; he said they picked him up in Merrimack."

Colleen's brow furrowed. "Are there even any charm schools in Merrimack?"

"A few," Aaron said. "But from what I've heard, they're pretty divey —not like the big clubs in Ad Astra."

Imogen snorted a laugh. "Oh, I assure you, some of the places in Ad Astra are plenty divey."

Aaron bent his head in acknowledgment, feeling a little sheepish. "Yeah, I guess that's fair."

Just then, a large burp sounded from the sofa, followed by a deep sigh. They all looked over to see that Kirby had apparently finished gorging himself and was now succumbing to post-meal sleepiness. Which made sense, Aaron mused—he'd had a big night.

Imogen put her glass down on the stage and got to her feet. "I'd better go check on him so he doesn't end up falling asleep with his nose in that peanut butter jar."

She walked over to the sofa and began speaking softly to Kirby, helping him to move the ruins of his feast so he could lay down. Colleen and Aaron sat quietly, watching her.

"He doesn't have anything to do with charm schools," Colleen said finally. "Does he?"

"No," Aaron replied. "He's just a punk adept no one would miss."

"How'd the sanatorium people find him, do you think?" Collen said, and Aaron let out a long breath.

"He was probably sleeping on the street, running afoul of the local kids. When they saw what he could do, they probably got scared, and that made them cruel. Word gets around. If a copper or some RPC loyalist caught wind of it, it wouldn't have been hard to tip somebody off."

Colleen sat very still, clearly processing. A moment later, she got to her feet and began walking around the perimeter of the room, inspecting the jumble of items hung on the walls. Glancing over at the sofa, Aaron got up and followed so they could keep talking without bothering Imogen and Kirby. Out of habit more than anything else, he made his way behind the bar, propping his crossed arms on the worn surface as he watched Colleen ramble.

In the course of her wanderings, she came to an intricately detailed wooden cabinet against the far wall. Roughly waist height, the cabinet sported a pair of doors topped by a pane of etched glass with dials set to either side. Colleen paused, cocking her head.

"What is this?" she muttered, seemingly to herself, but Aaron answered anyway.

"It's an audiophone."

She turned her head to look at him. "A what?"

"An audiophone," he said. "You put a coin in and it plays a record."

Colleen brightened. "Oh, yeah! I've heard of those. Never seen one in real life before, though."

She returned her attention to the cabinet, running her hand over the top of it in an appreciative way. Then she kept walking.

After a long beat, she turned abruptly to Aaron.

"How'd you do that back at the sanatorium?"

Aaron raised his eyebrows. "Sorry?"

"The guard," she said. "How'd you knock him out like that?"

Aaron rubbed the back of his neck, feeling sheepish. "Well, I started thinking about this time that Oliver got some good weed. We all went up to the roof to smoke it—we've fixed the roof up really nice, there's benches and blankets and stuff—and I just thought about how relaxed we all felt-"

"Whoa, whoa, whoa," Colleen cut in, holding up a hand. "You mean to tell me that instead of, I don't know, strong-arming his will into submission... you just got him high?"

"Well, it doesn't sound very impressive when you put it like that," Aaron replied. "But yeah, pretty much."

Colleen stared at him, slack-jawed, then snapped her mouth closed with a shake of her head.

"Unbelievable," she murmured.

She continued to wander aimlessly for a while longer, then drifted back over towards the bar, coming to a stop in front of Aaron. She laid her palms flat on the bar top, sweeping them out in wide arcs before bringing them back in towards her body. She looked up at Aaron.

"Don't you ever get angry?" she asked.

Aaron shifted on his feet, caught off guard by the non sequitur.

"Um, yeah. Of course I do. Why wouldn't I?"

"You could have fooled me," she said. "You seem so even keeled." Her mouth quirked up. "At least, in those brief periods when I haven't managed to get under your skin."

He rolled his eyes. "Yes, those periods are quite brief."

"Seriously, though," she said, sobering. "How do you do it?"

"Well, who actually likes walking around angry?"

"Nobody," Colleen said. "And yet people do it all the time. What makes you different?"

Aaron spread his own hands out on top of the bar, echoing her movement of the moment before, as he gathered his thoughts. "They want us angry," he said finally. "They want us just as filled with fear and hate and rage as they are. And I don't want to give them that much power over me. That view of the world is a prison, and I won't put myself in it."

"I wish I had that kind of moral clarity," she said.

"It's not moral clarity. It's survival. It's what gets me through the day."

She paused, looking at him until she seemed to come to some sort of decision. Then she hopped up onto one of the barstools.

"Make me a drink."

His eyebrows shot up. "What?"

She rolled her eyes. "Oh, you heard me. Don't make a big deal out of it."

But the thing was, it *was* a big deal. He just stood there for a moment, frozen by the uncertainty of how to respond, until she gave him a look of perplexed despair. Then he stepped back and cast a discerning eye on the bar, relieved to have somewhere to look besides at her.

The relief was short-lived.

"It's pretty slim pickings back here," he said mournfully. "Not a lot to choose from."

He crouched to inspect the shelves underneath the bar, hoping to find some glassware, but it was in vain. The disappointment he felt was silly. There was plenty in the kitchen; their own water glasses were just across the room on the table. But he felt oddly reluctant to leave this strange bubble they seemed to have created. He didn't want to break whatever fragile spell they'd cast.

He caught a soft gleam from the corner of his eye and let out a huff of triumph as he pulled out a copper mug. Not a proper vessel for anything he'd be able to make with what was on hand, but it would have to do. He placed it on the bar in front of Colleen with a flourish, then turned to examine the meager collection of bottles lined up against the wall.

Eventually, he grabbed a bottle of bourbon—mediocre at best, but what he had to work with. Next, he picked out a bottle of sweet vermouth and another of bitters, placing them beside the mug and reaching for a shaker.

"So, I'm going to attempt something approximating a boulevardier."

Colleen looked up from the bottles. "A what?"

"It's a drink that's popular in Belleterre," Aaron explained. "No clue if it's actually going to work. They don't have the right kind of bitters here, so I'm improvising with another type of aperitif, which should do the trick, but the flavor profile is different, so it's a crap shoot."

"I don't know what any of that means," Colleen said as he inspected the inside of the shaker, verifying that it was reasonably clean. He raised an eyebrow at her.

"Didn't you grow up in a bar?"

"I didn't spend much time *behind* the bar," she said. "And our clientele was mostly beer and whiskey drinkers—not much call for fancy cocktails."

"Fair enough," Aaron conceded, but he kept fidgeting. Colleen reached out and laid her hand on top of his, just as she had in the car.

"I'm sure it will be fine."

Aaron swallowed, then withdrew his hand and began pouring out the various ingredients, measuring them with an expert eye. He could have just stirred the drink, but he didn't see any of the long spoons intended for that purpose, so shaking it was. "Just keep in mind that these are supposed to be made with ice. I also like to add an orange twist, but there's not much in the way of fresh produce on hand."

"Aaron," she said, her voice so soft and gentle, he could practically feel it. "It's OK. I trust you."

And he knew that, somehow, she did. The weight of it caught him in the chest, and all he could do was nod as he gave the mixture a final shake and whisper of intent, then poured it into the mug.

"Your beverage, my lady," he said, sliding it toward Colleen.

Collen lifted the drink to her nose and sniffed it then took a long sip, grimacing against the burn. She stared down into the remaining liquid as she ran her tongue around the inside of her mouth.

"How will I know if it worked?"

"Oh, you'll know," Aaron said, amused and anxious in equal parts.

She took another experimental sip and seemed to turn her focus inward, searching for the imminent effects. With his practiced eye, Aaron saw the telltale signs—the loosening of her shoulders, the dilated pupils and slightly glassy quality in her eyes. After a moment, she took a third sip, no sour face at all this time, and set the mug meticulously back on the counter. Then she held out a hand, palm up, and looked at Aaron.

"Give me a nickel."

Aaron gazed at her, startled. "What for?"

She huffed in annoyance. "Just give it to me."

"But you haven't won the bet," he said, grasping at straws. "At least not yet."

When she spoke again, her voice was softer, but no less compelling.

"Give me the nickel, Aaron."

For a moment, both of them were still, the air between them charged with uncertainty. Then, as something slow and hot bloomed in his chest, Aaron reached into his pocket and pulled out a small collection of change. He poked through the coins until he found a nickel, then held it out to her. He might have expected a coy grin and snappy remark about giving in, but she took it from him almost solemnly, hopped off the stool, and crossed the room to the audiophone. He heard the soft clunk of the nickel landing inside the machine and saw Colleen fiddle with the dials to make her selections. Then the music began, something playful and bouncy with a lot of rollicking clarinet, though not raucous enough to disturb Imogen and Kirby, who both seemed to be dozing.

Colleen paused for a moment, just listening, then nodded, corners of her mouth lifting in a small, secret smile. As the first verse began, she moved to the center of the room, where she toed off her shoes. She shook out her arms and legs, presumably stiff from being in the car for hours, and did a few springy, impromptu dance steps before assuming a position that Aaron recognized from watching Paloma— one foot placed several inches behind the other with her toes pointing in opposite directions, knees bent. He could see her concentrating, searching for some cue in the music, and then she leapt into a spin, one leg bent, toe pointed at the opposite knee. It wasn't a particularly graceful movement, but she completed two rotations before going back to her starting position, and she didn't fall over, which was impressive since he could tell the drink was kicking in. She looked over at him with a satisfied expression.

"I didn't know you danced," he said.

"Four years of lessons in the smelly gym at the Ogygian Society. Traditional dance, too, but I always preferred ballet." She slid her back foot up to meet her front, bringing her to a regular standing position, then bowed with a flourish. Aaron clapped, unable to fight back a smile as she came back to the bar.

"Why'd you quit?" Aaron said, and Colleen shrugged.

"Got too busy," she said. "I really wanted to go to college, but there was no way we could have afforded it with Da gone. So I started taking every odd job I could find that was even loosely related to journalism. I barely had time for school, let alone something like dance classes."

"Did you miss it?" Aaron said.

Colleen shrugged. "Didn't matter. I had to do what I had to do."

Aaron wasn't quite sure how to respond to that, but just then, the song moved into the bridge, the clarinetist really went to town, executing a series of trilling runs and bombastic high notes.

He raised his eyebrows, letting out a whistle.

"What?" Colleen said.

"That solo is… something."

She shrugged. "Maybe he just wanted to make sure we got our money's worth."

"Not everyone had to plug a coin into an audiophone to hear it."

"Still," she said. "I like it. If you're going to do something, you ought to do it up big." To emphasize her point, she lifted her glass and knocked back the rest of the drink, giving an exaggerated "Ahhh" as she set the empty glass back on the bar.

Aaron chuckled. "I suppose."

The song wound down to its conclusion, and there was a click from the audiophone as a second record slid into place. A moment later, another song began, this one slower, more insistent. Colleen glanced over her shoulder, then looked back to Aaron.

"Come on," she said. "I need a partner for this one."

Aaron held up a hand. "Oh, no. Trust me, you will live to regret it."

She let out a huff of irritation and grabbed the hand still hovering in the air between them, dragging him out from behind the bar. Ignoring his protestations, she pulled him out to the center of the floor. Turning to face him, she moved the hand in her grasp to her waist and laid her own now-free hand on his shoulder. Instinctively, he reached for her other hand, raising it to roughly shoulder height.

While she had seemed fairly assured in getting him out there, now that they were so close—close enough for him to catch another whiff of that perfume, to notice the even more pronounced difference in their heights, now that she was in her stocking feet—she appeared to falter a bit. Feeling some urge to step into the breach, he literally took the lead, shifting his weight from one foot to the other to set them swaying. As the singer crooned about truth and consequences, Colleen began to relax, and soon they found a comfortable rhythm.

"I love this song," she said, voice dreamy.

Aaron swallowed. "Yeah."

They swayed together through the rest of the verse, and then, without warning, Colleen stepped in even closer, resting her head on Aaron's chest. Knowing she'd be able to hear everything going on in there, he did his best to keep his breathing steady, to stop his pulse from racing, but he worried it was a hopeless endeavor. The debacle in the closet had gotten his heart pumping, too, but this was different. It felt natural. Intimate. He was exquisitely aware of her, from the warmth of her skin radiating through his shirt to the stray hairs ticking the underside of his chin. Tightening his grip on her fingers, he pulled their joined hands in closer to their bodies, until their knuckles rested only inches from her face. Distantly, he remained conscious of the room around them—Kirby snoring softly on the sofa, breeze whistling through cracks in the windows—but mostly, his world had shrunk to the circle of their arms and the rocking movement of their feet. He inhaled deeply, almost a gasp, but if Colleen noticed that it shook, she didn't say anything.

As the tempo of the song slowed, the singer's tremulous voice giving way to the low wail of a saxophone and then a final, winsome tinkle of piano, Aaron had to surrender to a truth he now recognized with utter clarity.

He was in way, way over his head.

CHAPTER 15

COLLEEN

The next morning, Colleen was awakened by sunshine streaming through the high windows. As her eyes fluttered open, she became aware of both a chill on her face and an absence of one on her body. Looking down, she saw that she had been covered with some sort of white fabric that was keeping her tolerably warm. Upon closer inspection, the fabric seemed to be a tablecloth, and a hazy memory from the night before emerged from her still sleepy brain. She had been tired, but Aaron hadn't wanted her to lay down on the bare floor, so he'd poked around the hall until he'd uncovered a stack of linens. He'd spread one out of the floor for her to lay on, then covered her up with another, and she'd been out within seconds. Reflecting on it now, she wondered where exactly Aaron was and got her answer when she tried to shift and her blanket tablecloth didn't move. Aaron was lying on top of the other half, still deep in sleep himself. Colleen paused for a moment, taking in his peaceful face and the way he had his hand tucked up under his cheek almost like a little boy. The sight caused a not unpleasant pang in her chest.

Slowly, she wriggled out from under the tablecloth and eased herself into a sitting position, taking special care not to disturb Aaron's rest. She turned her head from side to side, working out the stiffness in her neck, and took stock of how the rest of her was doing. She was surprised, if pleased, to realize she didn't feel any symptoms of a hangover; in fact, aside from a few other muscle complaints and the ache in her hip where she'd landed on it the night before, she felt rejuvenated and refreshed. She observed that whatever Aaron had given her, he should bottle it; he'd make a fortune. Almost as soon as she finished the thought though, she felt a surge of self-recrimination. He couldn't bottle it. It was too risky. And even if it weren't, there were many people who would be leery of anything touched by magic. Because they were afraid—as she had been.

Shaking off that grim train of thought, Colleen noted that Imogen and Kirby were still asleep on the sofa and, also, that she desperately needed to pee. Pushing up to her knees, she draped her share of the tablecloth blanket over Aaron, then got to her feet and looked around for a bathroom. Finding a tiny one tucked into the back corner of the hall by the bar, she quickly took care of business, then paused in front of the mirror, taking in the dire state of her hair. She tried to smooth it back out with some water from the sink but quickly gave it up for a lost cause. Between that, the runs in her stockings, and the bumps and bruises she'd acquired in the course of committing what were probably multiple felonies, any hint of feminine glamour was long gone. She had more or less reverted to the scrappy tomboy she'd been at twelve.

With a sigh, she opened the bathroom door and returned to the silent expanse of the dining room. She'd only been gone a minute or two, but in the space of that time, Aaron had woken up. When she saw him, her step hitched ever so slightly, but then she resumed her pace until she reached their makeshift bed.

"Hi." she said, her voice sounding overly bright in her ears.

"Hi," Aaron replied, looking up at her from where he still sat on the floor. It was hard to tell from just that one syllable, but she thought his voice sounded hesitant—guarded, even. It struck her that it didn't suit him.

"Do we know what time it is?" she asked, rubbing her arms, and

Aaron pulled a watch out of his pocket, pressing the button to pop it open.

"7:30," he said, snapping the watch shut and putting it back in his pocket.

"Do you think it's safe for us to start heading back to Ad Astra?"

Aaron nodded, then stretched before rising gracefully to his feet. "Probably so. Truck drivers should be out now, and commuters. Daytrippers going into the city for the day." He gave another decisive nod. "We should be able to blend in well enough."

Over on the sofa, Imogen and Kirby had begun to stir, perhaps roused by the conversation. Collen nodded in their direction.

"Do you think they're doing all right?"

"Probably as well as can be expected," Aaron said, and when she turned back to him, he was looking at her intently. "How about you?"

"Me?" she said, and she hated that it came out squeaky. She took a breath to collect herself. "I'm fine. Better than fine, actually." She cocked her head, examining him. "What did you put in that drink anyway?"

Aaron licked his lips, and if she wasn't mistaken, he looked nervous, but when he spoke his voice was even. "I gave you ease."

Colleen's chest went tight, though she couldn't have said why. "Ease? What does that mean?"

Aaron shifted his weight, his eyes sliding slightly to the side, so they weren't quite meeting hers. "I just kind of... took away your worries for a little while. Lifted the weight. So you could kind of, I don't know... be the you you wanted to be."

Colleen stared at him, ears ringing. Because, now that she was fully awake, she had a pretty clear memory of the night before. And apparently, being the her she wanted to be meant dancing with Aaron. And then falling asleep next to him.

And she simply did not know how she felt about that revelation.

Luckily, Imogen and Kirby were also approaching full wakefulness, and they either couldn't tell or didn't care that Colleen and Aaron were having a significant moment.

"Good morning," Imogen said, stretching. "Is it time to leave yet?"

"Yes," Aaron said, and if Colleen was not mistaken, he also seemed pretty relieved to be changing the subject. "We were just discussing that. We should be OK out on the road now that the sun's up."

"Can we stop and get something to eat?" Kirby said, rubbing sleep from his eyes, and Aaron raised an eyebrow.

"Why don't you see if there's something left around here to tide you over until we get to Ad Astra?"

Kirby scowled at the suggestion, but that didn't keep him from going over to the remains of his feast and scavenging a few crackers and the last of the pickles. When he was finished, the four of them set about putting the lodge back to rights—throwing away the trash, washing all the glasses, just generally trying to erase any sign that someone had been there. The exception was the money that Colleen saw Aaron leave behind on the kitchen counter to pay for the food—even though that had been her idea.

The drive back to Ad Astra wasn't quite the panicked flight of the previous night, but nor was it exactly relaxed. Aaron kept a tight grip on the wheel and an eagle eye on the speedometer, wanting to avoid any altercations with stealthy traffic coppers. Kirby kept twisting around to peer out the back window, pointing out vehicles that struck him as suspicious. As this was most of the vehicles on the road, it started to wear on everyone's patience rather quickly.

"Do you think that's them?" he said, for what must have been the third time in the last ten minutes.

"No," Aaron said tightly.

"But how can you be sure?"

"Because I'm fairly certain secret society goons don't drive ancient pickup trucks with crates of chickens in the back."

"Face front, Kirby," Imogen said. "I'll keep watch for a while."

Kirby frowned, but he complied easily enough. Imogen did turn her attention to the window, but only as a glance over her shoulder. Facing front again, she cocked her head.

"So, where exactly are we going when we get back to the city? You never actually said."

"To our friends," Aaron said, and Imogen rolled her eyes.

"I mean, I know, but where are they? In some secret lair, like in the pulps?"

"No," Aaron said. "At the Hierophant."

Imogen blinked. "What, seriously?"

"Yep," Aaron said, popping the p.

"What's the Hierophant?" Kirby said.

"A fancy place," Imogen said, with more than a little disdain in her voice. "For people with money." People, the implication was clear, who were not like she and Kirby.

"Well," Aaron began, preparing to launch into some sort of defense, but then he fell silent again, apparently realizing that there wasn't much of a defense to be made, since the Hierophant did, in fact, overtly cater to people with money. Colleen could practically see the wheel turning in his head, trying to figure out how to spin this particular fact. Finally, he just muttered, "It's complicated."

"Mm-hm," Imogen said, and then they were all quiet again for a while.

IT WAS early afternoon when they finally reached Ad Astra. All four of them were pretty miserable at that point—sticky with heat, stiff from the ride, and just generally desperate to get out of the car.

"Do you want me to drop you off at the Independent?" Aaron said to Colleen as they crossed into the city, ignoring Kirby's whining about something inconsequential thing or other. "Or your boarding house?"

"No," she said. "You don't need to,"

"Are you sure? I don't mind."

"I'm sure," she said firmly. "I'm not about to miss out on whatever happens when you show up with these two at the club."

She was prepared to argue her case if he tried to refuse her, but he only nodded and turned his attention back to the traffic.

At long last, they turned the final corner to get to the Hierophant. Aaron parked the car in a discreet lot not far from the building, then led the three of them around to the back door. Colleen couldn't help but notice that Imogen made a point of keeping Kirby close, while the boy he just looked confused, presumably because Imogen had described the Hierophant as "fancy" and nothing about the neighborhood supported that assertion. When they all stepped inside the kitchen, a pretty girl standing at one of the counters looked up, and her eyes went wide. Abandoning her work, she rushed over to where they all stood.

"Gods, Aaron!" she said, wringing her hands. "We didn't know what had happened to you!!"

"I'm fine, Claudia," he said, but Colleen could hear the note of fondness in his voice.

Finally, the girl stepped back, taking in the rest of the group.

"Who are they?" she said, gazing at Imogen and Kirby. Then, eyes going impossibly wider, she said, "Did they come from that place?"

"Listen, I'll tell you all about it later," Aaron said calmly, "but right now, we need to see Esme, all right?"

Claudia frowned but nodded, and Aaron gave her arm a gentle squeeze before leading them down the hall to Esme's office.

He knocked softly, then opened the door. Esme was sitting at her desk, forehead propped on her hand, looking tense. When she heard them, she looked up and practically sagged with relief.

"Oh, thank the gods," she said, getting to her feet and pulling Aaron into a tight hug. "We were so worried." Then, to Colleen's shock, Esme reached for her, too. The gesture was surprisingly affecting, and Colleen swallowed down a lump in her throat as she stepped out of the embrace.

"And who do we have here?" Esme went on, turning on to where the escapees stood, Imogen's arm wrapped protectively around Kirby's shoulders. "New friends?"

"Yes," said Aaron. "This is Imogen and Kirby. They were being held at the sanatorium against their will."

"It's nice to meet you both," said Esme. "Please know that you are welcome here, and we will do our best to keep you safe."

"Um... thank you," Imogen said, shifting nervously, while Kirby just watched them all with wide suspicious eyes. Colleen couldn't really blame him; Esme was taking their sudden appearance in remarkable stride.

"Why don't you have a seat?" Esme said, gesturing to the empty chairs and chaise lounge across the room. "Can I get you some coffee? Or perhaps tea?"

"Coffee, if it's not too much trouble," Imogen said uncertainly as she steered Kirby over the chaise, where they both perched gingerly on the edge. Esme picked up the phone and murmured softly into it, then replaced the receiver.

"There now," she said, smiling at Imogen. "That should be here soon." Imogen nodded, giving a tentative smile of her own.

"Has there been any word yet about Ocean Serenity?" Aaron asked. By way of answer, Esme simply picked up a newspaper that had been sitting on her desk—not the Independent, Colleen couldn't help but note—and handed it to him. Colleen scooted closer so she could see the story even as Aaron read it aloud.

> Staff at Ocean Serenity sanatorium fear for the safety of two patients who went missing from their rooms overnight.
>
> Imogen Parker, 25, and Kirby Lancaster, 10, were present and accounted for during rounds yesterday evening. When staff conducted the standard check-in this morning, however, they were gone. A thorough search was conducted of the area, but the patients remain at large.
>
> Local law enforcement has asked that anyone with information related to this matter contact them immediately. Parker had been committed to Ocean Serenity for treatment of a mental disturbance, and staff fears for her safety as well as Lancaster's. Authorities urge citizens not to approach the missing patients directly, as Parker is possibly armed and dangerous.

Well. That explained why Esme wasn't particularly surprised by them showing up with two random adepts in tow.

"What does all that mean?" said Kirby

"It means they want everyone to think Imogen kidnapped you," Aaron replied.

Kirby gaped. "Well, that's some bullshit!"

"Kirby, language!" Imogen snapped, and he hung his head, chastened.

"Sorry."

Just then, the rear door opened, and Claudia came in with a tray that she carried to the low table next to the chaise. The tray was laden with a silver coffee service for Imogen as well as a pitcher of milk, presumably for Kirby, and a plate piled with snickerdoodles on one side and delicate almond cookies, their layers tinted pink and green, on the other. Kirby's eyes lit up at the sight of the sweets, but with a glance at Imogen, he carefully poured himself a glass of milk and placed a handful of cookies on a saucer balanced precariously on his lap before he started devouring everything with gusto.

Suddenly, the main door burst open and Oliver strode in, with Daniel and Cecily following more slowly. Imogen jumped to her feet, though whether this was because she'd recognized Cecily or just been startled by the commotion, Cecily couldn't tell. Kirby stood, too, a moment later, cramming a chunk of snickerdoodle into his mouth and chewing slowly as he watched the newcomers.

"All right," Oliver said to Aaron, seemingly oblivious to the fact that anyone else was in the room. "Explain to me precisely how a simple bit of reconnaissance managed to go so spectacularly pear-shaped."

"Oliver," Esme said warningly, but Oliver merely turned his ire from Aaron to her.

"Are you trying to tell me this *isn't* a complete disaster? I know Aaron is a soft touch, but I really didn't think he'd end up bringing home strays."

"That's enough," Esme said, a true edge to her voice, which finally seemed to bring Oliver out of his head. He appeared to notice Imogen and Kirby for the first time and turned to them, his manner shifting to something more formal.

"Please excuse me," he said, though he didn't sound particularly contrite. "Perhaps we should start again. My name is Oliver. And you are?"

Imogen crossed her arms over her chest. "Imogen. Imogen Parker."

Oliver raised his eyebrows. "You're the one from the Shooting Star, yes? You make fire."

Imogen nodded, looking wary. Oliver's gaze shifted to Kirby for a moment, then he glanced at Aaron.

"Well, I don't think this one was working at a charm school. Not unless someone has seriously lowered their standards."

"I have a name, too," Kirby piped up with a scowl, and Oliver looked amused despite himself.

"Of course. Please enlighten me."

"Kirby."

"And what's your story, Kirby?"

When Kirby didn't answer right away, Aaron put in, "We think he's like you."

Oliver looked at Aaron sharply, then turned back to Kirby with an odd expression, something like doubt and pity and protectiveness all at once. He took a few steps forward until he was standing in front of Kirby. He couldn't crouch or bend to talk to the boy, so he merely stood and watched, as Kirby stared up at him defiantly.

"Why don't you tell me what you can do?" Oliver said finally, and his voice was gentler now, though not patronizing.

"I can tell how people feel," Kirby said. "Like, right now, I can tell you're interested in us, but also kind of annoyed."

The corner of Oliver's mouth quirked up. "And so I am." He cocked his head. "Is there anything else you'd like to tell me, Kirby?"

"No," Kirby said, then deftly changed the subject. "What's wrong with your leg?"

"I was born with a clubfoot. Do you know what that means?"

Kirby nodded, brow furrowed. "I've heard of that, but I thought it was something doctors could fix."

"They can," Oliver said. "If they get to it soon enough. But when I was young, we couldn't afford the operation. By the time we got the money, they could only fix it part of the way."

Kirby nodded thoughtfully.

"Does your cane have a sword in it? I heard about that in a wireless serial once."

"This one doesn't," Oliver said. "But I do own a particularly nice antique specimen from Avalon that has a hidden blade. The rumor is that it was used to kill a man in a duel of honor."

Kirby's mouth formed a silent "Whoa". Colleen shot Aaron an inquisitive glance, trying to determine if this was true; Aaron gave a small nod.

"Oliver," Esme said. "Perhaps you can show Kirby your cane later, but in the meantime, why don't you, Daniel, and Cecily take he and Imogen upstairs to get them settled, hmm? They must be very tired from the journey."

"Of course," Cecily said, taking a step forward. "There's a cozy little spot up there that I think will suit you just fine. Daniel used to live there. He even carved his name into the brick with a pocketknife."

Daniel didn't look particularly enthused by this revelation, but Kirby did. "Wow, really?"

"Really," Cecily said, gently steering him out of the room. "Come on, I'll show you." Imogen followed them, but paused just inside the doorway to look back at Esme.

"Thank you," she said, to which Esme responded with an elegant nod. Then everyone was gone except Esme, Aaron, and Colleen.

"Sit," said Esme, in a tone that brooked no argument. "And tell me what really happened."

Aaron gave her something approximating a brief rundown, with Colleen chiming in from time to time to correct him on hazy details. When they finished, Esme sat tapping a pen on her desk blotter, face pensive.

"So what now?" Aaron said, and Esme sighed.

"I don't know that there's much we can do tonight," she said. "They're exhausted, you're exhausted, and we could all use some time to think."

"You think it's safe for them here?" Colleen said. "With the authorities out looking for them?"

"I'd say it is for now," Esme replied. "Though I'm not sure how tenable it will be in the long term. We really need to figure out what the RPC is trying to accomplish with all this. That will go a long way toward determining our next move."

Without meaning to, Colleen gave a huge yawn, and Esme's expression softened.

"Your first order of business is going home to get some sleep. We can send a car for you in the morning and bring you back here to hash all this out."

Colleen felt her eyes prickle with the beginnings of tears. She had, of course, wanted and even expected to be involved going forward, but the way Esme treated it as a given made her oddly emotional. It must be because she was so tired. She took a deep breath to steady herself.

"That would be fine," she said.

Esme nodded and turned to Aaron. "Can you get a cab for the two of you? Or do you want me to get someone else to drive you?"

"No," Aaron said, getting to his feet. "I can get a cab." That course of action was far preferable to asking Daniel for another car, considering what he'd done to the first one.

Colleen got up, too, and they began making their way to the door, but just then, said door flew open, and Ebony came charging in, face stormy. At the sight of Aaron, she drew up short, then walked the few remaining steps to him slowly, until she was mere inches away.

And then she punched him in the shoulder.

"Hey," he protested. "What was that for?"

Rather than answering, she punched him again—three times, in fact. Colleen felt that she should probably be removing herself from the situation, but she was worried that moving would draw Ebony's attention, so she just stood there like a frightened woodland creature.

"How dare you?" Ebony seethed, finally giving voice to her fury, and Aaron sighed.

"Eb..."

"How *dare* you?" she said again, as if he hadn't spoken. "After endlessly lecturing me about staying safe, where do you get off staying out all night without calling in, after driving off to a building full of people who would happily see you dead? *Who gave you the right?*"

"Ebony," Esme said, with what Colleen was coming to recognize as her typical calm authority, though it seemed there might be a little alarm underneath as well. Unlike Aaron saying her name, which had only seemed to throw fuel on the fire, Esme's voice did seem to have some soothing effect. She took a deep breath and stepped back, still glaring daggers at her brother.

"You are the worst sort of hypocrite," she said. "Don't ever say anything to me about my choices ever again."

And without another word, she turned and swept out of the room.

Aaron stared after her for a moment, then let out a huff of breath. "I probably deserved that."

"Yes," Esme said. "I daresay you might have."

"Come on," Colleen said, feeling a strange surge of protectiveness towards him. "You said you'd see me home."

Aaron turned to her and nodded, then seemed to remember something.

"Should I have the cab drop me off first?" he said. "So your landlady doesn't jump to conclusions after you've been out all night?"

"You know what?" Colleen said, heading out into the hallway. "I don't even care anymore. Just get me to my bed."

CHAPTER 16

COLLEEN

The next morning, Colleen pushed through her boarding house door into the bright sunshine and made her way to the big black sedan that was waiting for her. It wasn't precisely the same make as the ubiquitous cabs that ferried people around the city, but it was close enough to pass for one at a casual glance. Colleen suspected that this came in handy for certain covert activities. It did make her feel better about descending the steps and climbing in while her landlady almost certainly watched from behind a curtain.

Although, no cabbie in Colleen's experience would come around to open the back passenger door for her the way Daniel did.

She pushed away an unexpected pang of disappointment that it wasn't Aaron who had come and returned Daniel's gruff nod as she slid past him into the back seat. It might have been pleasant, fun even, to have her own chauffeur, except that when Daniel got in himself and pulled into the flow of morning traffic, he remained almost defiantly silent, giving off a general feeling of disdain for the task at hand.

Colleen cleared her throat. "You didn't want to bring Aaron with you this morning?"

"Aaron hadn't gotten to the club yet when I left," Daniel muttered. "He doesn't usually come in until later."

"And you do?" Colleen said, hoping to prod him into further conversation.

"I live closer. And I don't sleep much."

Colleen waited for more, but nothing was forthcoming. She cocked her head, assessing the back of his neck. This surly pseudo-gangster had stolen the heart of the famous Snowflake? Did Cecily Dearborn harbor a soft spot for bad boys? Or was it Colleen in partic-ular who inspired the sort of charming reception?

"Do you have some sort of problem with me?"

The question seemed to catch him off guard, and he shifted in his seat.

"No. Why would I?"

"I don't know," Colleen said. "You just don't seem eager to put out the welcome mat, so to speak."

Daniel shifted again, and she saw his hands flex slightly on the wheel.

"We're almost there," he said finally, and then he didn't speak again.

When they arrived at the club, Daniel ushered Ebony up the stairs to the back entrance ahead of him, but before she reached the top, the door opened to reveal Aaron, smiling down at them.

"Hi," he said. "I was wondering when you were going to get here."

"Hi," Colleen said, feeling strangely self-conscious. "I'm, uh, here now."

Daniel pushed past them with an exasperated grunt. Aaron shot a glare at his retreating back, then waved Colleen inside. As he led her down the hall to Esme's office, she was acutely aware of how close they were, arms almost brushing as they walked. She felt her cheeks heat at the thought, not from ardor, but from embarrassment. What was she, twelve? Still, it was hard to deny that something had shifted between them after their night of adventure. It was the how that remained to be seen.

But first: tackling the criminal conspiracy.

Daniel had already settled into one of the leather club chairs in the office, while Leo and Esme stood talking quietly behind her desk.

Ebony was off to one side as well, Colleen noticed, but she seemed to be making a pointed effort to ignore them. Thankfully, their welcome from Esme was warmer.

"Welcome back," she said to Colleen. "Sleep well?"

"Yes, thank you," Colleen said, then nodded to the mess of newspapers spread out over the surface of the desk. "How are things looking? I only had a chance to look at the Independent, but it doesn't seem like the heat has come down on the break-in since yesterday."

Esme huffed a sigh. "It has not. They are, in fact, expanding the search south of Merrimack and up nearly to the straight. They really, really want their escapees back."

"Should we think about moving them?" Daniel said, and Esme pursed her lips.

"Not just yet. If the search perimeter actually reaches Ad Astra, we'll probably need to take that step, but there's still so much we don't know about what's going on up there. The two of them may have some critical information on that front."

"They do," a new voice cut in, and they all turned to see Oliver at the door, accompanied by Imogen and Kirby. The fugitive adepts had changed from their hospital uniforms into regular clothes, and though it had only been a little over a day, they seemed different to Colleen somehow. Less drawn and edgy. More likely, perhaps, to trust a kind word.

"We were just upstairs talking about the asylum," Oliver said, and Colleen could tell he was trying to rein in a tide of big emotion hiding behind the words, presumably for Kirby's benefit. "And Kirby said something very interesting. Something I thought you might want to hear."

Esme didn't move from behind her desk, but she did sit down in her chair. Bringing herself closer to Kirby's level.

"I'm sure I would," she said, her voice warm and calm. "Please, all of you, come have a seat. And Leo, maybe send word to the kitchen for some snacks, hmm?"

Leo nodded and walked out the door, just as Daniel vacated his seat so there would be enough chairs for the newcomers. Once they were all seated, everyone turned to Kirby, who ran his hands up and down the arms of his chair, looking like he was ready to bolt.

"Go ahead," Oliver told him gently. "Tell them what you told me."

Kirby had come an impressively long way towards trusting Oliver in just a day, but he still twisted his head to look up at Imogen for reassurance. At her nod, he faced them all again, took a deep breath, and began.

"So, most of the time, they made us stay in our rooms—I mean, unless we were at meals or exercising. But sometimes, they would take me to the medical wing and put me in a room down there. Only it wasn't like the other rooms on the wing."

"How so?" Daniel asked.

"There wasn't a bed or any medicine," Kirby replied. "Just a table with a wooden chair on each side, and some other chairs over in the corner. And the doctors, they made me sit at the table, and then they'd bring in different people to sit across from me."

"What kinds of people?" said Esme.

Kirby shrugged. "All kinds. Sometimes it was ladies, sometimes men. Some were old and some were young. I never knew what to expect when I went in there. But the doctors always told me to read the people and then explain what I saw."

"And what was that?" Esme asked.

"That was different, too," said Kirby. "Some of them felt proud. They were excited to be there, and that made them easy to read. But some of them were mad and didn't want to be there. I didn't like having to read them, because then I started to feel mad, too. But one thing that was the same for almost all of them was that they hurt."

Daniel raised his eyebrows. "Hurt? You mean physically? Or their feelings?"

"Both, I think," said Kirby. "But mostly physical. And usually in the same place—here." He pointed to his temple. "Or sometimes here." This time, it was the base of his skull. "And it was new hurt, not something that had had time to heal."

Aaron glanced at Oliver. "You can pinpoint things like that? In that kind of detail?"

Oliver nodded, his eyes still on Kirby. "It's difficult, but it can be done. Well, it's difficult for me—the kid seems to have an easier time of it. People respond emotionally to stimuli in their bodies, good or bad. If you're able to tap into that, and find the source, you can learn all sorts of things about what's going on with them."

"And what was going on, Kirby?" Daniel said.

Kirby shrugged again, beginning to squirm a bit. "I never could tell exactly. But then one day, the doctors left me in the room by myself and went out into the hallway to talk. I couldn't hear them at first, and I couldn't read much through the door—just that they weren't happy with each other. And then I could feel them getting madder, and their voices started getting louder, and I heard one of them say, 'Maybe he's just extremely skilled, and there's nothing we can do to block him', and then the other said, 'You know that's not good enough—Bradshaw said it was-' Um, impressive… impartial? No, that's not right."

"Imperative?" Esme suggested, and Kirby snapped his fingers.

"That's it! Imperative that they got a shield?"

They all looked at each other. "Sweetie, who is 'they'?" said Colleen.

"I dunno," Kirby said unhappily.

"And more to the point," said Oliver. "A shield for what?"

Claudia slipped in then, dropping off a tray of pastries and departing as quickly she'd arrived. No one paid the tray any mind except Kirby, who took a giant cookie in each hand.

Imogen cleared her throat. "They never let us talk much in the hospital. But sometimes we could exchange a few words in passing without the guards noticing. There were rumors going around that the research at the hospital wasn't just for adepts. That it was also for normal people who wanted to be protected."

"Protected from what?" Colleen said reflexively. But the others in the room were already exchanging meaningful glances. They knew. And then she knew, too.

"Seems a bit excessive," Daniel said darkly. "If they already have the benevolent gift of a cure lined up. Wouldn't you say?"

"I would," Leo intoned, voice grim.

"And it would have to target those with mental and relational powers, specifically," Oliver said, tapping his chin. "There's not much to be done about a burst of Imogen's fire, for example, short of walking around in an asbestos suit."

"There's conjurers," Ebony said quietly. It was the first time she'd spoken up so far, and everybody turned as one to face her. "They don't have any natural magic to cure. There's no need for a carrot. Only the stick."

That pronouncement hung heavy in the room, the gravity of it pressing down on all of them. Then Aaron let out a long breath.

"OK, this is all pretty dire," he said. "But what exactly are we supposed to do about it?"

Daniel puffed up with indignation. "Are you saying we should just leave all those adepts there to be experimented on? Let them develop this, this weapon"—because he was right, it wasn't a shield—"to go after all of you?"

"No," Aaron said, seemingly holding onto his patience by a thread. "I'm asking *what we should do*. Obviously, we need to figure out how to get the adepts out, but then what? All we have is Kirby's word for what is happening, and that's not much to go on." He glanced at Kirby. "No offense."

"None taken," Kirby said through a mouthful of cookie, crumbs spilling down the front of his shirt.

"We need information," said Esme. "Evidence of what is happening there."

"It wouldn't be a good idea to go back up there just yet," Oliver said. "Still too much heat."

"Agreed." Esme said. "But there's got to be something off-site— correspondence, reports, that sort of thing."

"But who do we target to find it?" Daniel said.

"Turner-Hoff, presumably," said Esme. "But I'm not sure who else, and I don't like putting all our eggs in one basket." She looked at Oliver. "We need to get you in a room with a group of the higher ups to get a better sense of what's going on."

Oliver shrugged. "That's an iffy proposition. Congress is out of session, and a lot of the Members are back in their districts until the convention next week. There's not much to work with there, and even if I tried going in, it would be hard to stay inconspicuous."

Colleen cleared her throat.

"There's a reception," Colleen said. "Tomorrow night."

Esme looked up. "What kind of reception?"

"For Vasilyev's debut," Colleen replied. "Ahead of the convention. Getting him to defect has been this big symbolic coup for Bradshaw, so she wants to bask in her glory. All the bigwigs are supposed to be there—Turner-Hoff, Sutterfield, Teasley's even rumored to make an appearance."

"What do you think?" Esme asked Oliver, and he cocked his head, considering.

"Could work," he said and looked at Colleen. "I'm guessing this reception is by invitation only?"

"Oh, definitely," Colleen said. "It all seems very exclusive and hush-hush."

"Not hush-hush enough, apparently." Daniel said sardonically.

"Well, that's not ideal, but we can make it work," said Oliver. Here, he turned his gaze to Aaron, then Ebony. "It would be a big help if one of you could come. Or both, if you could manage it."

Aaron was opening his mouth to accept when Ebony shook her head.

"Not me," she said. "But I have something else in mind that might help." And she pushed off of the wall and strode out of the room.

Aaron frowned and started to call after her, but Esme stopped him.

"Leave her be," she said softly. "She has her own part to contribute."

Aaron's frown deepened, but he held his tongue.

Everyone started talking at once, speculating and plotting, and it all became a bit much for Colleen. She was used to the clamor of the newsroom, but this was different, somehow. Plus, her head was spinning with all she'd learned. She'd known she was onto something from the very beginning. She'd realized it was even bigger than she'd expected after visiting the sanatorium. But this... She didn't even know what the repercussions of this were. It certainly seemed like the kind of thing that made careers for scribblers like her.

Suddenly, the office felt oppressive, and she urgently wanted out. Attempting to be discreet, she stood and headed down the hall to the back door. If she could just step outside for a minute, maybe she could clear her head.

Once outside, she went down to the foot of the stairs, feeling a little better as soon as the sun touched her skin. She tilted her face up toward it and took a deep breath. She hadn't even completed the exhale when Aaron appeared.

"Hey," he said, concern in his voice. "Are you OK?"

"Yeah," Colleen hurried to assure him. "Yeah, I'm fine. Just needed some air."

"I hear you," Aaron said, running a hand over his close-cropped hair. "There was a lot happening in there."

"So if I'm understanding this correctly," she said. "The experiments Imogen was talking about are meant to find some way of making people, what, immune to certain types of magic?"

"Sounds like," Aaron said grimly.

Colleen traced an arc in the dirt with the toe of her show, turning the information around in her mind. Now that she thought about it, she'd never really heard anything about defensive measures used against magic. The main strategies deployed to enforce the Embargo seemed to mostly involve locking up those magic users deemed especially dangerous and shaming everyone else into submission. This idea of neutralizing magic, whether by "fixing" adepts or creating some sort of inoculation against magic, seemed strange and unsettling.

"Would it even work?" Colleen said. "I mean, I know people in my neighborhood have wards over their doors and stuff like that, but I never put much stock in any of it. Are there ways to actually stop magic?"

"There are," Aaron said. "It's part of the reason there's historically been bad blood between adepts and conjurers—the conjurers were largely responsible for coming up with ways to keep rogue adepts in line. But even then. It was the community of magical practitioners regulating their own. This new stuff the RPC is trying to do using science…" He shook his head. "I don't see any way it doesn't end very, very badly."

She bit her lip. "Interesting…"

Aaron raised an eyebrow. "What's going on in your head?"

Colleen blinked. "What?"

"You have a particular look on your face," he said. "It usually means you're plotting something."

She frowned. "I wasn't plotting!" At his disbelieving look, she sighed. "Well, this story just seems to keep getting bigger and bigger. I'm trying to figure out how to frame it so that it has the greatest reach among readers."

Aaron went very, very still. It gave Colleen a creeping sense of foreboding, though she couldn't have said why.

"You still plan on running this in the paper?"

She cocked her head, her sense of apprehension growing. "Well, yes. Why wouldn't I?"

Aaron ran a hand over the back of his head. "It's just that you've seen what's up there now. You know what they're doing."

"Yeah, and other people should know it, too," she said, wondering exactly where this conversation was going.

"They should," he said with obvious forced calm. "But in due time. There's still a lot we don't know. Playing a hand too early could jeopardize our efforts to figure out what's really going on. I'm just wondering what the rush is."

On the one hand, Colleen had to admit this was a fair point—and one that stirred up just the tiniest bit of guilt inside her—but on the other, something about his tone kindled an ember inside her, one that had originally sparked in the years that she was a small girl forced to stand up to a bunch of brothers who tried to push her around. It put her hackles up, however reasonable his argument.

"And what if we don't play a hand soon enough, huh? Like you said, they're going to be moving fast now. What if we wait and by the time someone starts looking into the matter, all the evidence is gone?"

"That's why we're trying to get into the reception," Aaron said, eyebrows forming sharp slashes over his eyes. "But is that really what you're concerned about? Or is it something more enterprising?"

The heat in Colleen went suddenly, dangerously cold. She crossed her arms. "What exactly are you insinuating?"

"That this has more to do with your ego and making a name for yourself than it does keeping people like me safe."

"And who are you to make that determination?" she snapped. "You knew from the beginning what I was trying to do. That was our original bargain, right? That your scoop was bigger than mine? You said yourself that you wanted your nickel. So, why is it a problem now?"

"Because things are different now," Aaron said, throwing his hands up in the air. "My scoop *is* bigger than yours, more than any of us could have realized. I don't know why you can't see that!"

Gods, it really was like talking to her brothers. Why couldn't someone just have faith in her? Why couldn't they, just once, believe that she might have some idea of what she was doing?

"Why are you getting angry with me?" she said, voice rising. "Why aren't you getting angry with *them*?" She threw her hand out to indicate the world at large.

"I *am* angry with them," Aaron yelled. "But I don't know—I guess I just expected better of you than I did a bunch of dangerous bigots."

Colleen took a step back, stunned, and dropped her arms.

"Well, that was your mistake," she said finally, then turned and began stalking away.

Behind her, she heard Aaron sigh.

"Where are you going?"

"To work!" she shouted over her shoulder. "How else am I going to achieve my fiendish ambitions?"

"Colleen, you can't walk there—it's too far."

"I can make my own way, thanks very much!"

Because she could. It had worked well enough so far, right?

To hells with Aaron and his stupid tender heart.

CHAPTER 17

AARON

*A*aron stormed back into the club, fuming. When he returned to Esme's office, he found that Imogen and Kirby had left, but the others were still there. Oliver looked around and past him, then met his eyes quizzically.

"Where's Colleen?"

"Gone," Aaron spat, dropping into a chair.

"Gone?" said Esme. "What do you mean, gone? Where'd she go?"

"Back to work," said Aaron. "She has to get her story written up if she wants to make the morning edition."

"Wait, what?" Oliver said, sitting up straighter. "What story?"

"Oh, didn't you know? She's going to revolutionize the news biz with her expose of this sinister conspiracy that in no way affects her directly, even if it compromises the efforts of those it does affect."

Daniel swore and pushed himself out of the chair, prowling the room. "I knew it. I *knew* we couldn't trust her."

"Now?" Oliver said, voice rising in alarm. "She's really going to do it now? Even after everything-"

Esme laid a claiming hand on his arm, and he subsided, though his face was still stormy. Then she turned her gaze to Aaron.

"Do you really think she's going to run the story right away? Really?"

Aaron sank lower in his chair. Now that he wasn't face-to-face with Colleen anymore and had vented some of his frustration, he was starting to realize that he might have overreacted just a hair. Hells, this was why he didn't like getting worked up over things; it was so easy for the heated feelings to spiral out of control.

"Probably not," he admitted. "There's still too much she doesn't know. Even if she tried, I doubt her editor would run it without more concrete proof."

Esme's shoulders relaxed slightly. Huh—so the questions hadn't just been rhetorical. Aaron was dimly surprised. It was rare to see Esme anywhere close to ruffled.

"All right," she said. "In the meantime, we should focus on things we can control."

"Oh, we can control her all right," Oliver piped up. "Can't we, Daniel?" Behind him, Daniel gave an affirmative—and ominous—grunt. "We'll just head on over to the Independent offices and-"

Esme rolled her eyes. "Stop it, both of you. There have been more than enough abductions to go around as it is. Right now, we need to finish getting plans in place for tomorrow night. Leo's out trying to find a floor plan of the performance hall. Oliver, do you think there's any chance you can finagle an invitation to the reception?"

Oliver looked insulted that she would even ask such a thing. "Of course I can. Just give me some time to make a few phone calls."

Esme nodded, and Oliver headed to the office door with a preoccupied look Aaron recognized. He was strategizing, playing out likely outcomes to determine the best course of action. Aaron had no doubt he'd have invitations in hand within the hour.

"What about us?" Daniel said, and Esme sighed, dropping into her chair.

"Maybe go get some lunch?" she said wearily. "There's not much to be done before Leo and Oliver get sorted, and you'll need the fuel."

Aaron didn't like this suggestion much, and he could tell Daniel didn't, either. They both felt the need to do something—anything, really—right away. But Esme wasn't wrong, and they didn't seem to have any better ideas, so without any further discussion, they trekked down the hall to the kitchen and asked their friend Bao, one of the junior chefs, to fix them something.

Daniel was typically reserved as they waited, and for once, Aaron didn't feel the need to fill the quiet with chatter. He kept playing the final exchange with Colleen over and over in his head, alternately thinking up lethal retorts he could have used and wishing he'd thought of some way to redirect the conversation before it had spiraled out of control. He sighed, rubbing his tired eyes with one hand.

"What's she like?" Daniel said suddenly, and Aaron looked up, confused.

"What?"

"This girl, Colleen—what's she like?"

Aaron cocked an eyebrow. "I thought you had that figured out. You said we couldn't trust her."

"I don't trust her," Daniel said. "But you seem to. Or at least you want to. What is it about her that makes you feel that way?"

Aaron groaned and let his head drop into his hands. "Man... I don't even know. She's just... Colleen. She's fierce and hard-headed, and she has the best laugh, and..." He looked up. "I'm in big trouble, aren't I?"

Daniel reached over and clapped him on the shoulder just as Bao called out that their food was ready.

"Don't take it too hard," he said as he got to his feet to pick up their meal. "It happens to the best of us."

Thankfully, Daniel returned to being stoic and taciturn as they ate, and by the time they finished, Leo had poked his head into the staff dining room and said Oliver was ready for them. After returning to the kitchen, they went to Esme's office.

Oliver was standing in front of a makeshift easel where an architect's rendering of the performance hall had been tacked up, with a line of chairs facing him. Aaron wasn't entirely sure how Leo had managed to scrounge a blueprint up on such short notice, but then, Leo had been doing this a lot longer than any of them, so it really wasn't that surprising. Paloma was already seated before the easel, and she smiled up at Aaron as he claimed the chair next to hers.

"Did you somehow get roped into this insanity?" he said.

"Oliver said he needed a plus one for the ballet, and asked if I wanted to go," she said, eyes bright. "Which I do, *obviously*. I get to see Pasha in the flesh!" On the other side of Aaron, Daniel cocked and eyebrow at her, and she sobered slightly. "Oh, and help get to the bottom of this sanatorium thing, of course."

This nod to professional decorum did nothing to hide her excitement. Her eyes shone, and her knee was bouncing slightly, her fingers curled around a pad of paper where she evidently planned to take notes. She was getting her first taste of being included on a covert mission, and Aaron felt a strange pang in his chest at the sight of it. He'd felt that way once, but now he'd long since learned the cloak and dagger stuff wasn't all it was cracked up to be. And yet, here he was, ready to plunge into the thick of it. Again.

He heaved a deep sigh. He was so tired.

"OK," Oliver said once it seemed everyone was settled. "Here's the rundown." He explained that his society contacts had come through and he had managed to score three tickets for the performance that night—he and Paloma in the orchestra circle and Aaron in the lower balcony to get a broader view of the room. They would stagger their arrivals, making sure to allow enough time to note the seating arrangements of many of the RPC luminaries and their allies before curtain.

"And then what do we do during the show?" said Aaron.

Oliver gave him a patient look. "We watch the show. Anything else would look suspicious."

Next to Aaron, Paloma was unable to fully refrain from squealing with delight and clapping her hands. Oliver gave her a magnanimous smile, and even Aaron's mouth quirked up, but they didn't linger.

"During intermission," Oliver continued. "We can keep our eyes open for who's talking to who and how they seem with each other. That might give us some direction on who we should focus on. And then, once the second act is over, the real fun begins.

"We know that the reception is being held in the Starlight Ballroom." He swung his cane—a lightweight one, without embellishment, that Aaron suspected he had chosen for exactly this kind of flourish—up to point at the depiction of a round room at the top of the drawing. "My sources tell me that the primary security point for these sorts of things is here." He let the cane drop slightly, so that it was pointing at a spot on the mezzanine level. "That is where they will be checking for invitations, and where we are most likely to need your help, Aaron. I'll try to talk our way in so you'll be free to move around the opera house on your own, but if that doesn't work, you're tapping in." Aaron nodded. "From here, guests take an elevator to the top level of the building; it's supposed to open directly into the ballroom."

"Once we're in there, it should be a pretty straightforward stretch of mingling and picking up whatever information we can gather. Paloma and I will circulate, while Aaron keeps to the periphery doing more garden-variety spying, if he's still with us. In the extremely unlikely event that something goes wrong, there are corridors to either side of the ballroom with sitting areas and the like. At the far end of each corridor, there's a doorway to a set of service stairs that connect to all the back-of-house areas of the complex. We can go that way to get back to the main floor and call for Daniel if we need back-up."

Aaron raised his hand, then flushed at the impulse—he wasn't in school. "OK, but how are we supposed to call for Daniel? Presumably we'll be in a hurry and won't have time to find a phone."

"Ebony is working on something," Esme said from the desk. "Along with our conjurer friends. They'll be here before you all leave to get you up to speed."

Aaron blinked at her. The conjurers were coming here? The conjurers were going to play an apparently significant role in this dangerous bit of subterfuge? A jumble of emotions spilled through him, none of them good. This arrangement seemed like a particularly inauspicious collision of every currently stressful thing in his life. But no one else seemed particularly bothered, so he did his best to push the feeling of foreboding away.

"Sounds pretty straightforward," Daniel was saying. "What's our time table?"

"Ignotus said his people would be here around 6 to make sure everything is ready to go," said Esme. "In the meantime, you two"— she nodded at Paloma and Aaron — "can get things prepped for your backup coverage this evening."

"What about Daniel?" Paloma said.

"Daniel can do..." Esme trailed off as she glanced at Daniel's impassive face. "Whatever it is Daniel does for these things."

"Yeah," Oliver said, poking Daniel's knee with the tip of his cane. "Earn your keep, peon."

"That's right," Daniel grumbled as he got to his feet. "Harass the one responsible for your safety on the job. Solid plan."

Following Esme's instructions, Aaron went to the bar and immersed himself in the soothing routine of prepping for the night, making sure all the appropriate glassware was accounted for and all the bottles were topped off and ready to go. And then he did it again. And when that still left him with time on his hands, he poured himself a beer and settled into a banquet to brood.

He wasn't much a brooder by nature—that was more Daniel's department—but if there was an occasion that called for ruminating in the half-dark of the empty club, this was it.

Ever since he and Ebony had settled in with Aunt Ruth and found their places at the Hierophant, Aaron had had one goal: stay safe. He'd very intentionally tried to avoid anything that threatened the stability they'd managed to attain because he never again wanted feel as desperate and hopeless as he had when the two of them had survived by hustling cards and eating out of trash cans. And then Colleen had barreled in, and against his better judgement, he'd been drawn in by her spark, that uncompromising will to go after whatever she wanted. Only he'd underestimated just how uncompromising she would be.

He'd genuinely believed that seeing what was happening at Ocean Serenity with her own eyes, spending time with Imogen and Kirby and hearing their stories—would shift her priorities. And for that, he had no one to blame but himself. She had, after all, been honest about her intentions from the very start.

He resolved that it was a lesson he would only need to learn once.

CHAPTER 18

AARON

*A*s the time approached for them to leave, Aaron went into one of the dressing rooms behind the stage to change into his outfit for the night—an evening suit Oliver had picked up for him somewhere. As he worked his way into the many pieces that made up the ensemble, he became increasingly irritable. He was no stranger to formal wear—he sometimes wore a dinner jacket while he worked, though shirtsleeves with garters and a vest gave him more freedom of motion—but this was something else entirely, with a white tie affair with a tail coat, silk pocket square, and *gloves*. He was beginning to see why Daniel complained so much when he had to dress up to accompany Oliver to some event or other. And tonight's would be no exception—at first, Daniel thought he'd gotten a reprieve since he'd be posted outside, but then Oliver had pointed out that 1) he still needed to act as chauffeur and b) if he was needed, he could hardly come busting into the performance hall wearing a tweed coat and a flat cap; security would be on him in a heartbeat. So it was likely that he was at that very moment just as miserable as Aaron, if not more so. Somehow, this lifted Aaron's spirits a little.

When he arrived in Esme's office, Oliver and Paloma were already there, decked out in their own finery. Oliver didn't look all that much fancier than normal, but Paloma, who usually padded around the club in one of her costumes, trousers, or a robe, seemed transformed. She was wearing a dress of dark pink silk with beaded embroidery on the bodice and a skirt that swayed around her calves. In the front, it sported a demure neckline, but the draped back plunged past her shoulder blades, leaving her tan skin bare. Paloma was one of the few women in Aaron's circle without bobbed hair, and her curls had been worked into a roll at the base of her neck, the ends tucked into a jeweled headband that matched her dress. The effect was rather dazzling.

"You look stunning," Aaron told her, and she beamed, doing a little twirl to show herself off to full effect.

"You clean up pretty nicely yourself," Oliver said, sounding impressed and, Aaron couldn't help but feel, unduly surprised. "You could sub in for me as majordomo looking like that."

Aaron rolled his eyes. "No, thank you. I will continue to toil happily away behind the bar." He glanced at the clock, brow furrowed. "Weren't the conjurers supposed to be here by now? It's getting close to time."

Paloma cocked her head toward the hallway, where a sudden rumble signaled the approach of multiple footsteps. "I'm guessing they're on the way now."

She was not wrong. A moment later, the door swung open, and a contingent of conjurers swept in led by Ignotus, who, as usual, gave off the air of a particularly arrogant student living in a garret somewhere. At this point, Aaron was able to clock that the last part was an affectation; however rumpled he looked, his clothes were top quality and expertly tailored. Aaron would be surprised if he'd ever even seen a garret.

The arrogance, however, was genuine.

"Set up over here," he said to the other conjurers, gesturing to the table by the wall. They dutifully descended upon it and began unpacking the many bags they carried. Some of the items they unloaded were what Aaron would have anticipated—books, pages of notes, a scroll or two—but there were other things that seemed more mysterious and exotic: a large tuning fork, a stone mortar and pestle, some round slabs of what looked like black glass. Apparently satisfied, Ignotus turned to where Aaron and the others stood and pulled a face.

"Oh, Oliver," he said, old Avalonian accent ringing out over the hubbub. "There you are."

"Ignotus," Oliver said brightly. "How's tricks?"

"Tricks are marvelous, darling," Ignotus drawled, and Aaron was actually surprised by his restraint. Aaron knew from Ebony that referring to "tricks" in front of conjurers was considered disrespectful and likely to get the touchier among them foaming at the mouth about the intricacies of scholarly magic. Oliver must have known this, too, but Ignotus seemed reluctant to take the bait as he turned back towards the worktable.

"How is the mindreading?" he threw off in their direction, seemingly an afterthought. "Discovered anything especially tawdry lately? I know you enjoy that sort of thing."

Ah. There it was.

"It's not mindreading, and you know it," Oliver said, cheerfully hitting his stride. It was always like this between the two of them. Aaron found it exhausting. "Now, what grandiose magical gewgaw have you cooked up for us this time?"

As they bantered, Ebony walked in, and Aaron couldn't help but notice how... intent she looked. Purposeful. Confident in a way he had rarely seen her—and, he realized, with a sinking sensation, only when she was immersed in a magic much stranger and more complex than what she used at the card table. The knowledge sat like a weight in his stomach, resisting any effort of his to brush it away.

Ebony walked over to the table where she exchanged a few words with the busy conjurers and gathered up a few small, shiny objects before coming to stand next to Ignotus.

"Thanks the gods," Oliver said, with exaggerated relief. "Ebony, can you please translate what the maniac is saying into regular-people language."

Ebony shook her head good-naturedly. "With so many moving

parts to this plan, we thought it would be helpful for all of you to have a way to communicate in the opera house."

"You mean like the watches we had when we were looking for Cecily?" Oliver said.

"Same principle," Ebony said. "But more sophisticated, so you can send more detailed messages." She juggled the objects in her hands, then held one aloft with a flourish. "Behold!"

They all peered at it, but no one seemed to have any more of an idea of what they were seeing than Aaron did.

"It looks like a powder compact," he said finally.

Ebony rolled her eyes. "That's because it *is* a powder compact, you dunce. Or it was. But we made some modifications." She handed the compact to Paloma and made a "go on" gesture. Paloma found the tiny catch on the side with her fingernail and popped the compact open. Inside, the mirror had been replaced by a smaller piece of the black glass the conjurers had spread out over Esme's table, while the space that normally held the powder boasted a tiny metal rod filed to a dull point.

"So, what does it do?" Aaron said, and Ebony's eyes lit up as she began pointing to the various parts of the compact.

"You use the stylus here to write on the glass, and it transmits a message to a corresponding receiver glass." She gestured to the table. "Then the recipient can write their own message in reply."

"Well, that's quite handy," Oliver said admiringly, and Ignotus sighed.

"A master of understatement, as usual," he said, and Oliver scowled. "It is not *handy*. It is ingenious." He smiled benevolently. "Ebony's ability to synthesize natural and scholarly magic is quite remarkable. I haven't found documentation of anyone approaching her caliber in decades, possibly a century."

Ebony practically glowed at the praise, and the weight in Aaron's gut turned barbed and prickly.

"So one of us can talk to someone here," he said, knowing he sounded petulant but unable to stop himself. "How does that help us?"

Ebony shot him an irritated look and handed more of the objects over to him and Oliver—pocket watches,

"Each of you will have a device of some sort," she said. "You can only communicate with us, but we can communicate with all of you. So, if you split up and, say, Paloma needs to tell you something, she'll send the information here and then we'll pass it along. Kind of like a switchboard." She lifted her chin, tone turning defensive. "I know it's not ideal, but it's what we were able to do with the time available."

"It's great," Paloma said firmly, staring daggers at Aaron. "Can we get a demonstration?"

Ebony nodded and reached behind her to take one of the larger pieces of black glass and a stylus from a nearby conjurer. She nodded toward Aaron's watch, and he pressed the button on top to open it. Inside, as expected, the clock face had been replaced with a piece of black glass, and another of the tiny metal rods tucked into the lid.

Ebony scrawled something on her glass slab, and a moment later, a ghostly image appeared on the glass in the compact. It was admittedly a marvel, but Aaron's sense of appreciation was slightly undercut by the fact that Ebony had sent him not a message, but a crude drawing of a face with its tongue sticking out. He gave her a flat look.

Next to him, Daniel glanced at the real clock on the wall and spun his keyring around a finger.

"Time is getting short," he said. "Probably ought to head out soon."

"In that case, I should grab my wrap and clutch," Paloma said. "I'll be right back."

As she hurried off and Oliver started sparring with Ignotus again, Aaron drifted over to where Ebony had started fiddling with some of the items on the worktable.

"I thought there were no names," he said.

"What?" she said distractedly, not looking up.

"You said there were no names with conjurers," he said. "For safety. But they know your name."

Ebony paused then, finally looking up with a sigh.

"It's not a big deal, Aaron."

He crossed his arms. "Well, I think it is."

"I wasn't introduced to the group in the usual way," she said. "I met

155

some of them before any of us knew we'd be working together so closely. At that point, the ship had sailed."

"I still don't like it."

"It doesn't matter if you-" she began, then caught herself and took a deep breath. Exerting a visible effort to steady herself, she reached into her pocket, then held a closed fist out to Aaron.

"Here. Take this."

He raised an eyebrow, leaning forward slightly, but keeping his arms tight to his body. "What is it?"

"Just take it!"

Prodded by the urgency in her voice, Aaron held out a hand, and she dropped something smooth and heavy into it. Drawing it closer, he saw that it was a piece of ceramic shaped like a wheel, with spokes radiating out from a central point to connect to an outer circle. Strange characters had been drawn on the surface of the ceramic, and a leather thong had been threaded through one of the spaces between the spokes to make a necklace. Aaron looked up at his sister.

"But what is it?"

"An amulet of protection. In case your dumb ass ends up in a tight spot."

He blinked, then looked back down at the pendant in his head. His throat felt oddly tight.

"Did you make one for the others?"

The corner of her mouth quirked up.

"What? You don't think there are perks to being a twin?"

He didn't trust himself to answer. Instead, he looped the thong over her head and tucked the amulet into his shirt, smoothing his vest to hide any hint of a bump. Ebony gave a satisfied nod.

"Good hunting," she said, and he gave her a nod in return. Paloma appeared at the office door, trilling that she was ready, and so Aaron joined the others in heading to the car. He was only a little ashamed of how relieved he was to go.

Oliver kept up a steady stream of banter on the way to Hartley Center, but Aaron barely listened. The two of them and Paloma were tucked into the back seat of the club's big black sedan, the one that looked like a city cab, with Daniel at the wheel. The plan was for Daniel to drop Oliver and Paloma, with their attention-grabbing sparkle and sophistication, off first, then circle the block before depositing Aaron on the steps alone. A solitary man, lacking a plus one, might prove noteworthy, but they had decided it was best for Aaron to keep his distance so observers were less likely to connect the three of them. Ideally, they'd be in and out without making much of an impression on anyone, but better safe than sorry.

The lobby of the opera house was sleek and spare, but in a way that suggested that every elegant fixture and modern carpet was cripplingly expensive. A pair of curved staircases on either side of the theater doors swept up from the lobby to the mezzanine, and Aaron made his way up the one on the right to take his seat in the lower balcony. He couldn't help but feel self-conscious, like someone was about to call him out as an impostor, and then feel silly about that. These blithe, moneyed people were some of the same ones he saw at work every night, after all. But it felt different here. He didn't have the darkness and the bar to keep him safe and anonymous. He felt a sudden pang of longing for the Hierophant, but he brushed it aside. He had a job to do, and he intended to do it.

After a brief wait at the door, Aaron produced his ticket for the usher, who handed him a playbill and led him to his seat. It was not a long walk; even though he was near the front, the balcony wasn't all that deep. The orchestra circle sprawled out beneath him, packed to bursting with men in sober evening dress and women in riotous color, swathed in silk and satin and dripping with jewels. Even amid all the clamor, Aaron was easily able to pick out Oliver's bright hair and Paloma's headband. They were only a few rows back from the stage, chatting animatedly with a society matron in a frankly ridiculous tiara. Aaron's own neighbors, a young, serious couple, had their heads together over their playbill and seemed far more intent on murmuring about it to each other than engaging him in conversation, which suited him fine. Opening his own playbill, he held it up, ostensibly to read it, but really to use it as cover for scouting what was happening in the private boxes on the walls adjoining the mezzanine.

There were quite a few people who genuinely seemed to be there to enjoy the ballet, but the see-and-be-seen RPC contingent was also well represented. Off to one side, Aaron saw Turner-Hoff talking with Sutterfield, looking for all the world as if he had never so much as heard of an asylum up the coast experimenting on captive adepts. Clenching his jaw, he let his gaze drift across the stage to where Eleanor Bradshaw sat in a tasteful blue gown and understated diamond necklace. She was half-turned in her seat, speaking to someone in the rear of the box who Aaron couldn't quite see. He attempted to shift unobtrusively in his seat, but just then the lights dimmed, indicating that the show was about to start. Aaron closed the playbill, reluctant to press his luck much further as people ended conversations and settled into their seats. He'd have to wait until intermission to see much more.

He knew the basic plot of the ballet—a tragic love story involving a beautiful princess, the mysterious fairy prince who loves her, and her greedy father determined to keep them apart—and that was all fine as far as it went. But when Vasilyev came onstage as the star-crossed prince, even Aaron, completely ignorant as he was of ballet, could tell that something in the room shifted. Vasilyev was not a big man—more compact and wiry than physically imposing—but he had a command-ing, magnetic presence; when he was on stage, it was almost impos-sible to look anywhere else. Aaron started to understand why his defection was such a big deal. If the RPC could claim credit for bringing *this* to New Avalon, people would pay attention.

When the lights came up for intermission, the first thing that Aaron noticed was that Eleanor Bradshaw was no longer in her box. That alone seemed significant, but glancing at the box below that, which had been empty before the show started, he made another interesting discovery. Just as Colleen had said, Emerson Teasley had deigned to make an appearance at an event that didn't involve him standing at a podium and shouting at people. As it was, he seemed to be holding court with a collection of fawning sycophants, laughing and slapping backs. Had Bradshaw left her box to speak to him? Where was she? Had Oliver noticed?

He leaned forward in his seat, trying to spot Oliver and Paloma again, but he couldn't find them. They must have stepped out into the lobby. Racked with indecision over whether to go after them or stay put and watch what transpired in Teasley's box, he eventually settled on the latter. He sat there for the remainder of the break, nervously drumming his fingers on his knee, but as far as he could tell, nothing particularly exciting happened. When the lights signaled the end of intermission, the hangers-on trailed out of the box, and then they were all returned to the darkness to watch the princess die her gorgeous, heartbreaking death.

As soon as the final applause had faded after the curtain call, the couple next to Aaron gathered their belongings and stood, signaling that they were ready to depart. Aaron got to his own feet and stepped part of the way into the aisle to let them pass. Below him, he saw Oliver and Paloma sweep up the aisle towards the lobby, laughing merrily. He remained where he stood for another moment, shooting his cuffs and smoothing his coat and vest into place, then turned and walked to the mezzanine to wait.

He was only out there a few moments before Oliver and Paloma appeared at the top of the stairs and made their purposeful, unhurried way to the spot where a goon in a tuxedo that couldn't entirely hide his goonishness stood sentry in front of a discreet bank of elevators—just as Oliver had said he would be. Aaron stepped into the shadow of a potted palm and knelt, quickly untying and then retying his shoe. As he did, he watched Oliver and Paloma carefully, This was the tricky part. Ideally, Oliver would be able to talk their way into the elevator without Aaron's assistance, leaving him free to move around the opera house and see if he could sniff out anything interesting before it was time for all of them to go meet Daniel. If not, Aaron would need to intervene.

The mezzanine was still fairly busy, with people venturing to the various lounges for post-performance drinks, so Aaron wasn't able to make out specifics of what was happening with the goon, but based on his friends' facial expressions and body language, it wasn't going well. Aaron had devoted just about as much time as would be reasonable to tying his shoe and was wondering what else he was going to have to do to stall for time, when Paloma's hand drifted behind her back and made a loose OK sign, their predetermined signal for help. Getting to his feet, Aaron strode across the mezzanine to her side.

"-really is just a misunderstanding," Oliver was saying to the goon who held a typewritten list in a death grip "Bertie really did tell me that the invite wasn't necessary if our names were on the list, so I thought-"

"And again, sir," the goon said, not very patiently, "Your names are not on the list. Now if you'll just move along before I need to-"

"Oh, I think I may know what's going on here," Aaron said with more confidence than he felt. "Let me take a look."

The goon began to protest as he stepped forward to peer at the list of names, but then Aaron reached up to lay a casual, friendly hand on the man's arm and flooded him with agreeable, friendly energy. *These are the right sorts of people,* the energy said. *You want to help them. You want to let them in. It's just an oversight that they're not on the list. It's your responsibility to make it right.*

Aaron felt the tension in the man's arm ease, and his eyes took on the familiar glassiness. Oliver, who knew exactly what to look for, cleared his throat. "Does that clear anything up?"

"Yes, sir," the goon said, hostility giving way to a sort of vague politeness. "It seems you were right—just a misunderstanding. Please enjoy your night." And with a sweeping gesture, he ushered the three of them past.

Oliver gave him a gracious nod, and they crossed to the elevator bank, where an attendant was waiting to take them up. They didn't speak in the elevator, owing to the attendant's presence, but they exchanged significant looks, confirming that they each knew their role once they disembarked. And then the doors opened, and they stepped out into the Stardust Ballroom.

Aaron had thought he'd had some idea of what to expect, but the blueprint had not done the ballroom justice. It was just as sleek as the lobby, but it also had an air of otherworldly opulence, like something from a particularly sophisticated fairy tale. The bulbs in the sleek gold and crystal chandeliers were turned down low, allowing the floor—dark blue marble with geometric patterns traced in gold—to reflect their muted illumination along with the city lights visible through the floor to ceiling windows at far end of the room. Gilded arches rose gracefully to a cantilevered ceiling that employed some trick of acoustics to keep the voices of the assembled crowd from echoing off the hard, unadorned surfaces—instead, they merged a low hum, accompanied pleasantly by a pianist playing a baby grand over in a corner. A server approached them with a tray of champagne, and each of them took a glass with a murmur of thanks. Then, giving Aaron an almost imperceptible nod, Oliver led Paloma into the throng to mingle, leaving Aaron to retreat to the perimeter and observe.

Not that there seemed to be much *to* observe. People in fancy clothes drank copious amounts of alcohol and made banal conversation. It actually kind of was like being at work, only more tedious. But then a particularly obnoxious burst of laughter drew his notice, and scanning the room, he caught sight of presumed RPC presidential candidate Emerson Teasley deep in conversation with Eleanor Bradshaw.

Aaron took a quick swig of champagne, assessing the situation. That exchange definitely merited attention, but how? They were entirely too far away for him to get a sense of what they were talking about. Should he approach them? Had Oliver noticed them yet? He was surveying the room to find out when he suddenly felt the pocket watch tucked into his jacket get warm through the fabric of his shirt.

It was entirely unexpected, considering Oliver and Paloma were both in the ballroom with him, and for a moment, he could only gaze down at his chest in consternation. Was Daniel trying to reach them? What for? Finally, he shifted his champagne flute from one hand to another and reached into his jacket for the watch. As soon as he popped it open and caught sight of Ebony's familiar handwriting, however, inquisitiveness gave way to a lurching sense of horror. It wasn't a long message—just three simple words—but it was enough.

They have Colleen.

CHAPTER 19

COLLEEN

For the first block or two, Colleen was too preoccupied with seething to think about much else. Soon, however, she began to realize she might have been a bit hasty in making her dramatic exit. The spring sun was bright overhead, but the wind coming in off the harbor had a notable bite, and the shoes that had seemed just right to her that morning (not that she had been worried about impressing anyone in particular, how dare anyone suggest such a thing) weren't really designed for long-distance walking. Plus, the neighborhood surrounding the Hierophant wasn't exactly over-flowing with pedestrian traffic or, accordingly, cabs. Colleen had to trudge on for nearly half a mile, swinging her handbag and ignoring the blisters rising on the back of her heels, before she was able to flag one down and slouch into the back seat, tossing off the address to her boarding house to the driver.

She really had meant to go back to work when she'd stormed away from Aaron's disapproving gaze, but now, she found that she just didn't have the heart. She'd called Stewart the day before, letting him know that she was home safe and that she might need him to cover for her just a bit longer. He hadn't been happy about it, but he'd agreed, so it wasn't absolutely necessary for her to show up. She could lie to herself and say it was because she was tired and disheveled, but really, she was embarrassed. Because she'd just gone and blown the scoop of a lifetime.

Missing adepts had seemed big. Missing adepts with connections to a dark government conspiracy had seemed even bigger. But this new development, building some sort of medically enhanced police squad to crush any trace of magical resistance—this was beyond what she could have possibly imagined. This was a career.

And she didn't have enough of it to print.

The bitter tang of it made the fight with Aaron even harder to swallow. In her typical fashion, she had gotten carried away—first with the heady rush of the discovery, then with her pique at Aaron's judgment—and lost sight of the fact that the question of whether or not she would take the story to Mr. Whitaker was moot. She couldn't. The premise was so outlandish that without any proof, he would laugh right in her face. And she'd just thrown away her opportunity to get that proof because Aaron had bruised her ego.

She stewed over this point as she climbed out of the cab in front of her building, as she climbed the stairs to her room, as she threw herself onto her bed with a satisfying *whumph*. Laying there on her back, she toed the shoes off of her poor battered feet and stared mournfully at the ceiling, wondering what in the world she was supposed to do now.

Again, she cursed herself for a fool. There was no guarantee that the reception would have yielded anything useful, but at least she would have been there to find out. Because if she was being completely honest, she still wanted the story, but she also just wanted to *know*. After all, she had learned things over the last few days that more or less upended her entire worldview; she felt a need, deep in her gut. to understand the things that were happening and why, wholly apart from whatever was going between her and Aaron.

Wholly apart from Aaron…

She sat bolt upright in bed. So what if she wasn't with Aaron and the others? She could go to the opera house herself. Sure, she didn't have a ticket, but that wasn't an insurmountable obstacle for a real reporter. She could find a way in. A place that size—they couldn't lock down *every* point of entry.

So there it was. *To hells with Aaron,* she thought again, *and his smug self-righteousness, too.* She didn't need his permission to do her job however she saw fit.

With renewed energy, she jumped off the bed and started digging through her closet. Ten minutes later, nearly every garment she owned had been strewn across her bad, and nothing seemed quite right. She examined the carnage, biting her lip, then ran out to the hall and banged on her neighbor Helen's door. After some negotiation and pledges of eternal gratitude, she returned to her room with something constituting a suitable outfit: a gold fringed shift, long string of glass pearls, and matching headpiece with heavy beading and a jaunty feather. She placed these carefully in her now-empty closet and then settled in at her desk.

For the rest of the afternoon, she recorded everything she had learned about the disappearances, the sanatorium, and the experiments Kirby and Imogen had described. She made notes of outstanding questions—of which there were many—and points that merited further investigation. By the time the sun began to sink behind the skyline, she felt a little better—having the facts laid out in front of her like that made it all seem clearer in her head, and now she had a more specific idea of what she should be looking for at the opera house. Pushing back from her desk, she went to the window and stretched gazing out at the city. A small, traitorous part of her brain wondered what Aaron was doing just then, but she quashed that train of thought immediately. She didn't care what Aaron was doing. She had a plan to execute and a job to save. With a brisk nod, she spun away from the window and started getting ready for the evening.

It didn't take her long to dress. When she was done, she dug her fanciest handbag out from underneath the detritus on her bed and made sure it was stocked with the essentials—emergency money, lipstick, a handkerchief, room key. Looking over at the desk, she debated whether to take one of her pocket notebooks and a stub of pencil. It would be handy to be able jot down notes, but she didn't know exactly what she was walking into. She didn't want to incriminate herself by acting like an amateur. With a slight pang, she left the notebook behind and headed out to the street.

The street was busy with knots of people heading to dinner or the theater, so it took her awhile to find a cab, but she managed. As they moved closer to the Hartley Center, the traffic got thicker, so Colleen had plenty of time to take in the scene—autos lined up at the entrance to the opera house, searchlights arcing across the cloudy sky, the occasional flashbulb popping as some local celebrity went inside. And she had time to strategize. She knew she had to play this carefully, which was tricky, since she'd never been to the Hartley Center before. She didn't anticipate any trouble getting into the building without a ticket, but the actual theater was a no-go, and she didn't want to end up standing around in the lobby twiddling her thumbs once the show started. She'd heard that the cocktail lounges inside stayed open even during performances, so those seemed like her best bet. But how many were there? Where were they located? How might they afford her the opportunity to sneak into the more private areas and up to the reception?

Even as she turned all these questions around in her head, she realized she wouldn't really be able to answer them until she got inside. So when her cab finally had its turn at the curb, she paid the fare, took a deep breath, and went hunting.

It was hard to see much above the press of bodies, but before long she spotted a small group of society types roughly her own age who had apparently started indulging before they'd arrived. She had a hunch that if she followed them, she'd end up in one of the lounges, and she was correct. Making her way to the bar, she ordered a ginger ale julep, reasoning it looked enough like a real cocktail to help her to blend in while allowing her to keep a clear head throughout the night. As she hopped up onto a stool at a high table with a good view of the door, the lights flickered, letting everyone know the show was about to start. The lounge emptied quickly, leaving only a few stragglers behind.

A few minutes later, a group of young men came in, lamenting loudly that they had missed the beginning of the performance and would now just have to drink until intermission. One of them caught Colleen's eye and wandered over once he had his drink; one of his friends drifted over to join them, while the others stayed huddled around the bar. They were nice enough guys, if a bit full of themselves, and Colleen did her best to stay witty and charming while politely but firmly refusing offers of further drinks. As far as she could tell, not of them noticed her watching the lobby over their shoulders.

Intermission came and went, and still the boys stayed in the lounge, getting progressively drunker and louder. Eventually, she decided she'd had enough and made her escape, claiming she had to powder her nose. Once she was out of the lounge, she took a quick look around and decided to check out the mezzanine while it was empty. If she spent too much time wandering around, she'd look suspicious, but if she headed upstairs with purpose, she'd have a bit of time to see what she could find before going back to ground.

She took the staircase closest to her, the one on the left side of the lobby, up to the second level. Conveniently, there was a sign for the ladies' room pointing further to the left, so she popped in for a moment to freshen her lipstick. Then she went back outside, glanced around to make sure no one was watching, and walked further along the curving corridor, away from the lobby. She stopped when she heard voices coming from a back stairway and stepped behind one of the potted palms that lines the public areas. A couple of bulky men in tuxedos exited the stairwell, muttering what sounded like complaints to each other; Colleen thought she detected the words "Bradford" and "shindig" in the course of their conversation. Bingo. This was exactly the kind of lead she'd been looking for.

Deciding to bide her time—she couldn't exactly slip into the reception undetected if there was no reception yet—she retreated, settling into a lounge that had spied on the mezzanine level. Glancing down at the lower floor, she saw that her friends had left the first lounge, which was just as well. This seemed a much better place to roost.

She was most of the way through a second julep when the sound of applause leaked out through the theater doors, and a few moments later, crowds of attendees followed. Colleen took the final swig of her drink and dabbed her lips with a napkin, distracted from the mass of bodies by her racing heart. She kept an eye on the clock over the bar, and when 15 minutes had passed and the mezzanine was calmer but not yet deserted, she made her move.

Striding confidently, she headed to the bathroom she had found earlier. There were a few people milling around, chatting or waiting for their dates to finish using the facilities, but they all seemed to observe a sort of unspoken boundary—nobody strayed more than a foot or two past the bathroom door. Except, that is for Colleen. Without looking left or right, she retraced her steps down the corridor to the stairwell she'd seen earlier, pulled the door open, and stepped inside.

Where she came face to face with none other than Eleanor Bradshaw and Dr. Gavin Hayward, talking in hushed voices on the landing.

They looked as surprised as she was, but Dr. Hayward recovered first, his face darkening with rage.

"*You,*" he snarled and lunged for Colleen. She tried to jump backwards, but he was too fast for her, and he seized her wrist in one broad hand. She yanked and twisted, but his grip was like iron.

Bradshaw stood observing the scene with an expression of distaste. "Who is this, Gavin?"

"This is the one who snuck in and stole our reader," Dr. Hayward said. "Isn't that right, *Veronica*? Who are you really? Shining Light?"

"Gods, no," Colleen said, indignant despite herself. Shining Light was the infamous group of pro-magic terrorists who killed in the name of their cause. She just wanted information.

"So what then, press?" he continued, giving her arm a shake, but this time she knew to keep her mouth shut. Her gaze drifted to Bradshaw, and she saw that while the woman had just a moment before been radiating aloof contempt, now her eyes were filled with pure, hard malice. It was enough for Colleen to cease her struggle.

"Press," Bradshaw said slowly. "Hang on… you're that Crimm girl, aren't you? The one stirring up trouble over at the Independent?"

Still, Colleen said nothing, but she felt her insides grow cold. When Mr. Whitaker had told her she'd drawn the notice of the RPC, but it had been worrying, but also rather abstract. Nothing about Eleanor Bradshaw staring at her like that felt abstract.

There was a burst of laughter down the hall, and Bradshaw thankfully broke eye contact to glance over her shoulder. It ended up not being much of a reprieve, though.

"We have to get upstairs," Bradshaw said. "They're expecting us."

"What are we going to do about her?" said Hayward. "We can't just let her go."

"Well, obviously," Bradshaw snapped, voice icy. She gave Colleen one more bone-chilling look, then seemed to come to some sort of decision. "Follow me. I know somewhere we can put her until we have time to deal with this situation properly."

CHAPTER 20

AARON

*a*aron sat his drink down on a nearby table, taking pains to move casually though his heart was racing. Smoothing his jacket, he began making his way to the door, catching Paloma's eye as he went. He gestured to let her know that he was stepping out, and she gave a tiny, almost undetectable nod before turning back to her conversation.

Once outside the ballroom, Aaron scrambled to find a place that gave him a modicum of privacy, ending up in a rather garish restroom —wallpaper with palm fronds and toucans, really?—and locking the door behind him. He proceeded to exchange hurried messages with Ebony, becoming increasingly frustrated by the unwieldiness of the process—what he wouldn't have given for a telephone just then. Eventually, he was able to piece together the basics of what was going on:

- Daniel, keeping watch across the street, had seen Colleen encounter Bradshaw and an unidentified tall blonde man through a window, and they had dragged her off somewhere.

- No, Daniel did not know where they had taken her, and while Aaron had seen Bradshaw in the ballroom, Dr. Hayward was still unaccounted for.
- Yes, Daniel could have picked the lock on an exterior door and gotten inside to look for her, but without knowing where she was and what exactly he was walking into, it was too dangerous.
- Aaron needed to come down to street level to let him in, and together, they could go find Colleen.

Aaron gritted his teeth as he snapped the watch shut and tucked it back into his jacket. He took a steadying breath, then unlocked the bathroom door and began his descent down the service stairs.

The backstage portion of the hall was a dizzying warren of prop shops, wardrobe work rooms, rehearsal areas, dressing rooms, and on and on. He was actually making fairly good time getting through all of it, but from what he remembered of the blueprint he still had a ways to go. He just had to hope his luck would hold.

It didn't.

Just as he was approaching the mezzanine level, a door swung open, and a hulking man in a tuxedo lumbered in. Aaron thought fast, but there was nowhere to hide and nobody else around to provide a distraction. When the man caught sight of him, his eyes narrowed.

"Hey, who are you?" he growled, making a beeline for Aaron. "And what are you doing back here? This area is off limits."

"Oh, sorry," Aaron said, reaching out to give the man a friendly pat on the arm, the shoulder—really anywhere he could make decent contact. "I didn't reali-"

In a surprisingly fluid motion, the man grabbed Aaron's arm and twisted it up behind his back, shoving him face-first into the wall.

"How about you keep your hands to yourself and tell me what it is you're doing here?" he said. He gave Aaron's arm a twist for good measure, and Aaron hissed in pain.

"I'm... I'm just running an errand for my boss," he said, words muffled thanks to his mouth being flattened against the brick. "He's upstairs at the big do, and he needed me to get some reefer from the car." Hoping he could keep the guy distracted if he kept talking, he started slowly reaching backwards with the arm at his side, straining his fingertips to make even a little bit of contact. But it was hard to judge the pressure, and the man jerked as Aaron made contact with his thigh.

"What the-" he burst out. "Are you trying to feel me-" He cut off suddenly, understanding dawning. "Wait, are you one of the guys who works your sick magic on people by touching them? They warned us about you."

Aaron had a split second to wonder precisely who "they" were before the man spun him around and punched him in the face. The force of it knocked Aaron to the floor, and he barely had time to roll from his side onto his back before the guy was on him, pinning him with one hand and punching him again with the other. His eyes were burning with hatred and disgust, and that was almost worse than the pain, because as far as Aaron could tell, it meant he wasn't going to stop punching any time soon.

Aaron struggled, but it did little good; the hits kept coming. Until suddenly, they didn't. Instead, he heard a sickening *thunk*, and then the man's weight collapsed on top of him. He opened his eyes in time to see another man, also dressed in evening wear and holding a 2x4, plant his foot into the big guy's side and roll him over onto the floor. Then he looked up, and Aaron realized he recognized that face.

It was Pavel Vasilyev.

"You," he said in astonishment as Vasilyev tossed the 2x4 to the side and brushed his hands together.

"Ah," he said in a thick Ursan accent. "You know me. That is good. No need for introduction." He offered a hand to Aaron, who took it and got shakily to his feet. "But who are you?"

"Aaron," he replied, still reeling a bit. "I'm Aaron. But how did you-"

"I was on my way to the ballroom," Vasilyev said. "And I heard the scuffle. I got here and heard what he said about magic. I could not just stand there and let him beat one of us to death, could I?"

"Right," Aaron said. "Because you're an adept, too."

Vasilyev sniffed. "Yes, I think that is your word for it. Now, what are you doing here? Because I do not think you were really getting the reefer."

"I'm looking for a friend of mine," Aaron said. "They've hidden her somewhere, and I need to find her."

Vasilyev gave him a speculative look. "This girl, she has magic, too?"

"No."

"Then why would they hide her?"

Aaron paused, unsure how much to reveal in this increasingly bizarre set of circumstances. "She… is asking questions about things certain people want kept quiet."

A look of understanding crossed Vasilyev's face. "She is inconvenient."

Aaron choked out a laugh. "Yes. Inconvenient and stubborn and stupidly brave."

Vasilev looked at him for a moment longer, then gave a decisive nod. "Come. I might know where they put her."

He turned and began striding down the hall as Aaron stared after him, mystified. After a moment, he realized he was walking alone and looked back to Aaron, exhaling hard through his nose.

"Are you coming? Or shall I just go to the awful party upstairs and drown myself in vodka?"

Aaron shook off his stupor and hurried to catch up with the wiry dancer. "Why are you helping me?"

Vasilyev grunted. "Is long story."

Aaron waited a moment, but Vasilyev didn't seem inclined to continue. "Want to give me a rundown?"

"Not especially, no."

"Well, then how do I know I can trust you?"

Vasilyev stopped and shot Aaron a look of supreme annoyance, but eventually, the expression softened into resignation, and he started walking again with a sigh.

"Tell me, how much do you know about my country, Aaron?"

Aaron swallowed, feeling heat rise in his cheeks. "Not much, if I'm honest."

Vasilyev made a very Ursan sound of derision.

"I mean," Aaron jumped in, trying to save at least a bit of face. "I know your king was deposed. And there was a civil war. But that's about it."

Vasilyev nodded, seemingly mollified. "When the Serayan Army came for the king, they gave the country hope. I was just a boy then, but I could see it in my elders—this faith that life would be better now that we were free. It did not last long. All the sweet promises of a new Ursa crumbled once the army leaders got into power and decided tyranny was not so bad as long as they were in charge."

"But almost as much as the Serayan regime wants power, they also want to be seen as legitimate. Respectable. And one way to do that was through art. Ursa would have the greatest music, the greatest literature, the greatest dance. The world would stand in awe of us. To this end, they created the great Academy for the nation's most gifted children in Serdtse. And they searched the land for students to fill the academy's halls."

"We are an active people, Ursans. In my little village in the mountains, we did many of the same things our countrymen did throughout the land. We hunted and fished. We skated on the frozen lakes and ponds in the winter. And we danced.

"My mother said I danced before I walked. Everyone in my village recognized my talent, even as a very small child. So when the scouts came, I was the obvious choice to go to the Academy. They took me with them to the capital, and I never saw my village again."

"How old were you?" Aaron asked.

"I was eight years old."

"What happened then?"

"I went to the Academy, and they made me into one of the greatest dancers of all time."

His voice held a bitter note, but also, if Aaron was not mistaken, some pride.

"You still haven't answered my question," he prompted. "Why give it up? Why come here?"

"Have you ever heard the name Olga Romanova?"

Aaron searched his memory, but to no avail. "No, I don't think so."

Vassilyev sighed. "A crime. Everyone should know it."

"Was she at the Academy with you?"

Vasilyev nodded. "I thought the Academy a terrible place when I arrived. Everyone seemed bigger, smarter, better. I could not keep up. Olga was my first friend. I could not figure out why. She was brilliant, funny, charming, and I was a snot-nosed little peasant from the mountains. But one day, she chose me as her friend, and that was that."

"And then what?" Aaron said, caught up in the story in spite of himself.

Vasilyev opened his mouth, then snapped it closed again, casting a sidelong glance at Aaron.

"I don't suppose you would take anything I told you to the authorities?"

Aaron chuckled. "Considering I encountered you while breaking and entering in pursuit of details regarding a vast government conspiracy, no, I don't think that's anything you need to worry about."

Vasilyev didn't smile, but his expression somehow suggested wry amusement. He gave a single nod, conceding the point.

"It didn't last. At the Academy, younger students spend a lot of time together, but as we got older, we drifted apart. Once I got over my homesickness, I became obsessed with training, with excelling in all areas of dance. And it worked—I was the youngest featured dancer ever in the National Ballet. It was then, when I had left school behind to become a professional, that I encountered Olga again.

"I was at a party in Serdtse when I saw the most beautiful blonde in a long black dress. She noticed me and came over. I could not believe it was my little friend from the Academy. She had become a noted writer and painter in the city, even had an exhibit at the National Gallery. We talked all night, and I asked if I could see her the next day. She agreed. We saw each other that day, and the day after, and the day after that."

"You fell in love with her," Aaron said. Vasilleyev nodded.

"And she with me. For the first weeks, we were almost sick with it, the pleasure of each other's company. But it didn't last. I was told the National Ballet would be heading out on a six month tour, which would obviously keep us apart. But also, when Olga's exhibit had made some powerful people very angry. While I had devoted myself to the pursuit of greatness for the glory of Ursa, she had begun to question the motives of the Serayan regime. To believe that the party leaders weren't concerned for the people, but only for their own self-interest. And it showed in her work.

"People talked. The exhibit was shuttered a week before it was supposed to close. In the last days before I left on tour, I thought I saw men following us on the street. She told me I was being silly, that the whole thing would blow over, but I wasn't convinced. I begged her to be careful when I left, even urged to leave the city and stay with her family in the country, but she refused. Then, when we were performing in Ville du Soleil, I got a letter from her. A friend had gotten word to her that she was going to be arrested if she stayed in the city, and if that happened, she would almost certainly be sent to a labor camp. .

"What happened?" said Aaron, fully invested now.

"She did go to her mother's house then, but we both knew that was not a permanent solution. She was in their sights now, and they would get to her eventually." He ran a hand over his hair. "Olga, she has a heart condition, something she was born with. She would not make it through a winter at the camps. We needed a better plan. So I asked a friend in Belleterre for help. I stressed the importance of discretion, but let him know that I was open to any opportunities. He put me in touch with a contact at the New Avalonian embassy in Ville du Soleil. They offered Olga and me asylum, but only if we promised to abide by the Embargo, and to do so in a very public manner." He looked at Aaron and shrugged. "We had no other options. We accepted."

"Is Olga here with you now?"

"No," Vasilyev said, and his voice was cold. "She is in a safe house in Belleterre. Your foreign office said it would be too obvious if we appeared together in Ad Astra at once, so I would come first, and she would follow later. But what they really meant was it would be easier to keep me in line once I arrived.

"I am in the public eye here. People would notice if something unfortunate befell me. But it would be easy for them to quietly shuttle Olga back to Ursa. And that would be a death sentence for her. So I must act the part until they decide I've earned my keep."

Aaron was quiet for a moment. Then he said, "I am very sorry that all that happened to the two of you. But I am still not sure what it has to do with me."

Vasilyev smiled grimly. "I hate them, these people who run your country. And if this friend is inconvenient to them, I like her. Plus, it is good to do something that reminds me I am my own man."

Aaron nodded, considering. And then he let out a slightly hysterical chuckle. Vasilyev raised an eyebrow, temper flaring.

"This amuses you?"

"No, no," Aaron rushed to say. "At least, not the story itself. But it is kind of funny..."

"What?" Vasilyev prompted, anger giving way to curiosity.

Aaron shrugged, resigned. "That we both ended up here because of a girl."

To his surprise, Vasilyev barked out a sharp laugh of his own. "Yes, I suppose it is at that."

Aaron looked around at the hallway Vasilyev had led them into. They were well and truly off the beaten path now; they had made their way back up a couple of levels and into an area that had a strange air of disuse compared to most of what he'd seen backstage. It was hushed and still back there, eerily so.

"Where exactly are we going?" he said.

"Storage room," Vasilyev said. "It's mostly forgotten. No one goes there."

"Then how do you know about it?"

Vasilyev smiled grimly. "Because *I* go there. Sometimes—many times—after dealing with my 'hosts' and the idiot artistic director, I want to go somewhere quiet. I found this place, and it was very quiet, so I kept coming back. Nobody has ever found me. It drives them all crazy that they can't figure out where I go."

"And you think that's where Bradshaw and Hayward took her? How can you be sure?"

Vasilyev shrugged. "Can't be sure. But it would make sense. Best hiding place in the building. Even if she screamed, no one would hear."

Aaron felt a stab of cold nausea at that horrifying prospect, but there was nothing to do about it but get to her, so he just swallowed and picked up the pace.

Finally, they came to a halt before a door at the far end of the hall-way. Aaron took a deep breath and reached into his pocket for his lock picks, but Vasilyev laid a staying hand on his arm.

"Allow me," he said and put the other hand on the doorknob. He narrowed his eyes, concentrating for a moment, and then Aaron heard a click. He raised his eyebrows.

"You're a metal-worker?" he said, realizing that for all the buzz he'd heard about Vasilyev, he had no idea what his ability actually was.

"Disorder," Vasilyev said, a fierce gleam in his eye. "If there is a system or resting state in place, I disrupt."

"Like the tumblers in the lock," Aaron said, and Vasilyev nodded. "Huh. Impressive."

"Thank you," Vasilyev said. "Now let's go find your girl, yes?"

"Yes," said Aaron, and he turned the knob.

CHAPTER 21

COLLEEN

*C*olleen was both surprised and dismayed to discover just how excruciatingly boring it was to be held captive. She couldn't help but think that if she was going to be in peril, it should at least be interesting.

Instead, she was sitting on the floor in a pitch dark room, alone, handcuffed to a water pipe, and questioning every decision that had led her here. She knew she should be afraid, and she was, but the longer she sat there, the more abstract the threat became. Mostly, she was just annoyed at herself. And bored. Her mind drifted to the moving pictures she'd seen where criminals in striped uniforms sang sad songs inside their prison cells or made their displeasure with the situation known by dragging a tin cup across the bars. But she didn't have a tin cup at her disposal, or bars, for that matter, and her singing voice was so frightful, she didn't even want to subject herself to it. So that left sitting in the strange limbo of knowing she was likely doomed, but not knowing how.

Just as she was once again questioning every decision that had led her here, she heard a scuffling noise in what she thought was the direction of the door and went very still. There was a muted hum of voices followed by a click of the lock, and then the door swung open.

The light spilling in from the hallway was a sickly yellow, but after the time spent in total blackness, Colleen flinched away from it anyway. Then the overhead light came on, and she forced an eye open, bracing herself for the prospect of Eleanor Bradshaw and Dr. Hayward rounding the pile of junk in the center of the room to sweep her off gods only where. Only it wasn't the two agents of evil she saw.

It was Aaron.

"It's you," she breathed, unable to keep the happiness and relief out of her voice. Then, identifying the figure striding along behind Aaron she did a double take. "And you brought Pavel Vasilyev?"

"I'll explain later," Aaron said and, turning to the man the adoring crowds called Pasha, gestured at the handcuffs. "Could you?"

"Of course," Vasilyev said and laid his hands on the cuffs. A moment later, there was a click, and they fell off Colleen's wrists. Reaching down, Aaron helped her to her feet.

"What are you doing here?" he said as he checked her over for damage. "What could you possibly have been *thinking*?"

Grateful or not, she did not appreciate being spoken to that way. "I'm fairly certain you're capable of putting that together yourself."

He stared at her, nonplussed, then gestured to the cuffs on the floor. "You know, we can put those back on you."

"Clock is ticking, Aaron," Vasilyev muttered. "Don't dawdle."

"Right," Aaron said, surveying Colleen one last time and turning to face him. "You need to get to your big event."

Vasilyev grimaced. "I do. And you need to get her out of here. I will try my best to grab everyone's attention up there, keep them focused on me rather than going anywhere. But there will be others like our friend downstairs in the building. Be careful."

"We will," Aaron said, guiding Colleen around a pile of clutter on the floor. "Thank you."

"Aaron." Aaron paused, struck by the urgency in Vasilyev's tone. He saw that the dancer's face had turned serious and a little sad. "When you talk to your friends, the other adepts... explain that I didn't want to bend the knee. Explain why I did it."

Aaron's face went solemn. "I will," he said, voice slightly husky, and reached for his hand. Vasilyev shook it and gave a sharp nod.

"And you, inconvenient girl," he said turning to Colleen. "What is your name?"

She blinked. "It's Colleen. Colleen O'Cremin."

He nodded, as if this satisfied him somehow. "Well, Colleen O'Cremin. Go forth and give them hells."

Colleen glanced from Vasilyev to Aaron and back. "Um, who exactly?"

Vasilyev's smile was wicked. "All of them."

Colleen returned the smile and darted forward to kiss him on the cheek. Then she allowed Aaron to lead her away towards freedom.

They took the first set of stairs in hurried silence, but then Aaron couldn't seem to help himself anymore.

"I really *can't* believe you, coming here by yourself," he groused. "You could have gotten yourself killed."

"And I can't believe you're pressing this point again, now that you don't have a chaperone," Colleen snapped. "It's not your call. I get to make my own decisions about where I go and what I do. I don't need to get your stamp of approval."

He shot her an irritated look.

"Is 'You're not the boss of me' just a universal card that all sisters play?"

"Well, maybe we wouldn't need to if brothers weren't forever trying to be the boss," she shot back and gestured at his face. "Besides, you don't exactly seem to be having a safe and wholesome night, either."

He glowered at her. "This all happened because I was coming after *you.*"

This caught her by surprise. "Me? How did you even know I was here?"

"Daniel saw you from the street, when you had your run in with Bradshaw and some tall blonde man?"

"It was Hayward," she said, scowling, and Aaron sighed.

"Of course it was. Did they say anything about what they were going to do with you after locking you up in that storeroom?"

"No," she said. "Just that they had to get to the reception and they'd figure out the rest later." She cocked her head. "Is Oliver up there now?"

"Yes, with our friend Paloma," Aaron said. "I was with them, too, but then I got the message about you."

Her brow furrowed. "Got the message? How?"

"It's a long story," he said. "And speaking of…" They had reached a landing, and Aaron pulled Colleen to a halt and pulled out what looked like a pocket watch. Only when he popped it open, there was no watch inside; instead he used a tiny rod to scribble on some dark, shiny surface, then popped the rod back into the lid and returned the "watch" to his pocket.

"OK," he said to Colleen. "We should be good now."

"What was that?" Colleen said, now unable to help herself, despite their haste.

"A communication device my sister and her friends dreamed up," he said. "I sent her a message that she was able to relay to Daniel out on the street, so he knows I have you and we're on the way."

Colleen's eyes widened. "Well, that's pretty nifty."

"It is," Aaron said, and she heard pride in his voice, along with something a bit more complicated. Instinct told her now was not the time to press this particular point, so she switched tack.

"So, are you going to tell me how one of the biggest celebrities in the world ended up coming with you to unlock my handcuffs?"

As they continued their descent, Aaron gave her a quick rundown of what had happened. It was, perhaps understandably, light on details, and Colleen hoped she'd have a chance to dig a little deeper on that front when they weren't essentially running for their lives. Because it was a fascinating story.

"So, he's what, a hostage? A puppet for them to dangle around on a string?"

"Pretty much," Aaron said. "At least until he figures out a way to get Olga out of Ursa. Or until they decide they don't have any further use for him.

"Bastards," Colleen spat, and Aaron gave a huff of agreement. They took another half-flight of stairs, and slowly, her anger turned to something cooler, more thoughtful.

"It was really decent of him to help us," she said. "And decent of you to come after me. With everything else going on."

Aaron glanced over her, seemingly unsure of how to accept something approaching a sincere apology from her. "Well, it wasn't like I could just leave you there."

"I know."

"And I still think it was foolish of you, charging in here by yourself like that-"

Colleen held up a hand, cutting him off before he could derail the conversation entirely.

"While it was *my mistake to make*," she said, pausing for emphasis, "I do appreciate you coming to help me sort it out. So thank you."

Aaron still looked wary, but he didn't press the argument any further.

"You're welcome," he said, and she nodded. Then they continued down the stairs.

After what seemed like an eternity, they reached the ground floor.

"Are we almost there?" Colleen said, slightly breathless from the descent.

"Should be," Aaron said. "From what I remember, we only have to make it to the end of the corridor and take one last turn—then we should see the exterior door." He glanced back over his shoulder at Colleen, and she saw a host of emotions cross his face—relief, triumph, and, if she wasn't mistaken, a hint of her own excitement. The thrill of their escape, no matter how much he'd grumbled about the rescue. She couldn't help but smile then, a big, honest smile, and seemingly by reflex, he reached for her hand as they approached that final, critical corner.

Then Dr. Hayward stepped into their path, pointing a handgun directly at them.

CHAPTER 22

AARON

*a*aron threw an arm out, pushing Colleen behind him. For a
moment, there was only the sound of the three of them
breathing, but then Hayward finally spoke.

"How is it," he said in a tone that was equal parts annoyance and
genuine curiosity, "that you two *just keep turning up?*"

Neither Aaron nor Colleen volunteered an answer. Hayward
shook his head.

"You know, all you're doing here is proving our point."

Aaron felt Colleen take a breath to respond, but he beat her to the
punch, hoping to hold Hayward's attention. "And what point is that?"

"That magic only serves to divide us," Hayward said. "Look at us.
You two have caused all manner of trouble over the last few days, and
now you're standing here at the point of my gun, and for what? All of
this could have been avoided if magic weren't an issue."

"It's not an issue," Aaron said. "It's a part of who we are, and you
shouldn't be able to take it from us. Aren't you a doctor? Didn't you
swear an oath to help and not to harm?"

"But I am helping," the doctor said. "That's what you don't understand. Your abilities are mutations, like cancer. They make you sick.

And we are developing a way to heal you, so you can live a full life and all of us in society can thrive."

"And what about this shield you're working on?" Colleen said. "Is that supposed to help someone heal, too?"

Some of Hayward's bold righteousness faded, and he swallowed.

"That part of the project is actually not in my purview. Mrs. Bradshaw brought in other doctors to oversee it."

Aaron was unable to fight back a laugh. "You don't even know what it's for, do you?"

"It doesn't matter," Hayward said, with the urgency of someone who doesn't really believe what they're saying. "It's all part and parcel of Mrs. Bradshaw's vision, of our vision. I don't need to bother with all the details."

Colleen gave a huff of disgust. Over the course of the exchange, Hayward's aim had wavered, but now he pulled his arms up straight and steady.

"Enough discussion," he said. "Time to go."

Aaron's heart began to pound, though he'd suspected this was where they were headed when Hayward hadn't shot them on sight. "We're not going anywhere with you."

"I'm not giving you a choice," Hayward said. "I can't let the two of you just walk out of here. No, Mrs. Bradshaw would like a word. She's starting to lose patience with you magical folk gumming up the works. Because she knows it's you—some underground network connected to the charm schools. And you're going to help her stop it."

Somewhere in the innards of the building, Aaron heard a door creak. Thinking quickly, he figured that meant one of two things: a means of escape, or a person who could help. Very quietly, so only Colleen could hear, he murmured, "Run."

"I'm not leaving you," she whispered back.

"Now," Hayward said, pulling back the hammer on the gun. "I'm not going to ask again. Start walking."

Aaron paused, taking stock. Then he reached back, shoving Colleen as hard as he and yelling at her to go, before lunging for Hayward.

He wasn't trying to use his ability this time; he just wanted to get Hayward to drop the gun or at least point it away from Colleen. Hayward was taller than Aaron, though, and broad through the chest —he was strong and had a longer reach. They wrestled for a moment, but then Hayward pushed Aaron away, pointing the muzzle directly at his chest.

Aaron heard Colleen scream and closed his eyes, bracing for the shot.

Click.

Aaron waited, but he remained on his feet, decidedly not bleeding out from a gunshot wound. Cracking one eye, he saw Dr. Hayward shaking his gun in consternation, and in the same moment, he felt a warmth against his chest. The charm.

Ebony's ward had worked. His little sister had just saved his life.

Aaron didn't linger a moment longer. He lunged at the doctor, who was still distracted by the malfunctioning gun, and the two of them tumbled to the floor. The gun slipped from Dr. Hayward's hand as they fell, but Aaron soon lost sight of it amid the tangle of flailing arms and legs. The doctor fought like a wildcat; as they grappled and punched, Aaron felt his lip split open and something crack ominously near his nose. But while Hayward was bigger, Aaron was younger and faster. And angry. Oh, he was so very angry.

Finally, Aaron had the doctor pinned to the floor, straddling his chest. The doctor struggled, but Aaron punched him in the face once, twice, and then the man groaned and went slack, his breathing heavy. With a snarl, Aaron pressed his hands to either side of the man's face, ready to fill him up with all the anguish and fury his "treatment" of adepts had caused. And then he heard his name.

He looked up to see Colleen gazing down at him. She had picked up the gun, but instead of pointing it, her hand hung slack at her side. She looked so tired, and the expression on her face was stricken.

"Aaron," she whispered again. "Don't."

Aaron realized his own breath was coming in ragged gasps as he turned back to the doctor, whose eyes were wide with horror. Because after all, he was just a man. A weak, petty, contemptible man.

And he would not get the satisfaction of breaking Aaron, of making him into the thing the world feared he was.

But Aaron wasn't going to let him off the hook either.

Pressing his fingers against the doctor's temples, Aaron sent waves of emotion into his skull. But it wasn't pain or rage, anything meant for straightforward torment.

No—he gave the man fear.

He drew on everything he knew about what it meant to be an adept under the embargo, stories from his friends, people they'd helped, even strangers he only knew from secondhand accounts. He pulled together accounts of parents dragged bodily from their children to be taken to a containment center, teenagers being thrown out of their houses because they couldn't keep their abilities under control. He called up the feelings of constantly being on alert, of wondering if the next person you saw on the street was going to sense the magic on you and beat you or drag you to the authorities for a reward. He recalled Oliver's moods when the burden of other people's lives became too much, Cecily's panic at stumbling onto a crime engineered to seal her doom, Mrs. Paulson's suppressed pain, Kirby's forced bravado, Imogen's fierce protectiveness. He thought of his own desire to keep his sister safe and how it had been squeezing the life out of her.

He gave it all to Dr. Hayward, all at once.

Hayward's back arched, his body thrashing as if he was having a seizure. Finally, Aaron let him go, and he went limp, eyes glassy and gasping for air. Pushing himself off the doctor's chest, Aaron nearly collapsed himself; his limbs shook, and his insides felt strangely empty, hollowed out by his massive exertion of power. He'd never tried anything close to it before. He'd never even *imagined* trying anything like it. In the aftermath, he felt an almost overpowering urge to curl up on the floor and sob.

But then Colleen was crouching next to him.

"Aaron," she said softly, and he wanted to look at her, he really did, but he couldn't convince his body to move. Seeming to recognize some of what was happening, she took his chin gently in one hand and turned his face to hers.

"Are you all right?" she said, and this time, he was able to at least manage a nod. "Do you think you can stand?" That seemed ambitious, but he gave another nod anyway. With her help, he slowly got to his feet, putting a hand on the wall for balance. Once he was upright, Colleen let him go, but her hands still hovered near his body, ready to catch him.

"You good?" she said. After a moment, he nodded and let go of the wall. Then their eyes met.

She was a mess. Her headpiece had gotten lost somewhere along the way, her makeup was smeared, and she had bruises on her wrists from the handcuffs. He didn't even want to think about what he looked like. But they were here.

Colleen's lip trembled, and she reached for Aaron—carefully, so as not to knock him over, but obviously with great feeling—and pulled him into a hug.

He winced at the pain that shot through his cuts and bruises, but it passed soon enough, and he pressed his face into Colleen's hair, taking in what was becoming the familiar scent of her.

They stood there wrapped in each other until Dr. Hayward began to cough.

Colleen stepped away first, wiping surreptitiously at her eyes. "Is he OK? How long is he going to be like that?"

"I don't know," Aaron said. "I've never really done anything like that before." Reaching down, he checked Hayward's breathing, then rolled him into his side to keep his airway clear. It was the least he could do—and the most. He wasn't going to leave the man for dead, but he wasn't feeling particularly charitable towards him, either. Straightening, he took Colleen's hand.

"Come on. Let's go find Daniel."

They really had almost made it to the door when Hayward caught them, so it was only seconds until they were out in the balmy spring night. As Aaron drew in a deep lungful of fresh air, he heard footsteps and turned to see Daniel jogging up to them.

"Where have you two been? What took so lo-" He cut himself off when he caught sight of Aaron, his diatribe dissolving into a litany of swearing. He reached up to tilt Aaron's face into the light, but Aaron brushed him away.

"I'm fine."

"You're not fine," Daniel said. "That left eye is going to be swollen shut before too long; I wouldn't be surprised if your cheekbone is fractured. And you could very well have a concussion."

Just then, Oliver and Paloma hurried up, evening finery fluttering in their wake. When Paloma saw Aaron, she gasped and covered her mouth with her hands.

"I'm *fine*," Aaron said again.

"And I'm telling you again, you're not," Daniel said. "We need to get your checked out right away."

Oliver looked over at Colleen, the first one to acknowledge her. "How about you?"

"I'm OK," she said, but her voice sounded wobbly. Aaron pushed Daniel and Paloma off of him enough to glance over at her, and he could see right away that whatever fortitude had kept her going throughout their ordeal had run out. She looked small and tired, her arms pressed tight to her chest. A sad, lonely girl who craved recognition and had just endured something terrible with him and managed to walk away. Seeing her like this made his heart ache.

But there was also the inescapable fact that they had had to endure it because she had come there that night, knowing what it might cost him, cost all of them. And he was having a hard time letting that go.

Their eyes met, and they stared at each other for a long time. Aaron didn't know what to say, but that kind of worked out, because everyone else was more than happy to fill the void.

"OK," Oliver said with authority. "Daniel, you and Paloma get Aaron to the auto. I'll put Colleen in a cab and come meet you."

Daniel nodded and took Aaron's arm to lead him to the auto just as Oliver did the same to Colleen, steering her towards the front of the building where a handful of taxis still waited to collect lingering ballet patrons. Aaron held back for a moment, watching them. Colleen looked over her shoulder at him once, then she and Oliver turned the corner and she was gone.

"Gods," Paloma said, voice tense. "What are we going to tell Ebony?"

CHAPTER 23

AARON

*A*s soon as they were inside the Hierophant, Daniel started calling out for assistance. A moment later, figures spilled out of Esme's office and down the hall to the kitchen. Esme got their first, gasping as she caught sight of Aaron.

"Oh, Aaron," she said, mournfully, reaching out to touch his cheek.

"Honestly, I'm fine," he said, and off to his left, he heard Daniel growl.

"Aaron, if you say that one more gods-damned time…"

Aaron scowled. Was Daniel getting soft? Aaron couldn't remember him being this much of a nursemaid before.

Oliver pushed his way to the front and let out a whistle. Dimly, Aaron realized it was the same reaction he'd had to Paloma's appearance earlier that night. Was that good or bad? Probably bad, he decided. Or not? Did the bodily injury give him a dashing air?

With effort, he pushed that train of thought away. Maybe Daniel was right about the concussion.

Esme had taken his arm and was leading him down the hallway. "What happened?" she called over her shoulder to Daniel. Aaron heard Daniel giving the basic overview of the night they'd managed to put together in the car as he was plunked into a chair in Esme's office, and the next thing he knew, Ignotus was leaning in uncomfortably close to examine his face.

"Let's see," Ignotus muttered to himself. "Lacerated lip, probable zygomatic fracture on the left-hand side..." The litany of injuries trailed off, but he kept shifting around to see Aaron's face from different angles, then reached up to prod gently at the back of Aaron's head. With a decisive nod, he stood and began rattling off a list of items that the other conjurers then scrambled to collect. While that was going on, Aaron let his gaze drift past Ignotus, where he saw Ebony standing in the doorway.

Her body was tense, arms crossed over her chest, but her face was unreadable. He opened his mouth to call to her, but she suddenly dropped her arms and turned to leave the room without a word. Aaron could only stare after her, feeling vaguely bereft. Was she really *that* angry? To just walk away and leave him there?

He was at least partially distracted from his musings by the arrival of Ignotus's requests. The conjurer poured a variety of powdery substances and some kind of oil into a stone mortar, then ground them together with the accompanying pestle. When he was satisfied with the result, he began dabbing the concoction on Aaron's wounds.

"This won't work instantly," he said distractedly as he worked. "It will still take some time for you to heal, but not as much. I'll give you some to take home, and you should apply it three times a day."

Aaron murmured his assent, and with another nod, Ignotus stepped aside to do more conjurer stuff. Aaron let his eyes drift shut for a moment, letting the sound in the room become a dull buzz.

The buzz was disrupted by the sound of someone flopping into the chair Ignotus had vacated. Opening his eyes, Aaron saw Oliver sitting there.

"Well, champ," he said. "You've gone and gotten yourself wounded in action. That means you've earned your stripes. If we did stripes. Which we don't. But good job!"

Aaron groaned, letting his head fall back against the chair.

"Is it really that bad?"

"Nah," Oliver said cheerfully. "You'll be sore for a few days, but

191

ultimately, you'll be fine. That stuff Ignotus makes is astonishingly effective."

"I just wasn't sure," Aaron mumbled, his eyes getting heavy. "The way Daniel was carrying on-"

Oliver waved a dismissive hand. "Oh, he's always like that when someone besides him gets hurt. He's a big mama bear."

"-and Ebony..." Aaron finished, remembering the strange, blank look on her face when she'd turned away from him. Oliver's face sobered a bit.

"Yeah, I admit she's having a bit of a rough time with this. But she'll be OK. She's tough."

Aaron didn't doubt that for a second. But he wasn't worried about her toughness. He was worried that she wouldn't forgive him for letting himself get beaten to a pulp. Although, he was having a hard time even focusing on that now that the pain and exhaustion were catching up with him.

"Did we at least get some good intel?" he managed to ask.

"No," Oliver said with a frown. "But we will."

Aaron's nod seemed to use up whatever energy he had left, and his eyes drifted closed again. He dozed until he heard Oliver say, "Come on, let's get you to the car" and felt a hand hoisting him to his feet. Oliver helped him down the hall and to the back door where Ebony was standing next to one of the club cars. She opened the passenger door, and Oliver eased Aaron inside. Oliver gave him a wave, and then Ebony came around to get in the drivers seat and take the two of them home.

They drove in silence, as Ebony still had not said a single word to him. When they reached their building, she helped him up to the apartment and then to his room. She eased him onto his bed, still fully clothed, then removed his shoes before slipping into the kitchen. She returned with ice wrapped in a clean dishtowel, which she pressed gently to his cheek.

"Keep ice on that for as long as you can," she said, raising his hand to hold the ice pack in place. "I have the salve from Ignotus; I can help you put it on in the morning. Get some rest OK?"

And then she turned to leave. Aaron blinked.

"Ebony-" he said, letting the hand with the ice fall to the table, and she stopped, but only to speak to him over her shoulder.

"Don't. Just... don't. We'll discuss it in the morning."

And she went into her room and closed the door.

WHEN AARON DRIFTED BACK to consciousness the next morning, it was less because of the pain, as he might have predicted, and more because of the frankly awful taste in his mouth. Gingerly, he sat up and ran a hand over his face, and oh, yup, there was the pain after all. Progressing slowly, he levered himself off the bed and hobbled over to where a framed mirror hung on the wall. Upon seeing his reflection, he let out a groan. He had been able to tell even without looking the swelling around his eye and cheekbone had gone down, and the cuts bore scabs that looked days, not hours, old, but even so, he looked horrible. How much worse must it have looked the night before? He shuddered to think.

After a few moments, his attention shifted from his injuries to the ruin of the evening suit he still wore. They'd stripped him of the tie, vest, and jacket at the club, but he still wore the torn, blood-spattered shirt and rumpled pants. Suddenly, he was desperate to get them off, and while he didn't think he could manage a shower, a fresh set of clothes seemed somewhat doable. Moving at roughly half his normal pace, he gathered clean underthings, trousers, and a soft, loose shirt and set about changing. The dirty clothes went into a dejected heap on the floor as he tugged them off. When he slipped out of his shirt, he noticed some odd stains mixed in with the blood and dirt on the shoulder–peach and black–and after a perplexed moment, her realized it was Colleen's makeup. He paused, remembering he face as she'd turned back to him that last time. Was she OK? She'd been OK, right? It was all kind of fuzzy in his head.

Kind of fuzzy in your heart, too, some morose part of his brain supplied, and he sighed, tossing the shirt away in disgust.

When he got down to his undershirt, something else unexpected caught his eye. It was the amulet Ebony had given him the night before. When she'd handed it to him, the marks on it had been etched neatly onto the surface, but now they were dark and smudged along the edges, as if they had been burned into place. He remembered the heat against his chest when Hayward's gun had jammed and marveled again at Ebony's ingenuity. When he put the new clothes on, he left the amulet in place, tucked under his shirt.

He heard a noise out in the apartment's common area, and when he opened the door, he was greeted with a wave of breakfast smells he was surprised he hadn't noticed earlier. Ebony was already up and dressed, puttering around by the stove as Randolph milled around her feet. When she heard Aaron, she glanced back over her shoulder, but her gaze didn't linger.

"You're up," she said to the kitchen wall and began heaping bacon and scrambled eggs onto a plate. As Aaron eased into one of the chairs at the table, she banged the plate down in front of him and turned back to the stove where a coffee pot was beginning to whistle.

"Ebony-" he began, but she cut him off.

"Eat what you want—or what you can, I guess." She poured out two cups of coffee but still didn't turn around. "When you're done, I'll take the leftovers down to Ruth."

"Hey, come sit down," he said. "We need to talk."

She slammed the coffee pot down so hard it made him jump.

"Why? So you can lecture me about how everything went wrong last night because of me?"

Aaron gaped at her. "Wait, what?"

"You heard me!"

"Hang on." He jumped to his feet and crossed to the stove, even as his body screamed in protest. "Is that really what you think?"

"Well, look at you!" she wailed, gesturing at his injuries but not meeting his eyes. "You're a wreck! You've never thought the work I've been doing with the conjurers was worth much, and it turns out you were right." She sniffled. "I had all these grand plans about protecting you, and you came back to us beaten all to hells. What am I supposed to think? I failed you."

"Ebony," he said. "You did not fail me. You saved my life."

Finally, she looked up at him, breath catching in a hiccup. "What?"

"When Colleen and I were almost out, Hayward, the doctor from the sanatorium, showed up with a gun. He had me dead to rights, point blank shot—and his gun jammed." Ebony's face had gone pale at this revelation, but he pulled the amulet from inside his shirt and pushed on, desperate for her to understand. "I felt this go hot against my chest when it happened. It protected me. *You* protected me."

Tentatively, Ebony reached up and touched the amulet, running her fingers over the darkened markings. With an effort, Aaron lifted the thong over his head and handed it to her.

"Really?" she said. "It worked?"

"It did," he confirmed. "If it hadn't, I'd have ended up with much worse than a busted lip and a black eye."

He could tell she was shaken by the way she didn't argue with the understatement. Sagging into one of the dining chairs, she took another long look at the amulet, then laid it on the table and pressed her hands to her eyes.

"Ugh, I hate this," she said, then dropped her hands. "It was so hard watching you walk out that door, knowing I wouldn't be there to help if you needed it. Is that how you feel whenever I go off to do conjuror things?"

"Pretty much, yeah," he said, and she slumped back in her seat, crossing her arms over her chest.

"Well, we can't just wrap each other up in cotton wool and stay inside all the time," she said. "What are we going to do?"

Aaron blew out a long breath. "I think we just have to trust each other to make the right decisions to come home safe."

Ebony made such an articulate sound of disgust that Aaron had to laugh.

"I know—it's not a perfect solution, but it's what we have to work with. And if it's the trade-off for the life we've managed to build here, well…" He shrugged. "I'd say that's fair."

Ebony cocked an eyebrow at him, considering.

"Do you ever regret it?" she said. "Coming with me? Leaving the family behind on the farm?"

"Never," he said without hesitation. "You and me are a team. Always."

"But-" she began, and he raised a hand to cut her off. Then he clenched the hand into a fist and pressed it to his heart.

"Dozie," he said, voice rough with emotion.

Ebony didn't seem able to respond at first, but then she mirrored his gesture.

"Dozie," she murmured. The two of them sat in unified silence for a moment, but then Ebony leaned forward, narrowing her eyes. Now that she wasn't avoiding his gaze, he realized, she'd gotten a good look at his face. And she apparently didn't like what she saw.

"OK, seriously, eat your breakfast," she said. "Then I'll help you put your salve on before I leave, so you can go back to bed."

Aaron scowled. "What are you talking about? I'm going with you."

"No, you're not," she said. "You need to rest. And don't try to argue —before we left last night, Oliver said he didn't want to see you again until at least this time tomorrow."

Aaron wanted very much to argue, but he also had to admit that going back to bed did sound appealing. "I thought my face looked better this morning," was the best protest he could come up with, but even he could tell it sounded weak.

"Better is not good," Ebony said. "Now eat up."

He did, and when he was finished and she had collected his dishes, she sat down across from him with the tin of salve in her hand. With a gentle touch, she began applying it to the damaged areas of his face.

"By the way," she said, overly casual. "What exactly is going on with the girl? *Colleen.*"

She made the name heavy with insinuation, and he did his best to glare at her from beneath her ministrations. Of course she would broach this topic with him when he was essentially trapped.

"There is nothing going on with the girl," he said, and Ebony snorted.

"Are you sure? The rumor is you've developed a bit of a *tendresse* for her."

He snorted. "Been practicing your Belleterran with Cecily? Your accent still needs work."

"Don't change the subject."

He considered holding out, but really, what was the point? He didn't have the energy.

"Spending all that time with her driving up to the asylum," he began and flinched when Ebony pressed a bit too hard on a sore spot. She murmured an apology and gestured for him to continue. "She's really something—fierce and determined. For a small person, she's got so much fire inside her. But that's kind of the problem."

"How so?"

"It makes her reckless. She dives headfirst into conflict without stopping to think first. I mean, if there has to be someone who's responsible for what happened last night, it's her."

"Is that really what you're upset about?" Ebony said, dabbing the last of the salve on his face. "Or is it that she makes you want to be fierce and reckless instead of playing it safe all the time?"

He glowered at her for a long moment, unable to speak.

"Has anybody ever told you you're very annoying?" he finally managed.

"It's a gift," she said, twisting the lid onto the tin of salve. "Now go get back in bed."

He opened his mouth to dispute the point, but when his argument turned into a gigantic yawn, he decided to cut his losses and obeyed.

CHAPTER 24

COLLEEN

*A*cross town, Colleen was sitting at her desk in the Independent offices, tapping the capped end of her fountain pen against her teeth and wondering how she'd gotten herself into this fix.

Setting aside that fact that she'd woken up feeling like death warmed over—something akin to the worst hangover ever, especially galling since she hadn't had anything to drink—she was now pretty close to despondent over her situation, which rested on e three basic unsettling truths:

1. She needed a scoop.
2. She had promised Mr. Whitaker a scoop.
3. She had no scoop.

Some of this was a practical matter. Haring off to the opera house on her own, buoyed by the righteous fury of what she could now see was basically a temper tantrum, had not, in the end, yielded any corroborating evidence of what was happening at Ocean Serenity. But even if it had, she found that she didn't have the stomach for it. The story wasn't a problem for her to tackle anymore, a mystery to solve.

It was a horribly real bit of treachery directed at real people—people who had been good to her and deserved much, much better.

She couldn't bring herself to do anything to make their lives harder. And so there she was, ostensibly staring off into the middle distance as the newsroom clattered along around her, but really watching her lofty ambitions crumble into dust.

Just as she was considering jabbing herself in the jugular with her fountain pen and ending this misery once and for all, a shadow fell over her desk.

"Sandwich?"

Looking up in surprise, Colleen was further discombobulated to see Edith Thompson standing there holding a paper bag and two steaming cups.

"Sorry?" Colleen said, wishing her brain would hurry along and explain what was happening.

"Would you like a sandwich?" Edith said. "I was heading out to the automat down the street earlier—I'm partial to their Rueben and often get it for lunch—when I noticed you looked like you could use a break and something to eat. What do you say?"

"Uh, thank you." Colleen said. "That's very kind."

Then Edith further surprised her by dropping into the empty chair next to Colleen's desk and setting down the bag and cups. "The automat has better coffee, but I wasn't sure those flimsy paper cups would survive the journey, so you'll have to make do with some from the office pot. Black OK?"

"Sure," Colleen said as she tried to shuffle the clutter on her desk around enough to make room for their meal. "I always take it black." Which is what happened when you had four annoying brothers and had started drinking coffee on a dare.

"Good then," Eleanor said brusquely. "Dig in." She wasted no time tucking into her own sandwich, while Colleen went a bit more cautiously. Her experience with corned beef upon moving to Ad Astra had been spotty at best; it rarely met her exacting standards, and on occasion, she found it downright inedible. But biting into her Rueben, she was pleased to discover that this corned beef was actually quite serviceable—not what she'd grown up with, of course, but it was rich and salty and melded wonderfully with the rye bread and all the fixings. As she swallowed her first mouthful, she realized that Edith had actually been right—she was famished. When had she actually eaten last?

She didn't have long to ponder this, though, before Edith started talking.

"I met her once, you know."

Colleen sighed inwardly, wishing Edith would stop being so infernally cryptic, but the woman had fed her, so she did her best to remain gracious and cordial.

"Met who?"

Edith had just taken a swig of coffee, but she inclined her head towards the picture frame on the desk, and Colleen's eyebrows shot up.

"What, Amity? Really!?"

Edith gave a single nod. "I was just a girl, but she made a big impression on me, even then. She was truly a remarkable woman."

"She was," Colleen said and looked at the familiar photo.

Edith popped the last bite of her sandwich into her mouth, brushed the crumbs from her fingers, and settled her hands in her lap.

"Now," she said. "I don't know what exactly is going on with you beyond some vague intimations Stewart has made, but you seem to be having something of a tough time, and I thought you might benefit from the perspective from another female journalist. Never mind that you have dismissed the significance of the women's page from the moment you passed through the newsroom door."

Colleen's jaw dropped. What was even *happening* with this conversation?

"But I didn't-" she stammered. "That is, I would never-"

"You have," Edith said decisively. "You are not the first of your generation to do so, nor do I believe you will be the last. All of you coming up now seem to have very high opinions of yourselves, as if none of the women who came before you had ever considered doing journalism properly. Or at least, none who didn't die tragically young, remaining forever beautiful and romantic in the public imagination."

Colleen glanced guiltily at the picture of Amity, but if Edith noticed, she didn't give any indication.

"But aside from a certain undercurrent of philosophical distaste, I don't let it bother me much. And would you like to know why?"

"Yes?" Colleen said, almost a squeak.

"Because I know my worth. I am damn good at my job, and they are lucky to have me no matter what anyone thinks. You have the makings of being damn good at your job as well."

Colleen blinked. "I do?"

Edith nodded. "You're a good reporter. You're tenacious in your pursuit of a story, your writing has flair, and, perhaps most importantly, Stewart thinks you're good people. Stewart and I go back a long way; I trust his judgment. He grasps the underpinnings of influence in this city and, by extension, the country, like very few people I have ever encountered, even in our profession. He knows how to manipulate the levers of power in a way that might not seem obvious at first glance. It's why he still deigns to do what the self-styled crackerjacks around here consider drudge work. The philanthropy, the galas—they all tie back to the machinations of the elite. The people who can decipher those stratagems truly understand the game. Stewart is one of them. He thinks you have the potential to be, too."

"That,,, that means a lot to hear," Colleen said. "Truly. But I'm not sure it's enough to keep Mr. Whitaker from firing me."

Edith sat back in her chair with a sigh. "Whit's a good sort, a real newspaperman of the old school. But he's set in his ways, and he doesn't like hassle. He puts up with a lot from malcontents like myself and Stewart because we've been around for a long time, and we have clout. You, meanwhile, do not. So, yes, if the higher-ups lean on him because they are catching heat from the RPC over you, there is a good chance he'll fire you."

Colleen pursed her lips. "So, you're saying I would do well to remember my worth as a reporter while I search for secretarial positions in the job advertisements of the paper I used to work for?"

"No," Edith said firmly, unimpressed by Colleen's perfectly legitimate conclusion. "What I am saying is that Whit is not the last word on your career—you are. So you lose your job—our foremothers endured far worse in their pursuit of this noble cause. There is nothing wrong with secretarial work, but if you settle for it because persisting is difficult... well, you'll have no one to blame for your dreary plight but yourself."

As Colleen cast about for an appropriate response, one of the cub reporters dashed by her desk, barely pausing to spit out a message in his rush.

"Colleen, Mr. Whitaker wants to see you in his office."

Colleen felt a sudden, overwhelming sense of doom.

"About what?" she called, but the cub was already gone.

Next to her, Edith began calmly collecting the remnants of their lunch.

"Have courage," she said. "Remember that whatever happens in there, the world will continue to spin on its axis." She inclined her head toward Colleen's coffee mug. "Are you finished with that?"

Colleen nodded absently, repelled now by the very thought of putting anything else in her stomach. There was no sentimentality in Edith's counsel, only frank matter-of-factness, and somehow, that actually did make Colleen feel a bit more courageous. She got to her feet, smoothing her hair and brushing stray crumbs off her dress.

"I'd better get in there," she said, mostly to herself. "But Edith-" She waited until the older woman looked up. "Thank you."

Edith gave her one last curt nod as she stood and returned to her own desk. Then Colleen took a deep breath and set out to brave the lion's den.

She had barely finished tapping the door with her knuckle when she heard Mr. Whitaker bellow, "Come in!"

Bracing herself, she opened the door and found her editor rifling through his desk drawer. He spared her a quick glance before returning to his rummaging.

"Ah, Miss O'Cremin," he said. "Have a seat. I'll be with you in a minute."

Colleen settled herself on the edge of one of Mr. Whitaker's wooden office chairs as he finally withdrew a cigar tube and cutter from his desk drawer. With quick, practiced motions, he unwrapped and cut the cigar, lit it with the heavy marble lighter on his desk, and tucked it into his teeth as he leaned forward and crossed his arms on his desk. And then he just stared at Colleen.

Colleen struggled not to fidget. She was already half-convinced this conversation would end badly for her, and the look on his face wasn't doing anything to ease her. But he had been the one to summon her, so by the gods, she was not about to let him off the hook for whatever terrible dictate he was about to make, especially after her conversation with Edith. She'd wait as long as she had to for him to crack.

It turned out to not be very long at all.

"Do you know, Miss O' Cremin, why I took time out of my busy afternoon to invite you here?"

"Um, no," Colleen said, and she hated that it sounded so much like a question.

"I just got off the phone with the director of the Ad Astra Ballet," he said, and Colleen's heart began to race in earnest.

"Oh?" she said, feigning innocence.

"Yeah," Whitaker went on, plucking the cigar from his mouth and waving it as he spoke. "And imagine my surprise when he told me that not only has Pavel Vasilyev finally decided to break his silence, but that he would only do so to one person." He paused for a moment, then jabbed the cigar at her. "You."

There was nothing feigned about her reaction now. "Me?! Why?"

"That was pretty much my response, too," he said, sticking his cigar between his teeth on the opposite side as before. "Vasilyev has been indecently tightlipped since he arrived on our shores, and now that he's ready to share his story with the world, out of all the reporters at all the rags in this city, he says he won't talk to anybody but Colleen O'Cremin. And he did his homework, because that's the name he used. Not Lena Crimm. "

"But," Colleen said hesitantly. "Isn't that a good thing? For the Independent?"

Mr. Whitaker exhaled heavily, releasing a cloud of smoke and resembling nothing so much as a harried, overworked dragon. "Honestly, I think the whole situation stinks to high heaven. Nothing about it makes sense; it feels like some sort of sick prank, except I'm not sure who's pulling it. Or who they're pulling it on, for that matter. But if it's legit, and there's a chance we get the scoop..." He sighed. "We have to take it."

He puffed away at his cigar, stewing in a fug of indignation. Colleen tried to wait him out, but ultimately, her curiosity won out over her reluctance to poke the bear.

"So I get to do the interview?"

Mr. Whitaker's frown deepened, and he thrust his cigar into the ashtray at his elbow.

"They're expecting you at 4. Don't be late and wear something pretty. You'll need to come straight back and type up the story for the morning edition. Is all of that clear?"

"Yes, sir," Colleen said, jumping to her feet. She considered initiating a handshake and decided against it, choosing instead to get out of his sight before he could change his mind. As she opened the office door, letting in the roar of typewriters and urgent voices, she heard him call her name one last time and glanced back.

"Don't screw this up," he growled, then jabbed the cigar back in his mouth and scowled down at a file on his desk.

"No, sir. I won't, sir." With that, she made her escape, rushing back to her desk with her heart racing.

She couldn't believe it. Somehow, just when she'd needed it, fate or luck or whatever power was responsible for these things in the universe had thrown her a lifeline. Maybe, just maybe, she'd be able to keep her job after all. Maybe this last week hadn't been a complete waste of her time.

You already knew it wasn't, a voice in her head whispered. The voice brought to mind the delight on her mother's face when they appeared on her doorstep. The set of Imogen's jaw as she took hold of her chance at freedom. Aaron's hand at her waist as they danced.

She didn't argue with the voice; after all, it was right. But she pushed the musings away all the same. They were too big, too much. If she got too caught up in them, she wouldn't be able to do her job. And she needed to do her job.

She was not about to let this possibility pass her by.

CHAPTER 25

AARON

The next morning, Aaron grudgingly had to admit that spending the previous day in bed had probably been the right call. He felt significantly less sore, and all of his wounds looked markedly better. Much of that, he conceded, also had to do with Ignotus's salve, which he dabbed on his face as he stood in front of his bedroom mirror. There was still a bit of faint bruising, but overall, he seemed more or less back to normal. Ebony must have thought so, too, because over breakfast (toast and coffee rather than bacon and eggs—apparently, her guilt had been assuaged), she had agreed to take him to the Hierophant that day to get an update on what, if anything, Oliver and Paloma had learned at the reception, as well as what the status was on Imogen and Kirby. When he stepped out into the common area, Ebony did give him one last searching look, but she was apparently satisfied with what she saw and led them down to the car.

She'd borrowed the auto from the club again, making the case that Aaron shouldn't have to worry about catching a cab or being jostled around on public transportation in his condition, which was true as far as it went, but Aaron suspected Ebony had leaned more heavily into the injured-in-the-line-duty angle than was strictly warranted.

He knew Daniel had probably realized this, too, but he'd still loaned her the auto, and Aaron had to admit—having it at his and Ebony's disposal was actually pretty nice. Maybe he should think about getting one. If there was any time he'd have significant leverage to negotiate a raise, this was it. Maybe he could channel a bit of Ebony's mercenary instinct and do it. But that was a conversation for later. He had plenty to deal with as it was.

When they reached the club, they took the back entrance, finding the kitchen and its environs unusually quiet, but the calm was soon shattered by a body hurtling into Aaron, wrapping its thin arms around him and knocking most of the air from his chest.

"Gently, Claudia!" Ebony said in alarm, and Claudia disentangled herself from him looking contrite.

"I'm sorry," she said, glancing back and forth between the twins before settling on Aaron. "I was just so worried about you when Paloma told me what happened." She narrowed her eyes, examining his face. "Are you OK?"

"I'm fine," he told her. At the skeptical cock of her head, he amended, "Well, I will be. It's a work in progress."

Claudia still looked dubious but nodded and retrieved an envelope from her apron pocket.

"This came for you this morning. Seemed important."

Aaron turned the envelope in his hands. It looked pretty unre-markable, just plain white paper with his name and the Hierophant's address typed on the front. He looked up at Claudia, eyebrow raised.

"Where's it from?"

She shrugged. "I don't know. A messenger brought it. He didn't tell me much, just that it needed to be delivered directly to you." Just then, Paloma's voice came drifting out from the bowels of the dressing rooms, shouting her sister's name. Claudie gave a martyred sigh and rolled her eyes. "I'd better go. But I'm glad you're back."

She leaned in to give Aaron another quick and much gentler hug then went off to see what Paloma was on about. Aaron began working the flap on the envelope open, then looked up at Ebony, who was watching him intently.

"Can I have a little privacy, please?"

"Absolutely not," Ebony said, without hesitation. "Now, hurry up—I have business to see to."

Aaron gave his own sibling-inspired sigh and eye roll, but dutifully finished tearing the envelope open. Inside, there were two pieces of folded paper, one of which had some sort of small, heavy object tucked inside. He picked the rougher of the two first, leaving the object for later inspection.

Unfolding the paper, he realized it was a clipping from that morning's Independent, and his eyes went wide as he took in the headline and by-line.

PASHA SPEAKS!!!
    Ballet Superstar Breaks His Silence,
    Tells Harrowing Story of Defection

    by Colleen O' Cremin for the Independent

QUICKLY, he scanned the article, taking in the carefully curated version of the story Vasilyev had told him the night of the ballet. The dancer came across as poised, serious, grateful for the warm welcome he'd received from the New Avalonian authorities. But one passage at the end stood out to Aaron.

When asked how he pictures his future in New Avalon, Vasilyev was quiet for a while, then said that he only wants a quiet life where he and his loved ones can follow their dreams in peace and safety. This answer reveals much about the man, but perhaps most importantly, it shows that despite his remarkable story and his birth in a country far from our own, he cherishes the same values many New Avalonians hold dear. Family. Community. Possibility. As such, we should all be willing to welcome him with open arms so that he can have his quiet life, one rooted in dignity and freedom - freedom to grow, freedom to thrive, freedom from fear.

He stared at the last sentence for a long time before passing the clipping to Ebony who was practically vibrating with anticipation. As she read, he took the second piece of paper out of the envelope, careful not to let the object inside slip to the floor. It was an ordinary piece of stationery with no name or monogram, but it did boast a simple purple border, inside of which had been scrawled two words:

You win.

The object was a nickel.

Aaron swallowed around a lump in his throat as Ebony finished reading the article and took in the note and coin in his hand.

"What does all this mean?"

Aaron gave her a very brief rundown of everything that had transpired between Colleen and him over the last few days: the bet, meeting Colleen's family, the respite at Houseman's Hideaway, Vasilyev's assistance with their escape. For most of it, he kept his eyes on Colleen's handwriting and the nickel; when he finally looked up at the conclusion of the tale, the soppy look on Ebony's face forced a laugh at him.

"You have to go find her," she said, in a tone that brooked no argument, but Aaron found he was loath to give one.

"Yeah," he said. "I really think I do."

And so it was that, later that afternoon, Aaron found himself propped against the same wall he'd used to wait for Colleen only a few days before, waiting for her to leave for the day. It was a little disconcerting how much the things were the same and yet entirely different. The guy with the hot dog cart was breaking down, not setting up; an accordionist with an open case at his feet had taken the place of the organ grinder hoping for coins. Aaron's position was the same, but the shadows were different; the clock still tolled, but the hour had shifted.

He was different. Collen was different. Or at least he hoped she was.

Shortly after 5, he spotted her coming down the stairs in front of the building, wearing a grey dress with a long strand of purple and gold cloisonné beads and a deep purple cloche. Taking a deep breath, he pushed off of the wall and headed in her direction.

She was walking quickly towards the corner, and while traffic was humming merrily by, leaving pedestrians waiting at the crosswalk for the light to change, he didn't want to risk losing her, so once she was in earshot, he called out, "Miss O'Cremin!"

He thought he saw a catch in her step at the sound of her name, and she slowed until she was standing still in the middle of the pavement. Slowly, she turned until she was facing him, her gaze locked on his. He saw trepidation there, and, he thought, possibly hope.

"Mr. Dozie," she said as he closed the distance between them. He came to a stop about a foot away, not caring that he was creating an even bigger snarl in foot traffic. Now that he was here, he didn't know quite where to start, so he just latched onto the nearest thing at hand, hoping that inspiration would follow.

"Where are you off to with such a purpose to your step?"

She shifted, moving her handbag from one arm to the other. "There's an automat down the street that I found out about recently. They make a tasty Rueben, and I thought I might pick one up for dinner."

"Would you mind if I walked with you?" Aaron said, and she swallowed.

"No," she said. "I think that would be fine."

Together, they walked the rest of the way to the corner, then stood in silence as traffic slowed, then stopped, allowing them to cross. This, too, was different from the first time they'd made this trip. Rather than him scheming to get Colleen to talk while she did her level best to ignore his existence, both of them seemed a little nervous, a little breathless. They didn't have agendas this time. They only had the tentative connection they had managed to build and the possibility it hadn't broken as completely as they'd thought.

The quiet between them held as they crossed the street and started down the sidewalk towards the automat. Aaron began to sweat a little, casting about for some bit of small talk, but Colleen beat him to it.

"Your face looks better," she said.

He reached up and touched his cheekbone experimentally. "Yeah, Ignotus really knows his stuff. I think I'll be back to normal in a day or two."

Colleen nodded, and the quiet descended once more. The two of them broke it at the same time.

"Listen, Colleen-

"I'm sorry -"

They stopped again based on the other's outburst and laughed nervously. But now that the floodgates were open, the confessions came spilling out.

"I hate that you got hurt. I'm sorry for any part I played in it."

Aaron sighed, wondering why no one seemed to recognize that he was a grown adult and capable of taking responsibility for his own ass-kicking. "It wasn't your fault."

"Maybe not," she said. "But if I hadn't been there... Or if I had been there but hadn't stormed off on my own..."

She stopped walking, taking a slightly watery breath to steady herself, and Aaron stopped with her.

"Hey, it's OK," he said and noticed suddenly that they were standing just outside the tiny corner park where they'd made the initial bargain that he'd set all of this in motion. Giving a wry shake of his head, he took her gently by the elbow and steered her into the park's cool shade. There was a stone bench nestled in amongst the greenery, and the two of them sat, Colleen facing forward and Aaron turned slightly toward her. She heaved a deep breath.

"Maybe we should start over," he said. "As you can probably tell, I got your clipping and your nickel."

Colleen sniffed and nodded. "I wasn't sure it would be welcome. But I had to know that you knew. After everything that happened, I thought you might steer clear of the Independent entirely. And I wanted you to see."

"I saw," Aaron said, feeling a swell of not just warmth and affection for her, but pride. "You set out to get your big scoop and you got it."

She snorted, looking away.

"That was luck, pure and simple. I mean, don't get me wrong—I am so, so grateful for it, and I wasn't about to waste the opportunity. But it wasn't because of anything I did."

"No," Aaron said firmly. "It wasn't luck. Vasilyev didn't give you the interview out of the goodness of his heart. He did it because he knew you'd be a pain in the RCP's ass, and that is entirely owing to you being stubborn and inconvenient whenever possible. You earned that confidence completely on your own."

Colleen laughed and ran a finger under her eye.

"How did that go, anyway?" he said. "The actual interview?"

Colleen shook her head in remembered wonder.

"He walked in that room and acted like he had never seen me before in his life. He was all clipped and cool, the way he always comes across in public, so much so that I started to wonder if I'd done something wrong. But when he got up to leave, he winked at me." She shook her head again. "I hope I did right by him."

"You did," Aaron said, and she looked at him with grateful eyes, then away. In response, he scooted closer and took her hand.

"Tell me something," he said. "If you hadn't gotten this story, would you have run with your Ocean Serenity piece?"

"No," she said, turning to meet his gaze.

"Why not?"

"Because I couldn't, not in good faith. And someone made me understand I didn't need to. She told me nobody had the last word on my career but me and that the big, flashy stories aren't necessarily the ones with the biggest impact. That you can do real good in the world with the drudge work."

"And that's what you want? To do good?"

"Yeah," she said, with renewed confidence. "I do. I want to make the world better for people like my father and my irritating brother, who don't get the lucky breaks to chase their dreams. I want to make it safer for you and your friends." She lowered her voice. "But, I think, especially for you."

Aaron's heart picked up speed, and he shifted closer to her on the bench.

"You know," he said. "When we danced the other night, it was great and all, but I couldn't help thinking it lacked a little something."

"Oh, yeah?" she said, and her eyes flicked to his mouth. "And what might that be?"

Slowly, Aaron leaned in and pressed his lips gently, but firmly to hers. She felt somehow both delicate and strong to him, something he'd recognized in their very first meeting but was brought home to him with stunning clarity in this moment. He shifted to deepen the kiss, and she made a little sound that almost undid him, spurring him to draw away a bit to catch his breath; the last thing this fragile, wonderful moment needed was the two of them getting cited for public indecency. But he didn't go far, letting his forehead rest against hers. He could see the flush on her cheeks from there and hear her rapid breath.

"You know," she said. "We could try dancing again. Any time you want. And throw some more of that in there as well."

"I'd like that," he said, reaching up to smooth a stray lock of hair out of her face.

"Just pick the time and place."

"Tonight, maybe?" he said. "I know this great little spot. The bartender is really something. Best drinks in the city."

"You can skip the drinks," she said, grabbing his tie to pull him closer. "The bartender will do just fine."

Aaron grinned and leaned in for another kiss. What exactly constituted public indecency anyway? Maybe that could be Colleen's next story.

But not just yet.

EPILOGUE

ELEANOR

As night settled over Ad Astra, Eleanor Bradshaw sat in a deep leather chair before the window of her penthouse study, idly swirling a glass of whiskey.

She had always liked this room. But then, it had always been hers, unlike those designated for her personal and professional use at her permanent residence and lake house. Those had been Stephen's first, back when they had both labored under the delusion that he was head of the household. Before Eleanor had taken over the family finances — including the underperforming investment portfolio —and banished the red ink from their ledger. Once the money had started coming in, Stephen had been all too amenable to stepping aside, leaving him free to devote his time to golf and horse racing (and, almost certainly, mistresses, but they didn't talk about that). The efforts required to make over those spaces to her own specifications had been satisfying, in their own way, but she'd been able to build this one from scratch. It was her refuge.

Or at least it had been.

Her gaze drifted to the family portrait over the hearth, as it often did when she was feeling especially melancholy. She'd commissioned it just before Matthew had left for boarding school, and neither he nor Stephen had wanted to sit for it, but she had insisted, and she would be forever grateful that she hadn't wavered. The painting was precious to her now. She always thought the artist had captured something so bright and hopeful in Matthew, just thirteen, his face a near-copy of Stephen's but softened by the last remnants of childhood and a mischievous glint in his eye. None of them could have known that all of that beautiful potential would remain unfulfilled.

She was aware of the things people whispered about Matthew's death behind her back–that he'd been drinking too much, that he was irresponsible and reckless. But she knew the truth. He had changed once he'd started dabbling in magic, spending time in charm schools and tracking down rare conjurer texts. The boy she knew had started slipping away, and then, suddenly, he was really, truly gone. She'd already been elected to the National Congress by then, but in her grief, nothing felt worthwhile–not her public service, not the charities and arts organizations she sponsored, certainly not her finances. The only thing that had given her some sense of direction, of purpose, had been the vow she'd made to herself that no other family would ever suffer as hers had because of magic. So she'd dedicated herself to it with a vengeance.

And it had seemed to be going well, at least for a while. She'd taken up with the Reason and Progress Coalition, and they'd been getting legislation passed and helping to sway public opinion. As she'd become more deeply embedded in RPC leadership, she'd also begun learning about the more obscure, esoteric steps being taken to suppress magic, shielded from undue scrutiny until the time was right, and they had seemed to have so much promise. But then that idiot zealot Vandermark had gone rogue. The loss of Fairchild had caused incalculable damage to the work, but Vandermark at least had the decency to get himself murdered. It saved her the trouble of dealing with him herself.

She knew from the reports that adepts had been involved–not just disgruntled individuals, but an organized group. It surely wasn't a coincidence that Cecily Dearborn had fallen in with a charm school crew once her name had been cleared. Eleanor had meant to keep closer tabs on that situation, but the agitators had kept their heads down, and she'd just had so much other work to do. Slowly but surely, the anti-magic efforts had started regaining ground. The program at Ocean Serenity had not only resumed but grown. They'd seemed to really be close to cracking the secret of the shield. And then that accursed reporter had shown up with an adept in tow and walked off with two of the test subjects.

Sneaking into the ballet two days later had taken moxie, Eleanor would give her that. It had actually seemed a stroke of luck at first, since once she and Hayward had stashed the girl in that storage room, all they'd needed to do was make it through the reception, and then they could have figured out what to do with her at their leisure. But when the reception was over, the girl had disappeared, as had Hayward. The former had struck Eleanor as the real problem initially, the latter more of a baffling irritation. That all changed once she got the call from Turner-Hoff.

Hayward's secretary, Mildred something, had apparently called him in a panic when she showed up for work not long after the ballet to find Hayward's office completely empty, save for a signed letter of resignation on his desk. He had left no forwarding address or other contact information, and visits to his house came up empty. That all would have been troublesome but manageable, if he hadn't released all the test subjects before he left and destroyed any records pertaining to them that had been kept on-site. But he had, so it was a disaster. Not as bad as Fairchild, but close.

The useless RPC agents still hadn't found any leads on where Hayward had gone, so she'd decided she needed to try another tactic to get to the bottom of what happened. There was no doubt in her mind that it involved the same adepts as the Fairchild incident, and Dearborn and the journalist were almost certainly associates, so that was a place to start. However, both of them had protectors in high places—Green would be apoplectic if anything happened to his new star reporter, and law enforcement got tetchy if anyone even thought about shutting down their flow of dirty money, which Dearborn's friends surely had a hand in–so she'd have to be careful. Even so, she was going to put a stop to their interference.

She didn't have the details she needed, not yet. But she'd get them. After all, the magical world was small, as was the one that opposed it. Word would get out, especially if this group was set on actually accomplishing something, unlike the buffoons in Shining Light. And she was fairly certain they were, so it would all come together in time.

But they'd lost so much time already. She couldn't help but feel she needed to take steps to hurry things along.

Swallowing the last of the whiskey, Eleanor crossed the room to her desk and pulled out her address book. She rifled through the pages until she found the entry she was looking for and, as always, cringed when she found it. *Colonel Peregrine Tiberius Calhoun.* No matter how many times she saw it, it never got any less ridiculous. But he had a part to play in this just as she did, whether she liked it or not.

With a sigh, she took out a sheet of stationery, uncapped her favorite fountain pen, and began to write:

Calhoun–

There have been some developments as of late that may require us to accelerate our timetable. As such, we need you to return to Ad Astra as soon as possible. I know you are in the thick of your season, but the situation is quite urgent. Keep me apprised of your plans, and I will make the necessary arrangements. The moment we have all anticipated for so long may finally be nigh.

Yours,

E.B.

She sealed and addressed the letter, then placed it on the designated tray for staff to pick up in the morning. On her way to the door, she paused, taking in the sprawl of the city once more. So many lives out there, so many dreams. She wouldn't stand for any of them to be crushed by magic–not anymore. She'd made a promise, and she intended to keep it.

The moment was nigh indeed.

THE ADEPTS of the Hierophant will return in 2026.

IN THE MEANTIME, you can sign up for my newsletter to get information about new releases, cool extras, and other fun stuff at www.reneeedward sauthor.com.

AUTHOR'S NOTE

$\mathcal{J}$ did a bit of research for *To the Stars*, the first book in the Powerful Prohibition series, but not nearly as much as I did for this one (or for my Sherwood & Jarvis novellas, which are set in Victorian England and which you should check out if you are into Sherlock Holmes, lady sleuths, and/or the fae—I'm just saying...). I ended up going down multiple rabbit holes, so if you, like me, are nerdy and enjoy hearing about that kind of thing, here are some of the highlights that helped shape Aaron and Colleen's story.

JOURNALISM

I tried to find as much as I could on both lady reporters of the early 20th century and journalism in general of that period (and earlier —Amity Bell is very much based on Nellie Bly and other "girl stunt reporters" of the late 1800s). That said, I still deviated a bit if I needed to. For example, journalists were largely anonymous to the reading public until much later in the century, closer to the '70s when bylines became customary. In the period that inspired this series —the 1910s-1920s — bylines were even rarer than this story makes them sound and carried a hefty amount of prestige. It would have been highly unlikely that someone of Colleen's stature would get one on a story, with the possible exception of the interview with Pasha. I fudged it because the byline angle was important to her character arc. Authors get to do stuff like that.

Some of the resources I found helpful on this topic:

- *The American Newsroom: A Social History, 1920-1960* by William T. Mari
- *Undaunted: How Women Changed American Journalism* by Brooke Kroeger
- *Covering America: A Narrative History of a Nation's Journalism* by Christopher B. Daly
- *Main Currents in the History of American Journalism* by Willard Grosvenor Bleyer
- *The Great Reporters* by David Randall

Sanatoriums

The Library of Congress came in particularly handy on this point, serving up this marketing brochure for the Jackson Sanatorium of Dansville, NY. It's dated a little earlier than my inspiration window, but I still relied on it heavily for my descriptions of Ocean Serenity and gave it a nod in the text, when Dr. Hayward gives copies of a similar document to Aaron and Colleen.

THE CATSKILLS and Bungalow Colonies

Some of the earliest sparks I had for this story were images of Aaron and Colleen taking the characters that would become Imogen and Kirby on the run and seeking refuge in a deserted hotel very much like Kellerman's, the resort in *Dirty Dancing*. (Later, it occurred to me that since this scene in the book involves the characters searching for food, this was likely due to the scene in the movie where Neil takes Baby to the kitchen for a snack—"Sweet gherkin?"—and she sees Penny crying. But I digress...) So off I went to research the Catskills and the Borscht Belt, and I discovered that while there were some big hotels up there (including Grossinger's, the model for Kellerman's), most of the Jewish families who spent the summers in the mountains did so in the smaller communal vacation spots known as bungalow colonies, so that's the hideout that made its way into the book. I still used the name to work in a *Dirty Dancing* reference, though.

Helpful resources:

- *The Catskills: Its History and How It Changed America* by Stephen M. Silverman and Raphael D. Silver
- *In the Catskills: A Century of Jewish Experience in "the Mountains"*, edited by Phil Brown

Dancing Defectors

Pavel Vassilyev was inspired by a number of Russian dancers who defected to the West in the 20th century, including George Balanchine, Natalia Makarova, and especially Mikhail Baryshnikov. One of the most useful sources I found on this topic was "Soviet Leap: Oppression, Defection, and Re-Envisioning Ballet" by GK Martin. Also, I'm not a ballet scholar, but I would encourage you to go watch videos of Baryshnikov dancing online. He was magnificent in his prime.

Miscellaneous

- The Hartley Center is modeled largely on Manhattan's Rockefeller Center (especially Radio City Music Hall) with a little bit of Lincoln Center thrown in for spice.
- "Audiophone" was actually a brand name for an early jukebox model produced by the J.P. Seeburg Company, but I liked the sound of it, so I gave it the Kleenex/Post-it treatment and made it a generic noun.

- Cocktails served in copper mugs weren't really a thing until the 1940s, but I wanted to keep Aaron behind the bar during the scene in the bungalow colony instead of having him traipse off to the kitchen for glassware. So, voila— copper mugs at his fingertips.
- The songs I had in mind when writing the dance scene were the Postmodern Jukebox covers of Depeche Mode's "Enjoy the Silence" and the Foo Fighters' "My Hero".

Renee Edwards
2025

ABOUT THE AUTHOR

Renee Edwards is a lifelong book person and trained librarian. Her favorite books to read are the kind with magic, adventure, and romance, so those are what she set out to write. She fiddles away on her laptop in Texas, where she lives with her husband, their basset hound Winifred Barkle, and their cat Piper Meowliwell. You can find out more about Renee and sign up for her newsletter at www.reneeed wardsauthor.com .

ALSO BY RENEE EDWARDS

www.ingramcontent.com/pod-product-compliance
Lightning Source LLC
Chambersburg PA
CBHW020939180626
46814CB00003B/861